BEA

Rebecca James was born in Sydney, Australia, in 1970. She has worked as a waitress, a kitchen designer, an English teacher in both Indonesia and Japan, a barmaid and (most memorably) a minicab telephone-operator in London. Rebecca lives in Australia with her partner and their four sons.

Praise for *Beautiful Malice*:

'A tense and psychological thriller . . . A dark and gripping story, confronting uncomfortable emotions and told with suspense. As the truth unfolds towards a devastating climax, no one escapes untouched. As a debut novel, one can only imagine what else Rebecca James has up her sleeve.' *Daily Mail*

'*Beautiful Malice* is a good teen mystery story, with hints of *Wuthering Heights* and *Gossip Girl* thrown in . . . we think it's gonna be big news.' *Sugar Magazine*

'The psychological grip . . . keeps the reader hooked.' *Sunday Telegraph*

'This is a captivating and exciting read that will have you glued from beginning to end . . . James has done a brilliant job in creating a really unique teen thriller, with echoes of *The Hand That Rocks The Cradle*.' *Teen Today*

REBECCA JAMES

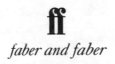

faber and faber

First published in 2010 by
Faber and Faber Limited
Bloomsbury House, 74–77 Great Russell Street,
London, WC1B 3DA
This paperback edition first published in 2011

Typeset by Faber and Faber
Printed in England by CPI Bookmarque, Croydon

A CIP record for this book
is available from the British Library

ISBN 978–0–571–25982–3

2 4 6 8 10 9 7 5 3 1

Part 1

I didn't go to Alice's funeral.

I was pregnant at the time, crazy and wild with grief. But it wasn't Alice I grieved for. No, I hated Alice by then and was glad that she was dead. It was Alice who had ruined my life, taken the best thing I'd ever had and smashed it into a million unfixable pieces. I wasn't crying for Alice but because of her.

But now, five years later and a lifetime happier; finally settled into a comfortable and routine life with my daughter Sarah (my sweet, oh-so-serious little Sarah), I sometimes wish that I had made it to Alice's funeral after all.

The thing is, I see Alice sometimes — at the supermarket, at the gates of Sarah's kindergarten, at the club where Sarah and I sometimes go for a cheap meal. I catch glimpses of Alice's glossy, corn-blonde hair, her model-like body, her eye-catching clothes, from the corner of my eye and I stop to stare, my heart pounding. It only takes me an instant to remember that she is dead and gone, that it can't possibly be her, but I have to force myself to get closer, to reassure myself that her ghost isn't haunting me. Close-up, these women are sometimes similar, albeit never, never as beautiful as Alice. More frequently, though, they look nothing like her.

Relieved, I turn away and get on with whatever I was doing before, but all the warmth will have drained from my face and lips, my fingertips will tingle unpleasantly with adrenaline. My day is, invariably, ruined.

I should have gone to the funeral. I wouldn't have had to cry, or feign despair. I could have laughed bitterly and spat into the pit. Who would have cared? If only I'd seen them lower her casket into the ground, watched them throw the dirt into her grave, I would be more certain that she was really dead and buried.

I would know, deep down inside, that Alice was gone for good.

1

'Do you want to come?' Alice Parrie is looking down, smiling. It's lunchtime and I'm sitting beneath a tree, alone, absorbed in a book.

'Sorry?' I shade my eyes and look up. 'Come where?'

Alice hands me a piece of paper.

I take it and read. It's a brightly coloured photocopy of an invitation to Alice's eighteenth birthday party. *Come one and come all!! Bring your friends!!* it reads. *Free champagne! Free food!* Only someone as popular and as self-assured as Alice would issue such an invitation; anyone more ordinary would feel as if they were begging for guests. Why me? I wonder. I know of Alice, everyone knows of Alice, but I've never spoken to her before. She is one of those girls – beautiful, popular, impossible to miss.

I fold the invitation in half and nod. 'I'll try. It sounds like fun,' I lie.

Alice looks at me for a few seconds. Then she sighs

and plonks herself down next to me, so close that one of her knees rests heavily against mine.

'You will not.' She grins.

I feel my cheeks begin to colour. Even though my entire life can sometimes feel like a facade, a wall of secrets, I'm not good at lying. I look down at my lap. 'Probably not.'

'But I want you to come, Katherine,' she says. 'It'd really mean a lot to me.'

I'm surprised that Alice even knows my name but it's even more surprising – in fact, quite unbelievable – that she wants me to come to her party. I'm practically unknown at Drummond High and have no close friends. I come and go quietly, alone, and get on with my studies. I try to avoid bringing attention to myself. I do well enough, but my grades aren't exceptional. I play no sport, have joined no clubs. And though I know I can't do this for ever – live my entire life as a shadow – for now it suits. I'm hiding, I know that, I'm being a coward, but right now I need to be invisible, to be the kind of person who arouses no curiosity. That way they need never know who I really am, or what happened in Melbourne.

I close my book and start to pack away my lunch things.

'Wait.' Alice puts her hand on my knee. I look at her as coldly as I can and she withdraws it. 'I'm serious. I really do want you to come. And I think what you said to Dan last week was fantastic. I really wish I could think of things like that to say, but I never can. I'm just not quick enough. You know, I never would have thought about that woman's feelings like that. Not until I heard you tell Dan off. I mean, you were great, what you said was just so right, and you really showed him up to be the idiot that he is.'

I know immediately what Alice is referring to – the one and only time I'd let my guard down, momentarily forgotten myself. I don't often confront people any more. In fact it's something I try very hard to avoid in my day-to-day life. But the way Dan Johnson and his friends had behaved two weeks ago had disgusted me so much that I couldn't help myself. We had a guest speaker talking about career planning and university admissions. Admittedly, the speech was boring, we'd heard it all a billion times before and the woman talking was nervous and so she stuttered and hesitated and talked in confusing circles, only becoming worse as the crowd became noisier, more restless. Dan Johnson and his group of creepy friends had taken advantage of her. They were so cruel and deliberately disruptive that the woman ended up leaving in humiliated tears. When it was all over I stood behind Dan in the hallway and tapped him on the shoulder.

Dan turned round with a smug, self-satisfied look

on his face, clearly anticipating some kind of approbation for his behaviour.

'Did it ever occur to you,' I started, my voice surprisingly strong, fuelled by anger, 'how much you've hurt that woman? This is her life, Daniel, her career, her professional reputation. Your pathetic cry for attention means a whole lot of humiliation for her. I feel sorry for you, Daniel. You must be very sad and small inside to need to bring someone down like that, someone you don't even know.'

'You were amazing,' Alice continues. 'And to be honest I was totally surprised. I mean, I think everyone was. No one speaks to Dan like that.' She shakes her head. 'No one.'

Well I do. I think to myself. At least the real me does.

'It was admirable. Courageous.'

And it's that word that does it: 'Courageous'. I so want to be courageous. I so want the coward in me to be obliterated and smashed and destroyed that I can no longer resist her.

I stand up and hook my bag over my shoulder. 'Okay,' I say, surprising myself. 'Okay, I'll come.'

2

Alice insists that we get ready for the party together. She picks me up in her car, a battered old Volkswagen, shortly after lunch on the day of the party and takes me to her place. She lives alone, she tells me as she speeds along, weaving in and out of lanes much faster than any P-plater is officially allowed, in a one-bedroom flat in the inner city. I'm surprised by this, astonished really. I'd imagined that someone like Alice would live in a comfortable house in the suburbs with her devoted parents. I'd imagined her being spoiled, looked after, coddled (just as I used to be) and the fact that she lives alone makes her suddenly seem more interesting, more complicated than I've given her credit for. It's clear that Alice and I have more in common than I'd imagined.

I want to ask her a million questions – Where are her parents? How does she afford a flat? Is she ever afraid? Is she lonely? – but I keep quiet. I have secrets of my own and have learned that asking questions only puts me at risk of being interrogated myself. It is safer not to be too curious about others, safer not to ask.

Her flat is in a square, very ordinary-looking brick block. The stairwell is dark and uninviting, but when we get to her apartment, breathless after jogging up four flights of stairs, she opens the door to a room full of colour and warmth.

The walls are a deep burnt orange and are decorated with large, brightly painted abstract canvases. Two enormous, soft-looking couches are draped with burgundy fabric and covered with colourful, ethnic-looking cushions. Unlit candles cover every horizontal surface.

'*Voilà!* My humble abode.' Alice drags me inside and watches my face expectantly as I look round the room. 'What do you think? I did it all myself, you know. You should have seen it when I moved in, so boring and plain. It's amazing what a bit of colour can do to a room, though. A bit of creativity and some bright paint is all you really need.'

'This is so cool,' I say. And I can't help but feel a little envious. Alice's flat is so funky, so much younger, than the modern, minimalist apartment I live in.

'Really? You really like it?'

'Yes,' I laugh. 'I really do.'

'I'm so glad. I want you to like it as much as I do because I plan for us to spend a lot of time together. And I can see us spending a lot of time right here, in this room, talking and talking and talking, sharing our precious secrets deep into the night.'

I've heard that charming, powerful people have the knack of making you feel as though you're the only person in the world and now I know exactly what that means. I'm not quite sure what she does, or how she does it – another person would have come across as overly eager, obsequious even – but when Alice gives me her attention like that, I feel golden, warm with the certainty that I'm fully understood.

For a brief, insane moment, I imagine telling her my secret. I picture it all clearly. Me and Alice in this room; both a little tipsy, both giggly and happy and ever so slightly self-conscious with the feeling you have when you've made a new friend, a special friend; I put my hand on her knee so that she is still and quiet, so that she knows I'm about to say something important, and then I tell her. I tell her quickly, without pausing, without meeting her eyes. And when I've finished she is warm and forgiving and understanding, as I hoped she'd be. She embraces me. Everything is all right and I am lighter for having told. I am free.

But this is all just a dream. A crazy fantasy. I tell her nothing.

I'm wearing my usual costume of jeans and boots and shirt and I've brought some make-up with me to apply before we go to the party, but Alice insists that I wear a dress. Her wardrobe is bursting with them, in all sorts of colours and lengths and styles. There must be at least a hundred, and some still have tags. I wonder where she gets the money, how she affords so many clothes, and I'm tempted, once again, to ask.

'I have a bit of a clothing habit.' She grins.

'Really?' I joke. 'I would never have known.'

Alice reaches into the wardrobe and starts pulling out dresses. She tosses them on the bed. 'Here. Choose one. I haven't even worn most of these.' She holds up a blue one. 'You like?'

The dress is pretty but I've already spotted the one I'd really like to wear. It's red and patterned in paisley, a wrap-around dress with a tie-waist, made from some kind of stretch material. It looks like something my mother might have worn in the 1970s and would go nicely with the long boots I'm wearing.

Alice is watching me. She laughs and picks up the red dress. 'This one?'

I nod.

'It's gorgeous, isn't it?' She presses it against herself and looks in the mirror. 'Expensive too. It's a Pakbelle and Kanon. You have good taste.'

'It's beautiful. Why don't you wear it? It's still got the tag on it, you've never even worn it. You were probably saving it.'

'Nup. I'm wearing something else. Something special.' Alice holds it up in front of me. 'Try it on.'

The dress fits perfectly, and as I suspected, goes well with my boots. The red flatters my dark skin and hair, and I smile at Alice happily in the reflection of the mirror. I'm excited now, glad that I agreed to come.

Alice goes to the kitchen and takes a bottle from her fridge. It's champagne. It's pink.

'Yum,' she says, kissing the bottle. 'My one true love. And hey, as of yesterday, I'm actually legal.'

She opens the bottle, aiming the cork at the ceiling, and, without asking if I want any, pours us both a glass. She takes hers into the bathroom to shower and dress, and when she's gone I lift my glass and take a tiny sip. I haven't had alcohol since the night my family was destroyed. Not a drop. But then, I haven't enjoyed myself with a friend since then, either, and so I tip the glass up to my mouth again and let myself enjoy the feel of the bubbles against my lips, on my tongue. I let another small mouthful slide down my throat and imagine that I can feel the effect immediately, the alcohol rushing through my veins, making my lips tingle, my head light. The champagne is sweet and easy to drink, like a cordial, and I have to force myself not to swallow it all too quickly.

I savour each mouthful, enjoying the way my body relaxes more and more as I drink. When the glass is

13

empty I am happier, lighter, more carefree – *a normal seventeen-year-old* – and I plonk myself down on Alice's colourful sofa and giggle at nothing at all. And I'm still just sitting there, smiling, enjoying the comfortable heaviness of my body in the chair, when Alice returns to the room.

'Wow. Alice. You look . . .' I shrug, unable to find an adequate word. 'You look stunning!'

She lifts her arms and spins on her toes. 'Why thank you, Miss Katherine,' she says.

Alice is beautiful; strikingly beautiful. She is tall, with generous breasts and long, shapely legs and her face is a picture of perfection: her eyes a deep and glorious blue, her skin golden and luminous.

I'm not exactly ugly, but beside Alice I feel completely unremarkable.

While we're waiting for our taxi Alice takes our empty glasses to the kitchen and refills them with champagne. As I stand up to get my glass, my head spins a little. It's not an unpleasant feeling – in fact I feel easy and loose and relaxed. And this feeling, this light-headed happiness, this sense that the world is a benign and friendly place is suddenly very familiar and I realise just how much this feeling scares me. It's the trick alcohol plays with your mind – convincing you to let your guard down, to trust the world to look after you – but I know that this feeling of safety is only a dangerous illusion. Alcohol encourages you to take risks that you wouldn't usually; alcohol means you make stupid choices. And more than anyone, I know how devastating the consequences of a single bad choice can be. I live with them every day.

I accept the glass but I only pretend to sip on it, barely letting the liquid wet my lips, and when the taxi arrives I tip the rest of it down the sink.

Alice has hired the ballroom at the top of the Lion Hotel. It is huge and grand, with enormous timber windows and magnificent views of the city. There are white balloons, white tablecloths, a band. There are caterers polishing champagne glasses, and platters of expensive-looking finger food. And because it's a private party nobody asks us for ID when Alice gets us both a glass of champagne.

'This is fantastic.' I look at Alice curiously. 'Did your mum and dad do all this for you?'

'No.' Alice snorts dismissively. 'They wouldn't know how to host a barbecue, let alone something like this.'

'Do they live in Sydney?' I ask.

'Who?' She frowns.

'Your parents.'

'No. No they don't, thank God. They live up north.'

I wonder how Alice can afford to live in Sydney, how she pays her rent. I had assumed that her parents supported her, but it now seems unlikely.

'Anyway,' I say. 'It's very nice of you to put on a big party like this for your friends. I don't think I could ever be so generous. I'd rather spend the money on myself. A world trip or something cool like that.'

'Generous? You reckon?' Alice shrugs. 'Not really. I love parties. Particularly when they're all about me. I couldn't think of anything better. And, anyway, I'm not interested in going overseas.'

'You're not?'

'I don't know anyone there, nobody knows me. What would be the point?'

'Oh.' I laugh. I wonder if she's joking. 'I can think of a few good things about it. Swimming in the Mediterranean, seeing the Eiffel Tower, the Great Wall of China, the Statue of Liberty . . . and not knowing anyone. Imagine how liberating that must be.' I notice that Alice is looking at me sceptically, 'Are you seriously not interested?'

'Nah. I like it here. I like my friends. I love my life. Why would I want to leave?'

'Because—' I am going to tell her of my intense curiosity about the rest of the world, the fascination I have with different languages and ways of living, with the history of the human race, but we are interrupted by the arrival of her first guests.

'Alice, Alice!' they cry and she is suddenly surrounded by people, some I recognise from school, older people I've never seen before. Some are dressed very formally, in long dresses and suits and ties, others are dressed casually, in jeans and T-shirts, but they all have one thing in common: they all want a piece of Alice, a moment of her time; they want to be the focus of her attention, make her laugh. They all, without exception, want her to like them.

And Alice spreads herself round, makes all her guests feel welcome and comfortable, but for some reason it's me she chooses to spend most of the evening with. She keeps her arm linked through mine, drags me from group to group and involves me in every conversation. We dance together and gossip about what different people are wearing, who they are flirting with, who seems to be attracted to whom. I have a wonderful time. It's more fun than I've had in years. And while I'm there I don't think of my sister once, nor of my devastated parents. I dance and laugh and flirt. I forget, temporarily, about the night I realised the awful truth about myself. I forget all about the night I discovered the shameful, grubby coward at the core of my soul.

3

After Alice's party, people are noticeably more friendly to me at school. I get smiles and nods in the corridors from students I don't recognise, and a few people even say *Hey, Katherine!*, surprising me by knowing my name. And Alice finds me at lunchtime, sits down beside me and makes me laugh with stories about the other students, gossipy pieces of information about people I barely know. It's fun and I'm more than happy for the company, glad not to be alone any more.

I don't question why she would want to spend time with me. I used to be popular, after all, and am used to being liked. Alice says she wants to be my friend, she seems to enjoy my company, she listens, intently, to everything I have to say. So I am grateful and flattered and pleased. And, for the first time since Rachel died, I feel something resembling happiness.

On the Thursday following her party I call Alice and invite her over for Saturday night. I live with Aunt

Vivien, my father's sister. I like living with Vivien, she's warm and easy-going and I'm grateful that I'm no longer in Melbourne, that I can finish high school where nobody has heard of Rachel or the Boydell sisters. I spend a lot of time alone because Vivien goes on so many business trips and if she's free on weekends she goes away with friends. She's always encouraging me to invite people to the apartment and clearly thinks it strange that I never socialise, but I've grown used to my own company, and enjoy being able to choose exactly what to eat, what to watch, what music I listen to.

'I'll make dinner,' I say.

'Awesome,' Alice says. 'Hope you're a good cook.'

'I am. It's one of my many secret talents.'

'Secrets, hmm?' Alice is quiet for a minute. 'Have a lot of them, do you?'

I laugh, as if the very idea is absurd.

I spend Saturday at the markets buying food. I used to cook a lot before Rachel died, when we were still a family, and so I know what I'm doing and what I'll need. I buy all the ingredients – chicken thighs, cardamom pods, yogurt, cumin, ground coriander, basmati rice – to cook one of my favourite curries. That way I can prepare it all early, before Alice arrives, and when she gets there I can let it simmer and grow more delicious as we talk.

I've become so used to keeping everything guarded

and private, so reluctant to let anyone close, that I'm surprised to realise how much I'm looking forward to Alice's company. I don't know when or how the idea of friendship and intimacy became so appealing, but all of a sudden the thought of having fun and getting to know someone new is quite irresistible. And although I'm still afraid of revealing too much, still conscious that friendship can be risky, I can't quell this feeling of excited anticipation.

I get home, prepare the curry, then shower and dress. I have an hour before Alice arrives so I call my parents. Mum and Dad and I all left Melbourne about a year ago. Too many people knew us there, too many people knew what had happened to Rachel. It was impossible to cope with the pitying stares, the curious looks and the conspicuous whispering wherever we went. I moved in with Vivien so that I could finish high school at Drummond, one of the largest high schools in New South Wales, a place so big that I could keep to myself, remain anonymous. My parents bought a house a couple of hours north, in Newcastle, near the beach. They wanted me to go with them, of course, and argued that I was too young to be leaving home. But I'd started to find their sadness overwhelming, their very presence suffocating, and so I convinced them that Drummond was the perfect school, that my very happiness depended on it, and they eventually relented.

'Boydell residence.' My mother answers the phone. I changed my last name when I moved and now go by my grandmother's maiden name, Patterson. It was surprisingly easy to cast off my old name – so easy, at least on paper, to become a new person. I miss my old name. But it goes with the old me, the happy, carefree, sociable me. Katherine suits the new, quieter version. Katie Boydell is no more. Rachel and Katie Boydell, the infamous Boydell sisters – both are gone.

'Mum.'

'Sweetheart. I was just about to call you. Daddy and I were talking about your car.'

'Oh?'

'Yes. Now don't argue, darling, please. But we've decided to get you a new one. They're much safer these days, what with airbags and the like. We've got the money and it just feels ridiculous to let you drive around in that old bomb.'

'It's only eight years old, Mum.' I drive her old Volvo, which is already a very new and conservative car for someone my age.

She continues as if I haven't spoken. 'And we've found this lovely Peugeot. It's quite compact, it's a darling car, really, but best of all it scored remarkably well on all the safety tests. It'll be perfect for you in the city.'

There's little point arguing. I don't want to upset her, or make a fuss. Since Rachel's death my parents have been quite obsessed with my safety, with doing as much as is humanly possible to make sure that I stay alive, and I have no choice but to accept their gifts, their concern.

'Sounds great, Mum,' I say. 'Thanks.'

'How's school going? Have your grades picked up at all?'

'Yes,' I lie. 'I'm doing much better.'

'I've been reading about the medicine course at Newcastle University. It's really quite progressive, you know, and has a reputation that is on a par with Sydney's. In fact it really seems to be *the* place to do medicine these days. And there are a lot of outstanding doctors teaching there. It's something I'd like you to consider, darling. For me. You could live with us, and you know how pleased Daddy would be if you did that, and you could really concentrate on your studies without worrying about rent or bills or food. We could take care of you, make it all easier.'

'I don't know, Mum, I don't know. I'm enjoying English right now, and History actually, the reading . . . Science isn't . . . anyway, I thought I might do Arts or something. And, Mum, I really like living in Sydney.'

'Oh, of course, you do. Vivien's place is perfect and I know she'd be more than pleased to have you stay on there. And an Arts degree is a wonderful beginning to your education. But it really is only a beginning, darling. You will need to get back on track. Eventually. When you're ready.'

Back on track. When you're ready. This is as close as Mum can get to mentioning what happened to Rachel, acknowledging our loss, the life we had before she died. I was in Year 10 and doing very well – the top of my year. I'd hoped to do well enough in Year 12 to eventually study medicine at university. Obstetrics had been my ultimate goal; I had everything planned. But when Rachel died, my plans fell apart, things went completely off track. The track itself was ripped from beneath me, torn from the ground, obliterated.

And I discovered, during that horrific time, that science and mathematics, all that concrete stuff that I used to love so much, were completely useless when it came to understanding grief, dealing with guilt.

And now, I doubt that I'll ever be ready to get back on track. I'm on another track now, just slowly, slowly gaining some momentum, and I don't think I can, or want to, make the sideways leap off.

'I'll think about it.'

'Good. And I'll post you some of these brochures.' She laughs then, but I hear the little catch in her throat, the sign that this conversation has made her want to cry. 'I've collected quite a few of them.'

I touch the mouthpiece of the phone, as if by doing

so I can give her some comfort. And yet there is no comfort to be given. Her life is lived only in degrees of pain.

'I bet you have,' I say, as warmly as I can.

'Oh.' Her voice is once again crisp, businesslike, all emotion under control. 'Listen to me hogging the conversation like this. I bet you want to speak to Daddy? He's not here, darling, but I can get him to call you later.'

'That's okay. I'm having a friend to dinner, actually. I might call tomorrow.'

'Oh, I'm so glad you're having some fun.' I hear that catch in her voice again, then a quick cough to bring her voice back under control. 'Have a lovely evening. I'll tell Daddy to call you tomorrow. Don't you call. It's our turn to pay.'

When I hang up I feel flat, all excitement for the evening ahead dissipated. I regret having made the call. It hasn't made me happy – and I'm certain that it has only made Mum more miserable. It's always this way with Mum nowadays. She's always talking, always planning, always full of ideas and pragmatic conversation. It's as if she can't bear to be quiet or to allow herself a moment's silence. This way she gives herself no space to remember, no room to think about what she's lost. It also prevents the person she's speaking to from getting a word in, from talking about something she would rather not, from mentioning Rachel.

The modern way to grieve, the supposedly correct way, is to talk about it, to let yourself cry and scream and wail. My counsellor said we must talk. And I tried, during that long, long first year after Rachel was killed, to talk about what happened, to *express* my sadness, to *verbalise* our loss, to *own* my despair. But Dad refused to listen and Mum would cut me off, change the subject, and if I pushed it she would start to cry and leave the room.

I gave up. I felt as if I was torturing her and I became thoroughly sick of myself, of my neediness. In talking about it I'd been seeking absolution, reassurance that Mum and Dad didn't blame me for what happened. But I was asking the impossible, I soon realised. Of course they blamed me – for my cowardice, for my escape, for my having lived. Of course, if one of their daughters had to die, it should have been me.

And I no longer believe that there is any better way to cope with bereavement. There is just a shitload of pain to carry – a permanent and dreadful burden – and talking about it doesn't take that load away or make it any lighter. Rachel died in the most horrific way imaginable. Words are useless against the harsh truth of that. Rachel is dead. She is gone for ever and we will never again see her lovely face, never again hear her music. She is dead.

Why we should need to wallow in this reality, go over it again and again, poke and prod and examine it until our eyes are bleeding, our hearts crushed with the horror and unbelievable sadness of it, is beyond me. It cannot possibly help. Nothing can help. If Mum needs to be stoic, to pretend that she is fine, to hide her despair behind a transparent veil of crisp efficiency and businesslike conversation, then that's okay by me. It seems as good a way to go on with her diminished life as any.

I press my forefinger into the small circular scar above my knee. It's the only physical evidence I have of the night Rachel was killed, the only physical injury I suffered. The wrong girl died that dreadful day in Melbourne. And though I can't actually wish that I'd died instead of Rachel – I am nowhere near brave enough to be a martyr – I am fully conscious that the better sister died.

4

Rachel walked onto the stage and the crowd grew immediately silent. She looked beautiful, tall and striking; her red velvet dress – which I knew Mum and Dad had paid a small fortune for – accentuated her height and stature. She was only fourteen but on stage she could have passed for a woman in her twenties.

Mum squeezed my hand excitedly and I turned sideways to smile at her. Oblivious, she stared up at Rachel on the stage, her lips pursed in the funny expression she made when she was trying hard not to break into an enormous smile, her eyes wet with happy, devoted tears. On the other side of her, Dad turned to catch Mum's eye, but met mine instead; we smiled at each other – amused at Mum's expression – bursting, both of us, with familial pride.

Rachel sat at the piano with the skirt of her dress draped elegantly over her legs and began playing. She started the recital with a Mozart sonata – a pretty, delicate piece, with a melody so familiar to me that I could anticipate every note, every *fortissimo* and *crescendo*. And I watched her, mesmerised as I always was by the music she created, but also by the transformation that took place when she performed. On stage all of Rachel's shyness and awkwardness disappeared. On stage she was majestic and commanding, so taken up with the performance and the music that she would forget herself. When she was playing it was impossible to imagine that she could be shy and uncertain, that she was still just a girl.

During the entire recital, which lasted over an hour, Mum didn't take her eyes from Rachel for a second. Whenever Mum listened to Rachel play she seemed to lose herself, become unaware of time and place and whoever she happened to be with, and go into an almost trance-like state.

I too played the piano. Technically I was quite accomplished, having passed the exam for seventh grade a year earlier, and I often won at school competitions and local eisteddfods. But Rachel was the one with real talent, and had been offered three different international scholarships. Whether she should accept a place in Berlin, London or Boston for study – to pursue her dream of becoming a concert pianist – had been the main topic of conversation at our house for weeks. For me the piano was just an enjoyable hobby and I had no desire to practise all day, every day. But the piano was Rachel's great love, her passion, and she worked at it tirelessly.

Rachel was eighteen months younger than me, and despite what people say about the eldest child being the high achiever, the opposite was true in our family. Rachel was driven and ambitious. I was far more interested in boys and parties and in hanging out with friends than I was in achieving any academic or musical brilliance.

Mum and Dad talked about Rachel's future as a concert pianist endlessly – they were devoted to her career. I know that people were sometimes shocked by what could seem like favouritism on Mum and Dad's part, their doting idolisation of Rachel and apparent lesser interest in me. I'm sure people even felt sorry for me in the mistaken belief that I must feel neglected. But I didn't feel that way; I didn't have to – Rachel and I always wanted such very different things. I was more than happy for Rachel to be the brilliant sister. I knew the hard work she put into being a prodigy, and it didn't appeal. I enjoyed my friends and my social life far too much. Rachel might have been a genius but I had a lot more fun – and despite what it might have seemed like to an outsider, I always felt that I had the better deal.

Rachel was different. She didn't seem to need friends

the way most people do. That wasn't to say she was cold, or didn't love people, because she wasn't and she did. She loved deeply and generously and was ferociously loyal to those she cared about. But she was shy; social events only made her become awkward and uncomfortable and she was dreadful at making smalltalk. She could be so quiet and self-contained that, to those who didn't know her well, she could seem aloof or indifferent. But when you did manage to draw her into conversation, she would surprise you with how much she had actually noticed of what was going on. She had a gentle and compassionate wisdom that belied her age and almost everyone who made the effort to get to know her grew to admire her. She was the only person I have ever met who was completely without envy, greed or malice; the only person I would ever compare to an angel.

And so, regardless of what the papers said when she was killed – all that painful speculation and misguided conjecture about our relationship – I never lost sight of how I really felt. I worshipped Rachel, both while she was alive and after her death. I was, and always will be, her number one fan.

5

Alice turns up for dinner on time and is so cheerful and full of energy that as soon as she walks inside and starts talking I feel better.

'My God,' she says in a low voice, looking round Vivien's apartment. 'This is totally lush. Your parents must be, like, super-trendy.'

'No.' I shake my head. 'No. This isn't my mum and dad's place. I live with my aunt. She's away for the weekend.'

'So it's just us?'

I nod and Alice jumps into the air and whoops with joy.

'Yay. God, Katherine, I'm so glad. I thought your mum and dad were here. I thought this was like some big "Come and meet my parents" deal.' She rolls her eyes. 'As if we were getting married or something. Thank *God*.' She kicks her shoes off and starts strolling round the room, looking at things, taking in the view.

31

I'm all ready to explain to Alice *why* I live with my aunt instead of my parents, something about the reputation and quality of Drummond High compared with the schools in Newcastle, which isn't actually untrue. But she's far more interested in the actual apartment itself than in how or why I live there.

'It must be fantastic to live in such style,' she says, wandering down the hall, peeking into rooms. Her voice is loud and echoes down the hallway as she shouts. 'Have you ever had any parties here? I bet you haven't, have you? Let's have one. This'd be the most awesome place. I know heaps of people we could invite— Ooh,' she exclaims suddenly. 'Look at this!' And she reaches up into Vivien's shelf and pulls down a fancy-looking bottle. 'Irish whiskey. Yum. I love it. Let's have some.'

'It's not mine,' I say. 'It's Vivien's.'

'Doesn't matter. We'll replace it. Your aunt won't notice.' And she brings the bottle into the kitchen, finds the glassware, and pours a generous serve into two glasses. 'Got any Coke?'

'Sorry.' I shake my head.

'Water will do.' She goes to the tap and fills the glasses with water and hands one to me. I take a tiny sip. The whiskey smells foul and tastes even worse – bitter and dry and very strong – and I know I won't be able to finish it.

Drinking alcohol wasn't a part of my plan for the

evening, I hadn't even considered it. But Alice's eagerness to drink makes me realise how out of touch I really am. Not everyone is as terrified of the world as I am – not everyone has been burned.

We take our glasses out onto the verandah and look over the view of the city. It's mostly Alice who talks, but I'm happy just to listen and enjoy her energy, her *joie de vivre*. And I'm busy remembering what it's like to have fun with someone my own age, busy reacquainting myself with a different version of me – a younger, happier version – the girl who took it for granted that life could be like this, that it should be like this: free and light and full of joy.

'Hello, world!' Alice leans over the verandah and shouts, her voice echoing around us. 'Hello, world!'

She turns back to me and leans against the railing, tilts her head towards the inside. 'When I'm older I'm going to have a place just like this. Only it's going to be even bigger. Fancier. All my friends will be able to come and stay. And I'm going to have lots of help, too.' She puts her nose in the air and talks in an affected voice. 'I'm going to have staff, *dahlink*. Housekeepers. Personal trainers. Butlers. The lot. I'll have someone who comes round every night just to pour champagne.'

'Of course,' I say. 'Otherwise you might break a fingernail. Or get sticky.'

'*Quelle horreur!*' She opens her eyes wide with

feigned alarm and looks down at her hands. 'There is such danger inherent in being occupied with the mundane. I aim to rise above it.'

I laugh. 'You'll need a personal barista, too. To make your coffee in the mornings.'

'And a chef to cook my food.'

'Your very own massage therapist.'

'A hairdresser.'

'A stylist to choose your clothes.'

'A gardener.'

'A chauffeur.'

'Yeah.' She sits down in the seat next to me and sighs dreamily. 'I'll never have to do anything. I won't get caught up in complaining about housework all day every day like my mother. I just won't do any. I won't even have to run my own bath.'

'What if you get sick of it? All those people round you all the time. You might start craving some time alone.'

'Nah,' she says. 'Why would I? Being alone is boring. I hate being alone. Hate it. My life isn't going to be serious and boring. It's going to be fun. A party. A massive, never-ending, lifelong party.'

I think, *Alice is just the type of person I need to be with – she lives for the present and, very conveniently, has an amazing lack of curiosity about the past.*

When Alice has finished several glasses of whiskey –

and I'm still sipping slowly, safely, on my first – she announces that she's starving and we go inside. Alice pours herself another drink and offers me one but I hold up my still-full glass and shake my head. Alice frowns.

'You don't like it?'

'It's all right, I guess.' I smile and take a tiny sip and try not to grimace. I could explain my fear of alcohol, use it as an excuse, but I would only end up sounding like a nagging parent, some kind of freakish puritan.

Alice stares at me for a moment, as if trying to work something out, but then she puts the bottle down and shrugs.

'More for me, then,' she says.

We serve up the curry and take our overflowing plates to the kitchen table. Alice's enthusiasm for the food is gratifying.

'Delicious!' she says, shaking her head in disbelief. 'You're amazing. You could open your own Indian restaurant.'

I demur, but I'm flattered and can't help but smile. My mood has improved dramatically. The feeling of gloom that I had after talking to my mother has completely disappeared.

'So.' Alice taps her plate with the back of her fork. 'What shall we do after this?'

'We could play a game. I've got Scrabble. And Trivial Pursuit.'

Alice shakes her head. 'Boring. I can't concentrate on Scrabble for more than a second. Too much like schoolwork. What about Pictionary or charades? Something fun.'

'But we need more people for those games.'

Alice is quiet for a minute, thoughtful, then she looks at me and smiles. 'I know someone who could come over. Entertain us a bit.'

'Really?' I force myself to smile, but I'm disappointed. I've been enjoying myself immensely and don't think we need any entertaining. The fact that Alice wants to invite someone else over makes me feel dull. 'At this time of night?'

'It's nine o'clock on a Saturday! The nightclubs haven't even opened yet.'

I shrug. 'Who?'

'Robbie.'

'And?'

'And what?'

'Who's Robbie?'

'He's a friend of mine. He works as a waiter in a really posh restaurant. He's got the night off. He's a total scream. You'll love him.'

Alice takes out her mobile phone and starts to dial before I get the chance to ask any more questions. I listen to her invite him over – her voice confident and deep and flirtatious – and wonder if she has ever felt shy or uncertain. It's difficult to imagine.

'He'll be here soon.' She stands up and stretches, rubs her belly contentedly. 'This was such a good idea, Katie. Awesome food, good company, and so much more fun to come.'

'Katherine,' I say. 'I'm not Katie. I'm Katherine.'

Alice tips her head to the side, looks at me quizzically. 'But you look like a Katie. You really do. You weren't always called Katherine, were you? When you were younger? Such a big, mature name for a little girl. And Katie is cute. Fun. It suits you.'

'No,' I say. 'I'm Katherine. Just Katherine.' I try to keep my voice light and friendly but it comes out sounding harsh, an overreaction. I feel like one of those uptight, precious people. I never used to care what people called me – Kat, Katie, Kathy, Kate, I enjoyed them all – but I can't stand any of the shortened versions of my name any more. That abbreviated, easy-going girl is gone. I am Katherine Patterson now, through and through.

A small frown crosses Alice's brow and she stares at me, almost coldly, but in a moment her face clears, she shrugs and smiles and nods. 'Sure. Katherine is more distinguished anyway. Like that old actress, whatsername, you know, they made a movie . . . Katharine Hepburn. And a longer name suits your air of mystery better.'

'Air of mystery?' I snort, glad to have an excuse to

37

laugh the uncomfortable exchange off. 'I don't think so.'

'Oh but you have.' Alice leans forward. 'Everybody at school wonders about you. So pretty and smart. So quiet and private and self-contained, but not because you're shy or scared or anything like that. It's as if you just don't want to get involved. As if you've, oh, I don't know, got some kind of big, dark secret and you don't want to make friends with anyone in case they find out. You have *everyone* intrigued and intimidated. Some people even think you're a snob.'

'A snob? Really? Well they're wrong. I'm not.' I stand up and start clearing away the table, avoiding Alice's eye. The conversation is starting to make me uncomfortable – getting too close to the truth. I do have a secret. A big, dark secret, as Alice put it. And though I'm not a snob, it's true that I don't want to participate and I have avoided making friends, for exactly that reason. Clearly I haven't been as inconspicuous as I'd hoped.

But Alice laughs. 'Hey, don't be upset. Come on. I'm only teasing. It's cool to be mysterious like that. I like it. You're aloof. And I'm probably just jealous. I wish I was a bit more like that myself.' She puts her hand on her chest and closes her eyes. 'A mysterious woman with a tragic past.'

I'm amazed at how close Alice has come to hitting

on the truth. I feel exposed and uncomfortable and have to fight an urge to run away and hide. Keep my secret safe. I'm afraid that Alice is going to continue with this conversation, interrogate me until she knows everything, but instead she shrugs, looks round the room and shakes her head.

'God, this flat is awesome. We absolutely *have* to organise a party.' She stands and takes the plates from my hands. 'You cooked. I'll clean up. Sit down. Have another . . .' she looks at my glass and shakes her head, 'milli-sip or two of your drink.'

Alice fills the sink with hot soapy water, starts washing, then comes back to the table to chat some more, tell me another story. There is a knock on the door.

'It's Robbie!' Alice claps her hands together happily and rushes down the hallway.

I hear her greet someone, giggle and exclaim. I hear the deep rumble of his response. And then he is in the kitchen.

He is tall and blond and very good-looking in a sporty, wholesome kind of way. He grins at me and holds out his hand.

'Katherine. Hi. I'm Robbie.'

'Hi.'

His handshake is firm and warm and dry. His smile is open and lovely and for the first time in what feels like a hundred years I feel a mild but unmistakable pull of attraction. I feel myself start to blush. I turn away and occupy myself with the dishes, most of which are still piled messily beside the sink.

'I'll just finish these. It'll only take a minute.'

'No. No.' Alice takes me by the shoulders and pulls me away. 'I'll do them later. Promise. Let's just have some fun.'

There is a lot of curry left over and Alice insists that Robbie try some.

'Is that okay?' He looks at me apologetically as she serves him up an enormous plateful.

'It's fine. Honest,' I say, and I mean it. I made far too much. Enough for six.

Alice asks Robbie if he'd like to 'partake of an alcoholic beverage', but he shakes his head, says something about soccer training, and pours himself a glass of water instead. He watches Alice pour herself another drink.

'Whiskey?' He says. 'That's a bit hard-core, isn't it?'

'Yep.' She winks suggestively. 'Hard-core. Just like me.'

The three of us go back outside onto the verandah and Robbie tucks into his food enthusiastically. I feel a little shy with him at first but he is so friendly and so nice about my cooking, and his conversation is so amusing, that it doesn't take long for me to warm to him. Robbie is twenty and he works at some up-market restaurant as a waiter, and in no time at all I'm laughing freely at his stories about all the obnoxious customers he has to deal with.

When it gets too cold we move inside and sit around on the floor in the lounge room. All the whiskey Alice has drunk is starting to show. Her cheeks are flushed and her eyes bloodshot. Her voice is noticeably slurred and she is speaking loudly, continually interrupting Robbie to finish his stories for him. He doesn't seem to mind, though, just smiles indulgently when she interrupts and lets her talk.

He loves her, I conclude to myself. *The way he looks at her, the way he was available on such short notice so late on a Saturday night. He's completely in love with her.*

Alice gets up and goes to the sideboard to look through Vivien's CD collection.

'My God!' she says. 'I should have brought my iPod. This is all so old. So 1980s!' But she eventually chooses a Prince album and slides the disk into the player.

'My mum loves this song,' Alice says. 'She dances to it all the time. You should see her dance, Katherine. She's unbelievable. She looks like some kind of movie star. She just looks so amazingly beautiful when she dances.' And she turns the volume up and starts swinging her hips seductively from side to side.

Alice is smiling, her eyes closed, and I can't help but wonder at this unexpected admission of admiration and affection for her mother. The few times I've heard Alice talk about her parents in the past, she has been dismissive, scornful, almost as if she hated them.

Robbie and I both stay seated and watch Alice dance. She's a good dancer, smooth and sexy, and Robbie stares up at her, smiling. He looks completely besotted and I think to myself how nice it would be to be loved like that, how exciting to have someone interested in me romantically. And for the first time since Rachel died, since Will, I allow myself to imagine that one day I might have someone like Robbie to love. Someone beautiful and kind and smart. Someone who will love me too – despite who I am and what I've done.

6

When the first song finishes, another comes on, one with a faster beat, and Robbie jumps up, reaches his hand out towards me and pulls me up. And so we dance, the three of us loose and easy with one another. We dance close, our bodies touching, our hips and thighs bumping, our arms round each other. Robbie puts his arms round Alice. He kisses her and I watch them, their bodies pressed tight together. They are both so beautiful, they go together perfectly. Alice notices me watching and smiles, then whispers into Robbie's ear. Robbie lets Alice go and wraps his arms round me, hugs me tight, then he puts his hands on my cheeks, bends down and presses his lips against mine. It's a chaste kiss, almost brotherly, but it's thrilling nonetheless. Alice smiles, nudges me, giggles. And then the three of us are hugging and laughing and I am deliriously happy. I feel liked. I feel attractive. I feel *young* again.

And when the small voice starts up in my head – the voice that tells me I don't deserve happiness, that I shouldn't take what Rachel can't have – I refuse to listen. I decide, at least for tonight, to ignore the side of myself that disapproves of everything that I want. I'm giddy and carefree. I am Katie Boydell. Just for one night. Young and happy and impetuous. *Katie*. Fun and adventurous. *Katie*. Just for this one evening, Katherine is gone and I can be me.

So we giggle and dance and hug to song after song until our faces are shiny with sweat and we become thirsty and need to go to the kitchen for water. When we've finished dancing we pull the cushions from the sofa and set up a makeshift bed of pillows and blankets and collapse on the floor. We don't stop talking until after 3 a.m. – and our sleep is the sleep of the exhausted, heavy and deep and still, the three of us close, legs entwined, faces down.

When I wake, Alice is curled up next to me. She is on her side in a foetal position, her hands clenched in fists in front of her face. She looks like a sleeping angel getting ready to fight, a strangely innocent-looking boxer. She is breathing quickly and shallowly and I can hear a little high-pitched squeak from her nose as the air rushes in and out. Her eyelashes flutter and I can see her eyeballs roll beneath her lids. REM sleep. Dreams.

I extricate myself slowly and as quietly as I can. I'm

still dressed in my skirt and T-shirt. I go straight to the bathroom and take my clothes off and get into the shower.

When I'm finished I get dressed and go to the kitchen.

Robbie is at the sink, washing dishes, and has almost finished the pile left over from the night before – the mess Alice promised to clean up.

'Hey,' I say. 'Thanks. But you shouldn't be doing that.'

'Good morning.' He looks up and grins, and despite his messed-up hair and bloodshot eyes, he still looks incredible. 'Don't worry about it. I don't mind washing up. Actually, I kinda like it. I remember being a kid and watching Mum do it. I always thought it looked like fun. All the bubbles. The water.' He lifts a bubble on the palm of his hand, blows it off so that it falls back into the bowl 'How are you feeling? Tired? We only had about four hours' sleep.'

'Yeah, I know. I *am* a bit shattered. How about you?'

'Excellent. All ready for a day of soccer training and a long night serving arseholes at the restaurant.'

'You poor thing. You should go back to bed. Get some more sleep.'

'Nah.' He shrugs. 'I'm used to it. You want a cuppa? I put the kettle on.'

'I'd love one. But I'll make it. I'm very fussy about my tea.'

45

'Oh?'

'I only drink the proper stuff, you know, the whole tea leaf and teapot thing. People think I'm crazy. My fussiness annoys everyone. It's always easier if I just make it myself.'

'That's cool. I like the good stuff best too. It has a much nicer taste. My mum hated teabags. She used to only drink the real deal as well.'

'Used to?'

'Before she died.' He looks down at his hands, which are immersed in the water. 'Just over a year ago.'

'Oh, Robbie, I'm so sorry. I didn't know.'

'No,' he says. 'Of course you didn't.'

I could leave it at that, change the subject and talk about something happier, something less intense, but I remember the way people used to do that when Rachel died. I remember how bizarre and hurtful it felt to have the subject of her death brushed off and discarded as if it had no more importance than a conversation about the weather. So I don't change the subject.

'You must really miss her?'

'Yeah.' He looks up and his eyes are wet with tears. He smiles sadly. 'Yeah, I do.'

'And your father? How's he going?'

'He's okay, I think. But it's hard to know for sure, isn't it? I mean I don't want to just come right out and ask.'

'Why not?'

'Because what if he's not okay? What then? What can I do about it anyway?'

I know better than to offer up meaningless platitudes, to tell the lie that words can heal. Because I know that they don't, they can't. Words are just words, collections of sounds that are powerless against the force of real pain, real suffering.

'Nothing,' I say. 'You can't do anything. Not really.'

'Exactly. And if you tell each other the truth, how sad you feel, then you're only going to feel worse because then you have to worry about the suffering of the other poor bugger, as well as deal with your own crap.'

'Yeah.' I shrug. 'It's probably better if you just deal with your misery your own way. And eventually, hopefully, it becomes less intense. Less at the front of your mind every day.'

Robbie nods his agreement. And then we're silent for a minute. I wait, giving Robbie the choice of continuing the conversation or changing the subject. His next words come out quickly, in a breathless rush. 'I was about to move out of home when she got really sick, but I stayed because I wanted to help out and because I wanted to be with her, you know, spend as much time with her as possible before she died . . . because we knew by then that she was definitely going to die, just a matter of when. But that was over two years ago. And I'm still there. I'm twenty years old and still living at home because I feel too sorry for my old man to move out. But the really stupid thing is, I don't even know if he actually wants me there. He probably wishes I'd just move the hell out so he could be alone, so he could wallow in peace. He probably thinks I want *his* company. It's just . . . well . . . it's just all screwed up, basically.'

'So your dad's still pretty sad, then?'

'Normally he's okay. Or at least he *acts* okay. Normally he's strong and really keen to get on with things, and make sure that the house is happy, clean, full of food, all that stuff. You know, we're always having friends over, pizza and beer nights, as if everything's jolly, as if life couldn't be better without a woman in the house. But then one night, about a week ago, I was heading to his room, I was gonna tell him something. And I just stopped for a minute outside his door, dunno why, maybe . . . anyway . . . I stopped and I heard him crying. Really crying, you know, that heartbreaking, noisy, sobbing kind of stuff. It was bloody horrible. I mean, sure, I know he really loved Mum, I know he misses her, but he sounded so . . . so helpless. Like a child. As if he had no control of himself. As if all this happiness and crap was just bullshit. Just a front for my sake. And I didn't know what to do so I just stood there for a second wishing he'd stop, that he'd shut the hell up. It was weird. The worst thing was that I felt no sympathy, I just hated him for it, for letting me hear that, for not keeping up the pretence that he was okay.'

'I know what you mean. Seeing your parents like that really makes you grow up, it makes you realise that the world's just a big scary place that they have no control over. And if they can hurt so much, if they can't control things, what hope is there for you?' The words are out before I realise what I'm saying, what I'm revealing.

'Exactly.' Robbie looks at me, suddenly alarmed. 'Shit. Your mum hasn't died or anything, has she?'

'Oh no.' I shake my head and laugh, as if the idea that I'm familiar with death is absurd. 'She's well and truly alive. I've just thought about this kind of thing a bit. And I've read some of my dad's books on bereavement and stuff . . . Morbid, I am. Crazy.'

'Well, you really nailed the feeling. Most people freak out when I say that my mum died. Most people get all upset or embarrassed and change the subject. And my counsellor's useless. She always asks me what I'm feeling and how I feel about what I'm feeling. And then she tells me that my feelings are perfectly valid while all the time there's this underlying message that I should really try to feel something completely different. I'd get as much insight talking to a roll of toilet paper.'

I'm about to reply when Alice calls out from the other room.

'Good morning?' she says, her voice raspy and deep from the late night. 'Peoples? Where are you? I'm getting very lonely in here.'

Robbie and I smile at each other and shrug, let the conversation end. We take the teapot and the milk, the sugar and the cups and go into the lounge room to join Alice.

7

I pick Sarah up earlier than usual from her child-care centre. I watch her through the window for a moment before she sees me, and am pleased to see that she looks perfectly happy. She's playing with a heap of bright green Play-Doh, alone, completely absorbed with patting and pounding it into a goopy, colourful mess. She's a solitary little girl, uncomfortable with people – just as Rachel used to be – and though I'm quite glad that she's cautious I also worry that this will make things difficult for her. After all, she has to mix with people, whether she wants to or not.

It's funny because I never saw Rachel's shyness as any kind of disadvantage. In fact, it was a trait that I found endearing. But for my daughter I want life to be perfect. I want everyone to love her. I want everything to be as easy and happy and smooth as possible.

People tell me that I'm over-protective, that I need to let Sarah go, give her space to make her own way in the world, but I don't believe there is any such thing as over-protecting your loved ones. I want to grab these people by the arm and shout *There is danger everywhere, you fools! You think you're safe, you think people are trustworthy? Nice? Open your eyes and look around!* But they would only think I was mad. They are naïve, oblivious, unaware that the world is full of people who wish you ill, and I'm amazed that they can be so blind.

Being a mother is difficult, contradictory, impossible. I want Sarah to be happy, to make friends, to laugh and feel joyful. I don't want her to be paralysed by fear and anxiety. But I also want her to be careful. To go into this dangerous world with her eyes wide open.

When I open the door and enter the playroom I stand behind her and wait for her to sense my presence and turn round. I love the moment when she first sees me, the look of pure delight that crosses her face, the way she'll forget, immediately, whatever it was she was doing, and rush into my arms. She only comes to child care two afternoons a week, Wednesday and Friday – painfully long, boring afternoons for me – and I'm always relieved when I pick her up on Friday afternoon, glad that another week is over, that we can be together for four straight days before it's time to bring her back.

I've come to collect her early today for our annual trip away. I'm taking her to Jindabyne, to the snow, and I'm as excited as a child at the prospect of Sarah's certain delight when she sees it. We can make a snowman, have snowfights, perhaps ride a toboggan. We can drink hot chocolate by the fire and enjoy the cold, enjoy also a little time on our own, away from my parents.

'Mummy!' she cries when she sees me. She stands up and rushes over, knocking her stool down in her haste, and wraps her arms round my neck. 'Are we ready to go?'

'I am. How about you?'

'Did you pack my things?'

'Yep.'

'My Sally-bear?'

'Of course.'

'But what about Nana and Pop?' She knows how much my parents depend on her, and it saddens me that at her age she already worries about them.

'They're going to have great fun this weekend too. They've got friends coming to dinner and everything.'

Her face brightens. 'Are they 'cited?'

'Very. Almost as excited as us.'

I bend over and scoop her up, collect her bags, sign her out and go to the car. The trip out of Sydney is quick and trouble-free, we're too early for the Friday-night rush hour. Sarah is quiet in the car. She sits staring out of the window, thumb in mouth, slumped and relaxed, trance-like. She has always been like this in a car, and driving was always the best way, when she was a small baby, to get her to sleep or to stop her from crying.

I drive carefully on the highway, keeping my car as far from others as I possibly can, taking heed of my father's lessons on defensive driving. Dad tried to dissuade me from taking this trip. *The roads will be terrible*, he said, *all the worst drivers, the bloody-idiot-maniacs, head down there on the weekends. And you're not used to driving in those conditions.* He spoke curtly. *Don't be such a fool.* But I noticed the tears in his eyes, the way his hands shook.

I understand his terror – people are killed on the roads every day. One small error, a mistake in judgement, a lapse in concentration – any of these could put us in the way of the many hurtling eighteen-wheelers that crowd this highway. Two more lives gone in an instant. An already-shattered family annihilated. My father knows, better than most, that the unthinkable happens. He knows that nightmares can and do come true.

So it's for his sake that I keep my eyes glued to the road, my hands firmly on the steering wheel, my mind alert. It's my father's fear that keeps me from pushing down on the accelerator as hard as I can.

8

'No no no no no. Not Coffs Harbour. No way.' Alice
shakes her head. 'It's so awful there, full of fat people.
And no good restaurants.'

'Full of fat people?' Robbie shakes his head. 'You can
be such a bitch sometimes, Alice.'

'It's just the truth. It's a hole. And if you want a
beach holiday, Coffs isn't the best place anyway. There
aren't actually any places to stay right *on* the water, you
know. There's a railway line between the houses and
the beach. It's crap, believe me. Coffs Harbour is full
of idiots, full of the type of people who eat margarine
instead of butter and iron creases in the front of their
jeans. My parents used to love it there. Which is just
about as big a condemnation of the place as you can
get.'

Alice hasn't told me much of any real substance
about her parents, and I wonder about her relationship with them. Occasionally she speaks of her mother

with a love and admiration that is almost palpable, and at other times she is derisive, almost cruel. When she mocks them – their poverty, their bad taste, their stupidity, I'm shocked that she can be so unfeeling towards her own flesh and blood.

The three of us are trying to organise a weekend trip away together. I'm excited and imagine a lovely weekend of swimming and eating and talking. But we can't agree on the best place to go – and we have a small budget, which makes it difficult because Alice is being fussy.

I feel a little guilty because my parents have a house in the Blue Mountains that they use for weekends occasionally. It's a lovely house, modern, all pale timber and stainless steel, open-plan, with spectacular mountain views. My father designed it and incorporated all the things he loves about houses: comfort and style, clean, straight lines, and most importantly, a great deal of light and air. There is also a swimming pool and a tennis court so there is always something to do, and it sits on five acres of land, tucked privately behind a dense screen of conifers.

My parents would be glad to let me have use of it, they often suggest that I take some friends up for the weekend, and I know they'd be thrilled to think of me enjoying myself there. But I don't think I could endure it. I've only been there once since Rachel died – a few months after her death, when Mum and Dad and I were still in shock, still behaving like a group of aimless, lost souls. And it was so incredibly painful being there without Rachel – her absence some kind of malign vacuum that sucked all the joy and beauty from the place – that I haven't been back since.

We used to drive up from Melbourne during the school holidays, and stay for a week, or sometimes two. It was a good, quiet place for Rachel to practise. The grand piano was always the focal point of the living space, and when she was still alive, Mum and Dad and I used to sit on the deck, sip on tea and listen to Rachel play. Apart from Rachel's music they were very quiet holidays – there was no television or radio, no outside source of entertainment – and so we spent the days walking and swimming, the evenings playing Scrabble or chess.

It's quite hard now to believe that I was often bored on those trips. It's painful to remember that I some-times resented being there: I missed my friends, my social life, whatever boy I had a crush on at the time, and was usually impatient to get back home. I wish now that I'd taken more notice, that I'd been more present. I wish now that I'd known how fragile it all was. If I'd understood how easily everything could be destroyed, I wouldn't have taken it for granted. With hindsight I can see so clearly how privileged we really were. With hindsight I'm ashamed of the fact that I had no idea.

bends down to kiss him tenderly as he takes it from her grasp.

'You're an angel, Robbie. A star,' she says. Robbie rolls his eyes, but he is pleased by her display of affection, it's obvious in his face.

She hands me my mug. 'And you, Miss Katherine. You're a total legend.'

I smile, sip on my tea.

Alice sits down, leans forward, her face animated. 'I was just thinking when I was in the kitchen. I was just thinking how cool it is that the three of us have found each other. I mean, I know it's probably corny to say so, but we really do get on well together, don't we? I mean, we just seem to fit together, like . . . oh, I don't know . . . like pieces in a jigsaw puzzle. We just totally get each other.' And she smiles, looks down, suddenly self-conscious. 'I just wanted to say that. Just wanted to say that you two are really important to me. My best friends in the world.'

There's a brief moment of silence before Robbie claps his hand on his knee and snorts loudly. 'Pieces of a jigsaw puzzle? Did I hear you right? Did you really say that?' He looks at me, and his face is transformed by delighted mirth, all signs of his earlier concern gone. 'Did she really?'

'She did.' I nod. 'I think she did.'

'Oh my God.' Alice covers her smile with her hand.

'Okay, I did. But in my defence I was brought up by a woman who ate *Days of Our Lives* for breakfast, lunch and dinner. I can't help it if I'm a walking cliché. You're being prejudiced and mean if you laugh at me, Robbie, and you're always rousing at me for that. You hypocrite!'

'Too bad!' Robbie shakes his head. 'There's no excuse for being such a dag. No excuse at all.'

'Okay,' Alice laughs. 'Okay. You've discovered my dirty secret. I'm a Coffs girl through and through. Can't help it. That's why I don't want to go there. I'm trying to free myself from its power over me.'

'I knew it. You're secretly a margarine-lover, aren't you?' Robbie says.

And the three of us laugh, clutch our stomachs, laugh some more.

'To be honest,' Alice puts her head down, feigns embarrassment, 'I love ironing creases in my jeans too. I have to force myself not to. It's hard, but I'm getting there. Overcoming it slowly.'

And we tease each other and laugh and make plans for our weekend away. I forget to wonder about what Robbie said about Alice, don't think to ask him again later. So Alice has a few minor personality quirks. Don't we all? I'm simply too happy to let that bother me. I'm having far too much fun to listen to the tiny little warning voice starting up in my head.

9

'And then what happened?' Carly leaned forward, her eyes wide with interest. 'Come on. You can't stop there.'

But Rachel was standing in the doorway. Her pyjamas were rumpled and her face red and blotched. I could tell she'd been crying.

'Rach?' I put my arm out. 'What's up?'

'I had another bad dream.'

'Oh. Come here. Come and sit with us.' I smiled at Carly in apology. I'd been telling her all about the night before, a night I'd spent with my boyfriend, Will. We'd kissed and touched one another, and ended up almost having sex. Carly had insisted on hearing every detail.

Carly was my best friend. She was loud and straightforward and funny. When she'd first started at our school I'd taken an instant dislike to her. I thought she was a show-off and that her jokes were obvious. She didn't like me much either at first, and told me later that she'd thought I was, in her words, 'a snotty, stuck-up rich bitch'.

Carly and I had become firm friends at Year 7 school camp; a torturous seven days of cold, damp, hunger and discomfort that was meant to help us 'find ourselves'. Carly and I were given the task of cooking together and we forged a strong friendship while battling each night to make something edible from very limited ingredients, and dealing with the constant, strident complaints of our classmates. I was impressed by Carly's ability to create a joke out of anything and Carly later told me that she'd admired my fierce determination to make the best of what we had. We'd been inseparable since.

Rachel sat down on the floor next to me and I put my arm round her shoulders.

'The same dream again?' I asked.

'Yes.'

'Rachel has been having this really awful dream,' I explained to Carly. 'She sees a girl that she thinks is very familiar, and the girl is smiling, so she walks up to her.'

'And then the closer I get,' Rachel continued, 'the more familiar this girl's face looks. And at first I'm really happy and excited to see her, I have this really kinda strong feeling of love, as if I know her from somewhere. But as I walk closer I start to think that maybe this girl is not as friendly as she looks, or that there's something really bad about her. And then, when I'm standing right in front of her, I see that she's actually me, that she's got my face, and then I just suddenly know what that means. To see my own face like that. It means that I'm going to die, and I'm just so scared suddenly . . . and I try to turn away, to get away from this girl . . . but she starts smiling, a really horrible, evil smile. And I try to run and she starts laughing and laughing and, of course, I can't get away. And then I wake up.' Rachel looked at Carly. 'It's really scary, I know it doesn't sound that bad, but it's terrifying. This girl, this me-girl, is like some kind of death messenger.'

'Erk, that sounds totally creepy.' Carly shuddered. 'No wonder it freaks you out.'

'Why don't you lie down in here for a while,' I said to Rachel. 'Try and get back to sleep. You've got that big rehearsal tomorrow. You need to rest.'

Rachel got into my bed. I pulled the covers up over her and went back to sit next to Carly on the floor.

'So?' Carly nudged me. 'Continue please.'

I shook my head. 'No,' I whispered. 'Wait till Rachel's asleep.'

'I know what you're talking about,' Rachel said from the bed. 'I know you're talking about boys and stuff. I heard you when I came in before. Don't stop because of me. I don't care. Honestly. I won't even listen.'

Carly raised her eyebrows as if to say, *See? No big deal.*

'You promise?' I said. 'Promise you won't listen, Rach?'

'I can barely keep my eyes open,' she said. 'I'll be asleep before you even say two words. And I don't want to know what you and Will do to each other, believe me. It's just gross.'

And so I told Carly what had happened between Will and me. I told her almost everything in a rushed and quiet voice so that Rachel couldn't hear. At least, I told her about the physical stuff, but I left out what we'd said to each other. I didn't tell her how we laughed with wonder and joy, how we whispered tender words and promised to be true. The loving words we'd exchanged were sacred and I kept them to myself.

The following day, Carly and I met Rachel after her piano rehearsal. We'd recently started drinking coffee, and enjoyed nothing better than going to a cafe and sitting over a cappuccino for as long as we could – watching the other patrons, gossiping about our friends. It felt like a grown-up thing to do, but unlike a lot of the other social activities we were starting to enjoy – parties and alcohol and all things to do with boys – it was also safe and comfortable. There was nothing secret or covert about it, and there was no one to try and impress, we could just be ourselves.

We took Rachel to the cafe with us and she talked about how excited she was about her upcoming concert. The other musicians were fantastic, she said, and they all saw completely eye to eye in how to interpret the piece. I liked talking about music, and I knew the people Rachel was talking about so I was interested, but after a while I could see that Carly was getting bored; her eyes were drifting, and she started tapping her fingers impatiently.

'Carly,' I said. 'Hello? Are we boring you to death?'

'Sorry.' Rachel put her hands on her flushed cheeks. 'I'm just going on and on about this, aren't I? It's just so exciting. Sorry. Let's talk about something else.'

Carly dismissed Rachel's apology with a shake of her head. 'What time do you two have to be home?' she said.

'No particular time for me.' I looked at Rachel. 'But you have to get home and practise.'

Rachel looked at her watch. 'Yes, but it's only just past four. There's plenty of time.'

'You know Jake and Ross and those guys?' Carly looked at me and I could tell by the way she smiled that she had a plan I wouldn't want Rachel to be a part of.

'Yeah.' I knew them vaguely. They were from the boys' school and were a grade ahead of Carly and me. They were in a band and were known for being very wild and very popular.

'They're having band practice this afternoon. At the old farmer's shed. Well, I think it was going to be a band practice but it's turned into more of a party. Apparently quite a few people are going to watch them play. Like, everyone in Years 11 and 12. You know, music, a few beers and stuff. It should be fun.'

'Sounds awesome,' I said.

'Band practice?' Rachel said. 'How cool. I'd love to hear them. Can I come?'

'They're seniors, Rach. They'll be drinking and stuff. You'll feel totally out of place.'

'Not if there's good music, I won't.'

'No. No way. Don't be stupid. You have to go home and practise.'

'Oh, come on, Katie. *Please*. Can't I just come and watch for a while and then go home? I know you think I'm just a big baby, but I'm not. And I need some fun. I'll be practising every minute of every day for the next few weeks. The music will inspire me. Please.'

'Inspire you?' I roll my eyes. 'Yeah, right. Amateur grunge rock? As if.'

'Please, Katie? Please? Just for an hour?'

'No.'

'Oh, for God's sake,' said Carly, looking irritated. 'Just let her come. What does it matter? We don't have time to sit here and argue about it.'

There was no real reason to keep saying no – we

could go for an hour and get home before Mum and Dad and Rachel would still have plenty of time to practise – I just didn't want her tagging along. But I couldn't say that without making Rachel cry, and if she cried now she'd ruin everything – I'd have to take her home, look after her, wipe her snotty nose. Despite what she said, she really could be a big baby at times.

'All right, then.' I kept my voice deliberately cold. 'You can come. But don't blame me if Mum and Dad crack a shit.'

10

Vivien tries to hide it but I can tell that she's surprised when I say that I'm going away with Alice and Robbie for the weekend. She hugs me tight before she leaves for work.

'You enjoy yourself, young lady,' she says.

We've decided to head south and we take my car, the new Peugeot, because it's the fastest and the most comfortable. We leave Sydney on Friday morning. Both Alice and I should be at school, but the teachers are fairly lenient with Year 12 students and probably won't even comment on our absence. In any case I've brought my copy of *Hamlet* and plan to reread it while lazing on the beach in the sun. Robbie has taken a rare weekend off from the restaurant and he drives because he's the only one of us not restricted to driving at 80 kilometres an hour. The three of us are excited and in good spirits and laugh and joke for most of the four-hour drive to Merimbula. When we arrive we go to the local supermarket and stock up on supplies, food for the next few days. Alice fills the trolley with chocolate and lollies, Robbie and I collect the more practical supplies – eggs and milk and bread and toilet paper. We put our groceries into the boot of the car and check our map, then head east on the little road that takes us towards the beach.

We've rented an old, two-bedroom timber cottage. We found the house listed on the net, and though there were a couple of photos of the interior – the kitchen and the dining room – we're not entirely certain what we're going to find. So when we arrive and see a charming whitewashed cottage with a timber deck overlooking the beach we are both delighted and relieved.

We rush inside and run through the house, laughing and exclaiming.

'This is perfect.'

'God. Look at that enormous old bath.'

'And look at the view. You can hear the ocean from every room. Wow. This is just gorgeous.'

'Oh, hey, come here and look at the bedrooms. These beds. They're unbelievable.'

We put our swimmers on and run down to the beach. We all run straight into the water without bothering to test the temperature, and dive under the waves. The water is icy but I am far too happy, far too high on life and friendship and the knowledge that there are three entire days of fun ahead, to worry about the cold. Alice and Robbie splash one another and embrace and laugh. Alice runs from him, laughing and tripping. He catches her but she pulls away and one strap of her costume comes down over her shoulder and her breast is exposed. This makes her laugh more, and she spins and squeals like an excited child, and pulls her other strap down so that both of her breasts are free. Then she cups them in her hands, lifts and squeezes so her nipples are pointed at Robbie.

'Bang, bang, you're dead,' she says.

'Oh. Aaaaah.' Robbie clutches his chest and falls backwards into the water.

Alice turns to face me, nipples pointed.

'No, no,' I laugh. 'Please. Have mercy.'

I see movement in the corner of my eye and turn to see a middle-aged man and woman. They are walking past, staring, their faces fixed in disapproval and disgust.

Alice follows my gaze and sees them. I watch her expression change from one of laughing amusement to one of anger. Suddenly she turns so that she is facing the couple directly. She reaches behind herself and tugs at the string of her bikini top so that it swings loose in her hand; then she puts her hand on her bikini pants and pulls them down, steps out of them and straightens up. She looks at the couple, naked and defiant, and smiles a cold, challenging smile.

The man and woman rush away, red-faced, muttering and shaking their heads.

Alice watches them go, then tips back her head and laughs.

We feast that night on fish and chips bought from a local takeaway. The chips are crunchy, the fish fresh and tasty, and the three of us stuff ourselves full. When we've finished we spread out on the sofas in the lounge room and talk lazily about nothing much at all.

'God, I hate people like that,' Alice says, out of the blue.

'Like what?'

'Like those narrow-minded, conservative, small-town hicks we saw at the beach today.'

'Narrow-minded? Really? You've got them all worked out?' Robbie looks at her curiously. 'After seeing them for a total of five seconds?'

'Yes, I think I do, actually. Small lives, bad haircuts and horrible clothes. Fat and ugly to boot. The kind of people that vote for conservative politicians and hate gays. The kind of people who say things like . . .' Alice puts on a broad Australian accent, '"She's a nice girl, even though she's black. I wouldn't say I'd go as far as having her round for dinner, though."'

I laugh at Alice's wicked satire, assuming that she's just joking. But Robbie doesn't laugh. He looks at Alice and shakes his head. 'You can be such a bitch sometimes.'

'That may be true, but I'm probably right about them.' She points at him. 'You're just too nice for your own good.'

'I'm not nice. You're just unfair. You just—'

Alice yawns loudly, interrupting, and stretches her arms up over her head. 'Maybe I am unfair. But who cares? The whole world's unfair, Robbie. And believe me, I know those kind of people. I know their type. They're exactly like my parents. Sad. Bitter. Ugly. And they're always concerned with what everyone else is doing because their own pathetic lives are so boring. I can see it in their eyes. I can smell the stench of them from a hundred Ks away.' She stands and stretches again, flashing her tanned midriff and her belly ring as her T-shirt lifts. 'Anyway, this conversation is getting boring. We've had it too many times before and we'll just have to agree to disagree. I'm suddenly very, very tired.' She blows us both a kiss and walks from the room.

Robbie and I smile at each other, listen to Alice mutter to herself as she undresses, hear the squeak of the bed as she climbs in.

'Don't get up to anything naughty without me,' she calls from the room.' Nighty-night, children. Be good.'

''Night, Alice.'

'Do you want to go and sit outside? On the verandah?' Robbie says after a while.

73

'Sure.'

I can tell by the expression on his face as he arranges our chairs and by the way he waits for me to sit before he speaks that there is something on his mind.

'I want to ask you a question,' he says.

'Okay.'

He sighs. 'I hate asking this type of thing. And I understand if you don't want to answer. Feel free to tell me to bugger off.'

'Okay,' I laugh. 'Bugger off.'

'At least let me ask the question first.'

'Sorry. Ask away.'

He looks back at the house before he speaks. 'Does Alice ever confide in you? About me? You know, tell you how she feels?'

'No, not really.'

'Not really?' Robbie looks at me expectantly as if hoping I'll elaborate.

But the truth is that when we're alone together Alice very rarely mentions him. Of course, if we have plans to do something together she talks about him in a practical sense, but she has never really talked about her feelings towards him. I asked her once if she loved him, if she considered him her boyfriend, but she just laughed dismissively, shook her head and said that she wasn't girlfriend material. And although it's obvious that Robbie doesn't feel so casually about Alice – he's quite clearly besotted – I'd always assumed they had some kind of understanding.

But Robbie wouldn't be asking me these questions if he knew exactly where he stood. Clearly he's hoping for more from his relationship with Alice than she's willing to give. I have a sudden urge to tell him to protect himself, to steel his heart, to look for another girlfriend if he wants something serious. But I don't; I can't. I really don't know what Alice thinks of her relationship with Robbie – perhaps she does love him but is reluctant to admit it, perhaps she's afraid of being hurt – and I don't feel entitled to give advice or make warnings when I'm just as much in the dark as he is.

'I've only known her for three months, Robbie,' I say.

'But you two have become pretty close, you spend so much time together,' he says. 'You must have some idea what she thinks. Even if she doesn't say anything directly.'

'But she hasn't said anything. Honest. And so, no, I don't know any more than you do.' And I look at him, puzzled. 'Anyway, I thought you said that Alice was bad for you? You compared her to some kind of unhealthy addiction. I thought you were . . .' I hesitate, trying to think of the right word, 'um, I don't know, in this with your eyes wide open?'

'More like my heart wide open, I think.' He smiles

sadly. 'Sometimes I can be rational about it and be happy to take whatever she's offering. Sometimes I can concentrate on all the bad stuff about our relationship and convince myself that anything serious with Alice would only make me miserable. Or at least I can do a good job of pretending that to myself. But the reality is that I want more.'

He sighs. 'Sorry. I shouldn't have interrogated you like that. It's totally boring when people try and talk about their relationships with a third person, isn't it? I hate it when people do it to me.'

'Don't worry. I'm not bored. Not at all. I just don't have any answers.'

'Perhaps I should go and see one of those people who can tell you the future. What are they called?'

'A psychic?'

'That's it. A psychic.'

'Why don't you just ask Alice? Talk to her seriously and ask her what she wants.'

'I've tried. I ask her what she feels, what she wants, all the time. She's an absolute master at avoiding questions, you must've noticed that about her? I tell her I love her and she laughs and changes the subject. If I get too serious she gets annoyed and tells me to be quiet.'

'Perhaps you need to be more direct?' I smile and put my hand on his knee and squeeze affectionately.

'Ask her if she wants to marry you and have your babies and live happily ever after,' I joke.

'I *would* marry her, that's the sad bit. The truth is that I'd marry her and get her pregnant and have six beautiful kids and buy a house and get a boring job and support them all for ever. The whole lot. I'd do it in an instant. I'd love to.' He sighs again. 'I love her. There's just no one else like Alice, is there? She's beautiful, funny, smart . . . and she's got so much energy for life. So much enthusiasm. She can make the most boring thing in the world seem like fun. She can turn an ordinary day into a party. Everyone else seems, just, so, well, lifeless and empty in comparison.'

'Gee, thanks.'

'Shit. Sorry. I don't mean you.'

'That's okay. I'm only kidding.' I laugh. 'It sure sounds as though you're in love, though.'

'Yep. Pathetically, ridiculously in love. With a girl who's afraid of commitment.'

I wonder if he's right. I'd always assumed that when someone said they were afraid of commitment that it was really just a convenient way of getting out of an unwanted relationship. A way of dumping someone gently, without destroying the ego of the poor soul being dumped. *It's me, not you, I just can't commit* is certainly a less bitter pill to swallow than *Hey, I just don't like you enough to hang around. See ya later.* But he may be right about Alice – there's definitely something about her, something secret and closed, and despite all her apparent warmth and openness this part of her remains hidden, untouchable.

'Did she say that?' I ask.

Robbie is staring out towards the beach, deep in thought.

'Robbie?'

'Sorry?' he says. 'Did she say what?'

'Did Alice actually tell you that she's afraid of commitment? Or is that just what you think?'

'She didn't say it as such. God.' He laughs. 'Imagine Alice saying something like that? No. She didn't say it, but it's pretty obvious, and it would make sense, don't you think?'

'I don't know. I don't know how you can tell these things.'

'I mean because of her mum and stuff,' he says. 'Her real mum. All that rejection. She's bound to be a bit wary of love.'

'Her *real* mum? What do you mean?'

'Oh, shit.' He stares at me. 'She hasn't told you?'

'No. She hasn't told me anything. What? Is she adopted or something?'

'Yeah. Bugger. I probably shouldn't say any more. I should probably wait and let her tell you herself.'

'You've practically already told me,' I say. 'Her real

mother rejected her and she was adopted. I already know she doesn't like the people who adopted her. Or, at least, I assume they're the ones she calls her parents?'

'Yeah. She hates them.'

'Now it all makes a bit more sense. I didn't understand before. I wondered how she could say such horrible things about her parents, call them fat and stupid and stuff, and then in the next breath turn round and say something really nice about her mother. It's because they're two different people. She has two mothers.'

'Yep. Her real mother, her biological mother, is called Jo-Jo.'

'Jo-Jo?'

'Yeah. Hippy for Joanne. She's a hopeless old junkie. A more selfish, self-absorbed woman you've never met.'

'But Alice—'

'Totally loves her,' he interrupts. 'Worships her. And Joanne's filthy rich. She inherited a pile of money from her parents. She lavishes it on Alice now. Gives her whatever she wants. And there's this weird snobbery stuff happening. Even though Jo-Jo is a junkie, she acts superior to the people who adopted Alice. And Alice totally buys into it.'

'So that's why she has all those expensive clothes, why she doesn't need to work,' I say. 'Jo-Jo gives her money.'

'Yep. Some kind of guilt thing, I reckon. She was

too messed up to look after Alice and her little brother when they were kids, so she throws a whole lot of money at them to make up for it.'

'Brother? Alice has a brother?'

'Yeah.'

'A brother.' I shake my head, astounded. 'Wow. I had no idea. She's never even mentioned him once. What's his name?'

Robbie frowns. 'I don't actually know. Alice goes funny when she talks about him. She gets all upset and stuff. Just calls him her baby brother. I know he's been in some kind of trouble with the law, something big, but I'm not exactly sure what. Drugs probably, like his mother.'

I'm astonished to learn that Alice has a brother, that she was adopted, that she has secrets almost as devastating as mine. Alice and I have more in common than I'd imagined and I'm suddenly certain that this all adds up to a coincidence so extraordinary that it can only be explained as some kind of sign: a sign that Alice and I were fated to meet, that it was in our destiny to become friends.

'What a mess,' I say.

'Yep.'

'Life can really suck sometimes,' I say. 'Poor Alice.' But what I really mean is poor *us*. All three of us have had terrible things happen – murder, cancer, abandonment – and for the first time I'm tempted to tell Robbie about Rachel. It's not the sympathy that I want but the credibility that comes with having faced and lived through something tragic. I can say that I understand, and I do, but to Robbie and Alice, who know nothing of my past, my words must sound hollow. The soothing but uncomprehending words of the fortunate.

But I'm afraid I may regret such an indiscretion in the morning. I say nothing.

I wake early the next day and despite the late night I feel refreshed and happy. Sun is streaming through the window onto my bed and I lie there for a while with just the sheet over me and enjoy the warmth of the sunshine on my skin. I can hear the deep rumble of the ocean and I can hear Robbie and Alice talking quietly and laughing in their bedroom.

I get up, put on my dressing gown and go to the kitchen. I make a cup of tea and take it to the verandah. I lean against the railing and stare out at the beach. The ocean is a beautiful, clear turquoise and the waves break gently on the shore. With my mug cupped in my hands I step off the verandah and walk towards the water. I finish my tea, put the empty cup on the sand, look back towards the house and up and down the beach to check that no one is watching. I undo my dressing gown and let it slip to the ground. I run into the water and when I'm deep enough I dive beneath.

The water is so calm that I'm able to float comfortably on my back and swim a smooth and easy freestyle up and down. When I've been swimming for a while and am both tired and refreshed I get out, put my dressing gown on again and head back to the house.

'Katherine?' Alice calls out when I go inside. 'What are you doing?'

I go to their room and stand in the doorway. Robbie and Alice are sitting up in bed, their legs tangled. When he sees me, Robbie pulls the sheet up to cover himself and smiles sheepishly. I grin at them happily. 'It's a beautiful morning,' I say. '*Beautiful*. I've been swimming and the water is perfect. You two should go. I'll cook us some breakfast. Eggs Benedict, if you like.'

'You're going to make me fat with all this gorgeous food.' Alice yawns and stretches her arms up over her head. 'Fat like my monster adoptive parents.' She looks at me and raises her eyebrows. 'Speaking of which . . .'

'Yes,' I say, and for some reason I'm embarrassed, as if I've been sprung doing something I shouldn't. I think it's the way Alice is looking at me – like an angry mother waiting for her child to admit to a crime she already knows of. 'Robbie told me about . . . that you're adopted. That you've got a brother. I hope you don't mind.'

But the cold expression has disappeared from her face and I'm not sure whether I imagined it. She shrugs indifferently and yawns again. 'It's not as if it's a big secret. I just never got round to telling you. It's nothing really, anyway. Hardly worth talking about.'

I notice a frown cross Robbie's brow, an almost imperceptible pursing of his lips. He sighs and rolls his eyes. 'Of course. It's nothing. Like everything else to you, eh Alice? Nothing. Nothing, nothing, nothing. Your favourite word.'

'Hey, Robbie,' Alice says, her voice hard and cold, the expression on her face one of anger. 'If you don't like the way I live my life, if you disapprove of the way I think about everything, then what are you doing here? Huh? Robbie? What exactly are you doing here?'

'I don't disapprove of the way you think. I didn't say that. I just think it's crap the way you brush off everything emotional as if it doesn't mean anything. It's some kind of act of bravado. Some kind of defence thing – and I think it's unhealthy.'

'What?' She stares at him incredulously as she slides off the bed and stands beside it. She puts her hands on her hips. She is wearing a white nightie, a modest and pretty, almost child-like gown, and a spot of colour has appeared on each of her cheeks. Her eyes are bright with anger. She looks innocent and beautiful and dangerous all at once and it's hard not to stare. She shakes her head and smiles bitterly. 'What are you on about, Robbie? What are you *talking* about?'

'I'm talking about you, Alice. Your family. Your mother and your brother. I don't even know your brother's name. Katherine didn't even know you *had* a brother. Don't you think that's a bit weird? You never talk about him. You never talk about your parents or your childhood. You never talk about anything.'

'And why should I, Robbie? Just because you think it's the right thing to do? What is it that you're so desperate to know, anyway? What sordid little detail is it that interests you? Huh? You already know that Jo-Jo is a heroin addict. You already know that I was adopted. I don't talk about my brother because I barely ever see him. Because he's not exactly available, is he? I don't talk about him because we didn't grow up together, because he was adopted by some stupid arseholes and he had a crappy life and now he's in prison, okay? I don't talk about him because people like you couldn't possibly understand what he's been through.'

I stand there, watching them. It's difficult to tear myself away, difficult not to listen. Alice has secrets. So do I. Why shouldn't we? I want to tell Robbie to leave her alone, drop the whole subject, but this is not my fight. I turn away and start towards the kitchen and Alice shouts my name.

'Don't run away,' she says.

Her tone is cold and demanding and it annoys me. When I speak, I'm equally cold. 'I'm not running away,' I say. 'I'm going to make breakfast. I'm hungry.'

'I just want your opinion,' she continues, as if I haven't spoken. 'Don't you think I have the right to decide what I do or don't want to talk about? Or is it wrong of me to keep things to myself?' She glares at Robbie, then turns to me and raises her eyebrows. 'Or should friends talk to each other about everything? Everything that has ever happened?'

'No,' I say, my voice quiet. 'Of course not.' *Of course you can have secrets*, I think, *I have secrets of my own. Let's bury them deep and try hard to forget about them and never ever talk about them. Ever.*

But I don't have a chance to say any more because Robbie interrupts. 'Let's just leave Katherine out of it. It's not her fight.'

'Yeah, well, she's standing there listening to us as if it is.'

'I am *not*,' I say, suddenly defensive and embarrassed. 'I wanted to go. You asked me for my opinion.' And I stop myself from continuing, before I start to sound like a petulant child. 'Anyway,' I shrug, 'I'm starving. I'm going to make breakfast.'

I turn round and walk to the kitchen. The door slams loudly behind me. I hear Robbie exclaim and then Alice's angry retort. I'm stung that Alice has been so unkind, and a little humiliated to be thought of as some kind of eavesdropper. I take the ingredients from the fridge – eggs, bacon, lemon, chives, butter – place them on the counter and slam the door shut angrily.

I make the hollandaise sauce first. I crack the eggs and separate the yolks from the whites carefully. I can still hear the hum of Robbie and Alice's voices from the room. They are much quieter now, and sound calmer, as if they might be making up. And as I'm whisking the yolks, one arm holding the bowl tight against my belly, my other arm moving briskly round and round, I find myself smiling. We've had a fight, I think, a real fight. Our first one.

Just the way friends do.

11

Sarah and I get to Jindabyne before five. I love Jindabyne; the slow, relaxed pace of it, the cool, brittle air and the beautiful man-made lake. It has become much more cosmopolitan since we used to visit as kids, with cafes and modern-looking restaurants lining the main street, but it still has a sleepy country feel to it. I think it's because of the wide streets, the slow pace of the traffic, the slightly abandoned feel of the town following the mid-winter rush.

I've booked into some self-contained accommodation near the lake, unimaginatively named Lake Cabins, but I'm pleased with our cabin when we arrive and have a look round. It's already warm, as the owner has been kind enough to turn on the heating in anticipation of our arrival, and it has a small timber deck that overlooks the lake.

'But where is the snow?' Sarah rushes to the window and looks outside.

'There's none here, sweetie. But we'll catch the special train up to the mountain tomorrow and we'll see lots and lots of snow.'

'Is it a magic train?'

'I think so,' I say.

'A magic *snow* train?'

'Exactly,' I nod.

'Can I play outside?'

'For a little while,' I say. 'It's getting dark.'

I help Sarah put on her fleece jacket and her gumboots and she sets off outside, squealing and excited to be in a new place.

'Don't go near the water without Mummy,' I remind her.

I get the box of groceries – milk, tea, sugar, Weet-Bix – from the boot of the car; and bring it in to unload. I can see Sarah from the kitchen and as I unpack and start the evening meal I watch her digging in the ground with a stick, talking to herself in a happy sing-song voice. I've brought basil, garlic and pine nuts, and the rest of the ingredients I need to make a pesto with spaghetti for dinner. I've also brought a lettuce and an avocado to make a green salad, and some balsamic vinegar to dress it with.

When I've processed the pesto, made the salad and put a big pot of water on the stove to boil, I put my jacket on and go outside. I sit on the verandah and watch Sarah play.

'Mummy?' she says after a while, without looking up from her game.

'Yes.'

'Mummy. Are you happy?'

'Of course I am.' I'm taken aback by the seriousness of her voice. 'I've got you, so I'm very, very, very happy. I'm the luckiest mummy in the world. You know that.'

'I know.' She nods seriously. 'I know you're happy about that part. But are you sad because you don't have a daddy?'

'But I *do* have a daddy. Grandpa is my daddy.'

She pauses for a moment, thinking. Then she looks up at me, her brow knotted in thought. 'I mean a daddy for me, that's what I mean. Are you sad that you don't have a daddy for me?'

'I'm a little bit sad.' My instinct is to approach Sarah, to pick her up and cuddle her and tickle her and smother her with kisses. I would much rather avoid these sad discussions; too intense, too painful, I think, for such a little girl. But I know from experience that she wants these questions answered and that she will keep on asking and asking until she's satisfied. 'I miss your daddy and I wish he hadn't died. But you make me so very happy that I'm much more happy than I am sad.'

She smiles – a small, tentative smile of relief.

And I wonder if it's true. Happiness is such a difficult

emotion to quantify. There are moments when I'm happy, certainly, moments with Sarah when I forget who I am and what has happened, moments when I can forget the past completely and enjoy the present. But there is a weight about me, a deep sadness, a feeling of disappointment with the capriciousness of life that is hard to shrug off, hard to ignore. There are occasions when I realise that days and weeks have gone by without my registering them, as though I've been absent, or living life on some kind of automatic pilot. Sometimes I feel as if I'm a robot programmed only to ensure that Sarah is looked after, responsible for the smooth running of her life, with no capacity to desire anything for myself. My main hope for happiness now is Sarah. If she's okay, if she can live a life free of tragedy and heartache, then I can consider myself satisfied. But that's the most that I'm willing to expect for myself now, Sarah's contentment; loving her is the only emotional investment in life that I'm willing to make.

12

'So we'll see you Friday evening, then?' Mum says.

'Yes.'

I'm just about to say goodbye and hang up the phone when she asks, 'Why don't you bring your new friend up with you? Why don't you bring Alice? We'd love to meet her.'

I doubt that Mum and Dad really want Alice to come; they no longer appear to enjoy any type of social interaction. It's a strain to laugh and smile and make conversation when the only thing you can really think of is the death of your child, a subject that is impossible to bring up without frightening people away. But I appreciate that she's making an effort for my sake, that she wants my life to be as normal as possible.

I've thought of introducing Alice to my parents, but I've always decided against it. Mum and Dad are so sad, so quiet, that it can sometimes be hard for people to know how to behave. And I haven't yet told Alice about Rachel. So she would doubtless find their intense seriousness, their inability to laugh easily, quite disconcerting.

'I don't know, Mum,' I say, 'she's probably busy.'

'Oh please, darling. Please just ask her, at least. I know we're dull, I know it's probably a drag, but it would be really nice to see a fresh face. And it would do your father a world of good to see you happy and having some fun with a friend your own age.'

It's so rare for Mum to ask something of me, and she sounds so genuinely keen for me to bring her, that I agree to ask. I promise to let her know the next day whether Alice will be coming or not. She wants time to get in some extra food.

Alice says yes, she'd love to come, and she laughs and says that she's been waiting for me to ask.

Inevitably, on our first night there, Rachel's name is mentioned. But I manage to change the subject quickly and so avoid the awkwardness of having to tell Alice what happened beneath the curious stares of Mum and Dad. They would certainly wonder why I'd never told Alice before.

But I know that I'm going to have to tell her. There's no way we can get through an entire weekend without Rachel's name coming up again. So when Alice and I say goodnight to my parents and go upstairs to bed I ask her to come into my room for a minute.

'Why?' she whispers, giggling. 'Have you got a secret store of drugs in there?'

'I just want to tell you something.'

Alice looks at me wide-eyed, obviously surprised by the serious tone of my voice. 'Okay,' she says. 'Just let me pee first. I won't be a sec.'

When she returns we sit on my bed, facing one another, our legs crossed.

'I had a sister,' I say matter-of-factly. 'Rachel. She was murdered.'

Alice leans forward, frowns. 'What did you say?'

I wait. I know that she has heard me and just needs time to process the information. It's always like this when you first tell someone. Always hard to believe at first.

'Tell me,' she says eventually.

And I start to talk, and as I talk I sob quietly. I tell Alice everything. The entire story, starting from the moment when Carly and Rachel and I were having coffee all those years ago, the moment I decided that we would go to the party. And I cry with remembered horror, but also with relief that I'm finally telling someone, and I talk and talk and cry some more. And Alice, for once, just listens. She doesn't say anything, or ask questions, but she keeps her hand on my knee the whole time.

'Oh my God,' she says when I finally finish. 'You

poor thing. Your poor family. Why didn't you tell me before? Oh my God. Poor Rachel.'

'Yes,' I nod. 'Poor Rachel. Poor Mum and Dad. It just sucks. It ruined everything.'

And Alice wraps her arms round me and holds me while I cry. Then, when I'm completely exhausted and my head is sore, when the bedside clock is flashing 2 a.m., she helps me into bed and lies down beside me, brushing her hand over my hair until I sleep.

I wake the next morning with Alice standing beside my bed, a steaming cup of tea in hand. 'I brought you this.' She puts the cup on my bedside table and sits on the bed. 'Have you had enough sleep?'

Alice is dressed. Her hair is damp on the ends and I can smell the citrus of her shampoo. I sit up, feeling rumpled and tired and stale. I pick up the cup and sip on my tea. It is hot and strong and sweet, delicious in my dry mouth.

'How are you?' I say after I've drunk half the cup and feel lucid enough to speak. 'What time did you get up? You must be exhausted.'

'No. I feel great. I got up early and had breakfast with Helen on the porch.'

I wonder why Alice has started referring to Mum by her first name. My parents are usually the Mr and Mrs type.

'We've been talking about Rachel,' Alice says.

94

'Oh.' I'm shocked. I can't imagine what they would have said to each other. Mum is usually so reluctant to talk to strangers about Rachel, so afraid of reducing her life and death to a story. 'Is that . . . I mean, how's Mum with that? Is she . . . did she actually do any talking?'

'Did she talk? My God, Katherine, she didn't draw breath. I think this is really what she's needed. It's been . . . um, what's that word . . . *cathartic* for her, I think. Helen's a lovely, brave, strong woman, but she needs, I don't know . . . she really needs some kind of outlet for all of this. It's obvious that she's just been holding it all in, repressing all her fury and misery for so long. I mean, don't get me wrong, this morning was completely exhausting, emotional for both of us. We laughed and cried and hugged. We even had a shot of rum in our coffee, we were both getting so emotional. I mean, she just opened up completely this morning, told me all this stuff . . . things that I don't think she's told anyone before.' Alice tilts her head to the side and smiles dreamily. 'And I gave her some different perspectives. A new way of seeing things. A more sympathetic and tolerant view of the whole situation. I think I really helped her, you know. Really helped her let go of some of the shit she's been bottling up inside.'

'The shit?' I say. I'm irritated but not sure why. 'What *shit* is that exactly?'

'Oh.' Alice blinks, then looks at me a little warily. 'Are you okay? You don't mind or anything, do you? It just kind of happened. I'm not even sure who brought Rachel up. I mean, I think *I* did initially . . . but I couldn't just sit there with Helen and not say anything about her. I kind of felt false or like I was lying or something. But, wow, once I mentioned Rachel's name, that was it. Helen just couldn't stop *talking*.'

The way Alice is calling my mother 'Helen' is infuriating and every time she says it I have to control the urge to tell her to shut up.

'I'll have to go and see if she's really okay.' I sigh. I toss the blankets off my legs and stand up, avoiding Alice's eye as I put on my dressing gown. 'She's become very good at hiding her true feelings since Rachel died. You honestly can't tell what she's really thinking unless you know her very well. And she can be ridiculously polite. To the point of self-destructiveness sometimes.'

I leave the room without giving Alice a chance to say any more. I know I'm being rude and probably overdramatic, but I'm sure that Alice has read everything all wrong – I'm certain that if they've been talking about Rachel Mum will be feeling bruised and upset. And something about Alice's attitude towards the whole thing seems oddly self-congratulatory. Annoyingly smug.

* * *

I find Mum in the kitchen. She's standing at the island bench, kneading some dough; there's flour covering the bench, a smear of it on her cheek. She is humming.

'Oh. Darling.' She smiles and puts her hand on her chest. 'You startled me.'

'How are you?' I look at her carefully.

'Oh! I'm feeling quite . . .' She touches her lip vaguely, leaving a smear of flour behind. Her eyes become teary and I think she's about to cry, but then she smiles. 'I'm feeling really good, actually. Alice and I had a lovely talk this morning. A really good, honest conversation about Rachel. It was, well, it was quite . . . quite *liberating* to get it all out.' She laughs then and shakes her head. 'I was swearing like a sailor, darling. I even drank rum like a sailor too.'

'Rum? Already?' I look up towards the kitchen clock. 'It's only just past ten!'

'I know. Aren't we wicked? Your friend Alice,' Mum shakes her head, smiles fondly, 'she's quite a character, isn't she? Such good *fun*.'

'I guess so.' I open the fridge, busy myself looking through it. 'Although it's hard to imagine you swearing.' I can't help it, I sound abrupt and disapproving.

'Well, I was.' If Mum has noticed my mood she's not letting on, she remains cheerful and bright. 'Those poor men. Their ears must be burning still.'

'Poor men? What poor men?' I close the fridge door, stare at her.

'Well, boys, really, not men. The boys who killed Rachel.'

'Poor? I don't think so. At least they're still alive.'

'That's right. They are. And they've got to live with what they've done for ever.'

'Good,' I say viciously. 'So they bloody well should.'

'Indeed.' Mum looks at me and smiles. 'It's okay. Get it all out. Swear if you want to.'

'God, Mum, I've already done all that.'

'Good. Well, that's good. I'm glad you have,' she laughs. 'It feels good to get angry, doesn't it? It feels good to behave badly sometimes.'

'I wouldn't call it behaving badly. I'd call it behaving like a normal human being.'

'Of course. You're absolutely right. Alice pointed that out.'

'And you're okay?' I don't know why I'm not relieved. But there's a strange and shameful part of me that's disappointed to find her looking so happy. I suppose I'm a little jealous that it was talking to Alice, not me, that made her feel this way. 'You're not upset?'

'Upset? Well, of course I'm upset, sweetheart. My daughter was murdered. But it just feels so good to . . . to have acknowledged how fucking *angry* I really am. To let a bit of that anger out.' She shrugs and gets back to her kneading, pushing into the dough furiously. 'It just feels so great to express it. I was so vicious about those men, those boys, those *bastards*, I almost started feeling sorry for them.'

'Oh. Well. That's—' I stop, turn away and go to the kettle, busy myself finding the sugar, a cup, scooping leaves into the teapot. I've never heard my mother swear before. Never. In almost eighteen years. And far from feeling happy that she's finally releasing some of this natural anger, far from feeling pleased to see her let go a little, I am close to tears. I feel hurt. I've tried so many times to get her to talk about Rachel, to express some anger, to scream and cry and rail at the unfairness of it all, but she's always been so stony and stoic, purse-lipped and unwilling to let herself be overcome by emotion.

Where I have always failed, Alice has succeeded – and so easily and quickly!

I finish making my tea silently and as I'm about to leave the room and head back up to my bedroom to drink it in aggrieved solitude, Mum approaches. She stands directly in front of me, puts her hand on my shoulder and squeezes. 'She's a lovely girl, your Alice. I'm so glad you brought her up this weekend.'

I nod and force myself to smile.

'And she clearly thinks the world of you,' Mum says. 'She really couldn't sing your praises highly enough.

I'm so glad you two have become friends.' And then she leans forward and kisses me on the cheek. She smiles and it is the happiest, most genuine smile I've seen on her face since Rachel died. Mum holds her arms open wide, I put my tea down and my arms round her. We hug, squeezing tightly for a long, long time, and by the time we let go all the anger I've been feeling for Alice has disappeared. She's made Mum happy and instead of feeling childishly jealous I should be grateful. I've been unreasonable and self-centred and petty. And as I head back upstairs I promise myself that I'll be much more generous and understanding towards Alice in future. After all, she has the best intentions. She's a good friend, a kind and giving friend, and her heart is always in the right place.

13

Rachel and Carly and I stopped at Carly's house on our way to the party. Carly took off her uniform and changed into a pair of jeans, a tight pink singlet top and a pair of flat gold sandals. She offered to lend us something to wear as well and I chose a pair of jeans and a striped T-shirt but all of Carly's clothes were far too big for Rachel.

'You'll just have to wear your uniform,' I said.

'I'm going to look like such a dag,' Rachel whined, looking down at herself. And though she had already removed her school tie and untucked her shirt, making her uniform look as casual as it possibly could, there was nothing she could do about the length of the skirt – a long, dark green kilt that hung well beneath her knees, an obvious sign of private school status. 'I'm going to stick out like a sore thumb.'

'Who cares?' I said. 'You're going to stick out anyway. You'll be the youngest person there, the only fourteen-year-old within a hundred kilometres.'

'But I—'

'Rach,' I interrupted. 'Stop complaining. You shouldn't even be coming, remember. These are my friends, not yours.'

Rachel and I both took our hair out and let it hang loose – Rachel's long and straight and golden, mine brown and curly-wild. We borrowed some of Carly's lipgloss and made our eyes dark with her mascara and eyeliner.

Carly took her mobile phone from her schoolbag and switched it off. She put it on her bed. 'If you don't want your parents calling,' she said, 'leave yours here too. I'll give them back at school tomorrow.'

Rachel looked at me, uncertain, waiting for me to make the decision. I shrugged, took my mobile from my bag, switched it off and tossed it on Carly's bed. Rachel quickly did the same.

When we'd squirted ourselves with some of Carly's mother's expensive-looking perfume – bottles of which literally covered her dressing table – we set off. We didn't have enough money for a taxi, so we decided to walk. After we'd been walking for five minutes, idly discussing which houses we did or didn't like as we passed, Carly reached into her shoulder bag and brought out a plastic drink bottle.

'Hold on a minute,' she said. She stopped walking,

twisted open the cap and took a big drink. The way her eyes watered and the way she gasped as she lowered the bottle indicated that she wasn't drinking water.

'Vodka.' She held it out towards me. 'With a bit of lemonade. Want some?'

I shook my head in amused disbelief, but took the bottle anyway. I should've known that Carly wouldn't go to the party without some alcohol. She was the first girl at our school to start drinking, the one who arranged for someone older to buy it for us whenever we needed it.

I lifted the neck to my mouth and took a tentative sip. It was strong. Much more vodka than lemonade. 'God, Carly, that's lethal,' I said as I handed it back.

'Rach?' Carly held the bottle out towards Rachel and lifted her eyebrows questioningly. Rachel looked at me as if for permission.

'May as well.' I shrugged. 'You won't like it, though. It tastes like petrol the first time you try it.'

Rachel took a small sip, and as I suspected, pursed her lips and screwed her face up with disgust.

'Yuck. That is *vile*,' she said.

'It's just a means to an end.' Carly shook her head when Rachel tried to hand the bottle to her and pushed it back into Rachel's hands. 'Have another go. The more you drink, the easier it gets. It'll help you relax, help you have a good time.'

Rachel did what Carly suggested and put the bottle to her lips and took another drink.

'Not quite so bad,' she said, making a face. 'But I think I still like normal lemonade better.'

Carly laughed. 'But normal lemonade won't help you enjoy yourself the way this will. Take my word for it.'

I'm not sure why I didn't worry about what Rachel was drinking. I don't know why I didn't take care of her better, monitor her drinking and make sure she stayed relatively sober. I guess the vodka had an almost immediate effect on me – on all of us. We shared the bottle as we walked, each of us taking frequent sips, and as our senses became more accustomed to the alcohol it started to taste better and we started taking larger swigs.

When the bottle was empty, Carly stopped walking.

'Hold on.' She put her bag on the ground and pulled out another bottle, larger and made of glass, turning it so that we could see the label: Stolichnaya. 'You didn't think I'd let us go short, did you?' She looked up and grinned. 'We'll have to have it straight now. There's no more lemonade.' She refilled the drink bottle and straightened up, holding it out to Rachel. 'You can go first. It's going to taste like fire again. But you'll get used to it.'

Rachel took a large swig. The expression on her face as she swallowed made us laugh.

The walk took almost forty minutes and by the time we arrived we were all quite tipsy. Rachel had a neat circle of flushed skin on each of her cheeks and a huge grin on her face. She looked pretty and innocent and very young.

'How do you feel?' I took her hand in mine and smiled. The vodka had dissolved all my earlier irritation, smoothed out all my rough edges. I no longer felt so mad at her for coming with us. It just didn't matter. 'Do you feel okay?'

We still hadn't entered the shed but we could hear the music, the *dum dum dum* of the bass, the sound of voices and laughter, young people having a good time. Young people with no adults around.

Rachel just stared at me, still smiling, and nodded. She started moving her body in time with the music. She raised her eyebrows and cocked her head, as if to listen more carefully to the notes.

'Come *on*.' Carly stood behind us and pushed us gently forward. 'We're not going to stand out here all afternoon. Much as I love you both, I didn't walk all this way just to hang out here with you two.'

It occurred to me as we were heading towards the entrance that I hadn't actually thought any of this through very carefully. We'd only planned to be gone for an hour. We'd planned to get Rachel home by five, with plenty of time to practise the piano. But we'd been at Carly's for a good ten minutes and the walk had taken another forty. And as I watched Rachel heading into the party, the bounce in her step matching the rhythm of the music, I realised that it was inevitable that we'd be home late. If Rachel had just gone home everything would have been okay. I could have rung Mum and Dad later and made up some excuse for my absence, said I was working on an assignment at Carly's house. They would have been annoyed but not as angry as they were going to be now that Rachel was involved. Rachel being home late would be a big deal, she was still only fourteen and was missing out on piano practice – and missing piano was always a major crime. And I had no idea how we were going to cover up the smell of vodka. One thing was certain; we were going to be in trouble, *big* trouble.

I may as well make the most of it, I thought as I followed Rachel inside.

14

Alice walks ahead of us. She's only a fraction in front, barely two steps, but it's enough to make it difficult to include her in a conversation, enough to make it clear that she's not in the mood to talk. I don't think she's unhappy or angry or upset – far from it, she's in good spirits, glowing with energy and beauty, clearly excited to be going out on such a beautiful autumn evening and enjoying the last of the warm weather.

But she gets like this sometimes; preoccupied and uncommunicative. Robbie and I know her well enough not to worry that she might be upset or offended about something; we understand that she is sometimes happier not to participate. Robbie even made a joke about it once. Robbie and I were talking animatedly of our shared love of music – from rock and pop to opera – when we discovered that Alice had fallen asleep on the sofa. We had no idea how long she'd been asleep. We'd been talking on and on, oblivious, for hours. 'I think she's tired of our constant gibbering, Katherine,' Robbie had said, laughing, when we found her. 'I think we talk too much. We're boring her to death.' And he was probably right. Robbie and I never run out of things to say to each other – our conversations can continue for hours and hours.

In fact, Robbie and I talk so much, and get on so very well, that I started to worry that it might be upsetting Alice. I wondered if she might not be jealous. But when I asked her if she minded me talking to Robbie so much, if she wanted me to back off, she shook her head and looked at me quizzically.

'Why? I love it that you get on. My two favourite people in the world. I'm thrilled that you've got so much to talk about,' she said.

'Oh, good. I was scared you might be . . . well, think that I was stepping on your toes, that you might be jealous.'

'Jealous?' Alice shook her head, looked thoughtful. 'I've never been jealous. Of anyone. Of anything. I can honestly say that it's not an emotion I'm familiar with.' And then she shrugged. 'It sounds like a stupid, futile little sentiment if you ask me.'

It's Friday night and the Higher School Certificate exams are starting in a few weeks and I probably should be at home revising. But I studied hard during the week and both Robbie and Alice begged me to come out.

The HSC is important, I know that, but right now my friendship with Alice and Robbie is more so. Right now, having fun, living the life I've denied myself for so long, seems more than important. It's crucial.

Robbie and I are talking about skiing. Robbie loves it and suggests that the three of us head down to the snow next winter.

'I'm not very good, though,' I say. 'I'll probably just slow you down, ruin your holiday.'

'I'll teach you,' Robbie says. 'You'll be good by the time we leave.'

'Such arrogance.' I laugh. 'You don't even know how bad I am. To teach me to be good at skiing would be something close to a miracle.'

'He taught *me*.' Alice turns round and slows her pace so that she can walk beside us. She shuffles between us so that Robbie and I are forced apart and she can walk in the middle. 'I couldn't even stand straight on the skis when we went to the snow last year, but a week later I was skiing like a champion.' She hooks her arm through Robbie's and smiles up at him. 'And you are so bloody sexy when you're skiing.' She looks at me. 'He's just so confident and in charge when he skis. So totally lovable.'

Robbie suddenly stops walking and looks down at Alice. He is frowning suddenly. 'Lovable, huh? You could have fooled me. That's not quite the impression I got when we were there.'

Alice laughs and pushes her body closer to Robbie's. 'Silly,' she says. 'You obviously don't understand me, then.'

Robbie doesn't respond to Alice's affection the way he usually does; instead he shakes his head in a gesture of irritation. 'We're here,' he says, unhooking his arm from Alice's and stepping ahead. He nods towards a bar doorway which has 'Out of Africa' written above it. 'This is the place.'

He pulls open the door and steps aside so that Alice and I can go in ahead of him. I smile at him as I pass and though his mouth curves upward the smile doesn't reach his eyes. And I can tell by the stiff way he holds himself that he is upset or angry or both.

Inside it is dark, lit only by small lamps on the walls and candles on the tables. It takes a moment for my eyes to adjust, but when they do I see that the walls are a deep red and that there are brightly coloured Moroccan-looking cushions on each of the chairs.

'I'll go to the bar and get us some drinks,' Robbie says.

'What an excellent idea,' says Alice. 'I'll have a bottle of champagne.'

'A whole bottle?' Robbie stares at her. 'Don't you think that's a bit—'

'No,' Alice interrupts. 'I think it's perfect. A bottle. Thank you.'

Robbie shakes his head and looks at me. 'Katherine?'

'Lemon, lime and soda, thanks.'

Alice rolls her eyes. '*Lemon, lime and soda, thanks.*' She imitates me in a high-pitched, mocking voice. 'No alcohol for Miss Goody Two Shoes.'

'I can't, Alice. I'm under-age. I don't have ID.'

'You don't have to explain yourself, Katherine,' Robbie says. 'I'm just going to have a soft drink too. I've got soccer tomorrow. Alice is going to be drinking alone.'

'Wow.' Alice sighs. 'What a load of fun you two are. Lucky me.'

Robbie frowns down at her, his mouth set, his eyes cold, before turning away and heading towards the bar.

Alice watches him walk away. 'I think he's mad at me,' she says, shrugging. She looks round the room, staring openly at the other customers.

I turn to watch Robbie, who is standing at the bar, waiting for the drinks. He is staring straight ahead, his face blank. He looks miserable.

'What just happened?' I say. 'Why is he suddenly so angry?'

'Oh, I think I reminded him of something when I talked about our snow trip. He got a bit upset when we were there. I spent some time with one of the ski instructors. Just one night. Robbie didn't like it.'

'Some *time*? One *night*? What do you mean?'

Alice doesn't look at me. She is staring at a couple at a table to the side of us. 'I mean exactly what I said.' She sighs and speaks in a clear, deliberate voice, as if I have difficulty hearing or understanding. 'Just one night. With another man. In his room. I'm sure you don't want the details? Robbie wasn't happy. He seems to have some kind of misplaced proprietary feelings towards me.'

I'm so shocked by what Alice has said that I can think of nothing to say, and I sit there stupidly for a moment, my hand over my mouth. I knew that Alice had a fairly casual view of her relationship with Robbie, I knew that she was far less committed than he. But that she actually spent the night with another man while on a trip away with Robbie is astounding. Either it was an act of unspeakable and deliberate cruelty or, just as shocking, it proved that Alice had some kind of bizarre inability to imagine how such behaviour would affect Robbie.

Before I have the chance to gather my thoughts and make some kind of intelligent response, Alice jumps up from her seat and starts waving her arms.

'Ben!' she calls out as she leaves our table and approaches the couple that she's been watching for the last few minutes. 'Ben Dewberry! It *is* you. I thought I recognised you. I've been staring and staring and then I heard your accent. I knew it was you, for sure, as soon as I heard you speak.'

Alice is so loud that there is a moment of silence in the restaurant as people stop talking to listen. Ben and the girl sitting opposite him – a tall girl with long, wild red hair and pale skin – stare at Alice in silence as she approaches. Ben looks shocked, almost frightened.

'Alice.' He stands up and extends his hand as if to shake Alice's, but she ignores his gesture and steps close to embrace him. She kisses him, hard and for a long time, on the lips. When she steps back, Ben's cheeks are flushed and he looks uncertain and embarrassed. 'Wow. What are you doing here?' He has an American accent.

'Having dinner, of course, silly. The same as you.' Alice takes hold of Ben's hand and turns back to face our table just as Robbie arrives with the drinks. 'Robbie, Katherine. This is Ben. Ben Dewberry, the first true love of my life.'

Ben looks over Alice's shoulder at his companion and shrugs, starts to say something, but Alice, who has her back towards Ben's friend, tugs on Ben's arm.

'Come and sit with us,' she says. 'Come on. We can all sit together.'

'Oh. I don't think . . .' Ben looks at his friend. 'Philippa and I . . .'

Alice spins on her heel and faces Philippa. 'Hello there. I'm Alice.' She lets go of Ben and puts her arm out towards Philippa. They shake hands. Alice grins and Philippa nods, smiling stiffly.

'You'll come and join us, won't you?' Alice says. 'At least come over and sit with us for a while. Ben and I haven't seen each other for years. We've got a lot of catching up to do.'

Philippa and Ben agree to join us and as they gather their things, Robbie looks at me, his expression one of irritation and disbelief, and rolls his eyes. The waitress helps us pull a table over and join it to ours to make enough room for the five of us.

Except for Alice, who seems oblivious to everyone else's discomfort and chats away happily, we are all very quiet and restrained as we sip on our drinks. Alice talks about the summer when she went out with Ben. Ben seems uncomfortable and embarrassed, and smiles at Philippa apologetically every time Alice mentions how much she enjoyed having an American boyfriend and how she used to love listening to his accent.

'Let's order some food,' Alice says suddenly. 'I'm about to die of starvation. You'll order for us, won't you, Robbs? You've been here before, you know what's good?'

'Oh.' Philippa shakes her head and looks at Ben with a panicked expression. 'No. We'd better go back to our own table now.'

'Don't be silly.' Alice reaches over the table and puts her hand over Philippa's. 'We're all enjoying your company so much. Please stay and eat with us. You know, the three of us were totally bored and irritable before you two joined us. We're all sick to death of each other really.' Alice tips her head back and laughs. 'We've spent so much time together lately that we can barely stand the sight of each other any more.'

Alice continues laughing but everyone else is silent. I stare down at the napkin in my lap and try to hide my burning cheeks. I feel humiliated and upset. I've been enjoying Alice and Robbie's company so much, feeling so happy to have such close friendships again, that Alice's comment – her obvious disdain of something I've come to value so dearly – makes me feel ridiculous, injured.

I'm sure that Robbie feels equally upset, and for this reason I'm unable to look at him. To see my humiliation reflected in his eyes would be unbearable.

Ben says, 'Sure, we'll eat with you guys. We're having a great time.' His voice is loud, over-enthusiastic. 'Aren't we, Philippa?'

'Excellent. Thank God for that.' Alice slaps her hand on the table triumphantly. Her champagne bottle is empty and she looks slightly drunk – her cheeks red, her eyes brilliant – and she's completely oblivious to the tension between everyone. 'Let's get some more drinks to this party,' she says. 'We're dying of thirst here, Robbie. What do you recommend next?'

Robbie clears his throat. 'I'm just going to have another

Coke.' He smiles at Philippa and Ben in a forced, un-natural way. 'What do you guys want?'

'More water?' Philippa lifts an empty jug. 'If that's okay?'

'Ben'll have a beer,' Alice says, nudging him, grinning. 'Won't you Ben? Huh? You're not a party pooper.'

'Sure.' He nods. 'Why not? A beer would be fine.'

'And more champagne,' Alice says, tossing a hundred-dollar note towards Robbie. 'Another bottle.'

'Could you come and give me a hand, Katherine?' Robbie asks as he takes the money. His voice is stiff and controlled. He looks furious.

'Sure.' I watch Alice as I get up. She's been so weirdly belligerent since we arrived that I'm afraid that my going to the bar with Robbie will incite another aggressive comment. But she's leaning towards Philippa, her eyebrows raised, and doesn't even glance our way as we leave.

Robbie and I walk to the bar in silence. When we reach it Robbie turns back to look at our table.

'Bloody Alice,' he says. 'She's got some kind of agenda tonight. This is going to end in tears.'

'What do you mean?' I feel a knot of dread tighten my lower belly. I don't want anything unpleasant to happen. I don't want Alice to behave badly, to be cruel. I don't want Robbie and Alice to break up, or for Alice to do something so horrible that I'm forced to question my friendship with her. The idea that this all could be over is too dreadful to contemplate and I have to control a rising sense of panic at the thought of a future without my friendship with Robbie and Alice, a future far too lonely and dull and miserable to bear. 'Let's just have dinner and get her out of here. Get her home to bed.'

Robbie looks at me. 'You haven't seen her like this before, have you?'

'Like this? I don't know. I haven't seen her be so deliberately unkind before, if that's what you mean.'

He shakes his head. 'This is different. I've seen her like this a few times now. It's really weird. And scary. She's on a self-destruct mission. There's no way we'll be able to get through to her tonight. She won't listen. Not to you or me or Ben or Philippa. And I'll bet you a million dollars she'll want to make a big night of it. And she'll drag Philippa and Ben along for the ride, you watch.' He laughs bitterly. 'She can be very demanding when she's like this.'

I'm not sure what Robbie is so worried about. What he's saying doesn't make a lot of sense, but I'm frightened anyway. 'So we'll just go out and have some fun. Go dancing or something. We can look after her, can't we? We can make sure nothing bad happens.'

'If I were you I'd bail out now while I could. I'd go home myself, but someone's got to make sure she makes it home alive. She's drunk or high or something.' He looks over at the table again. 'Or she's in some kind of psychotic state.'

Alice is talking animatedly to Philippa. Philippa has her arms crossed defensively over her chest and is leaning back, away from Alice. She isn't smiling.

We collect the drinks and as we are walking back to the table, Philippa jumps up. She walks quickly, her head down, towards the bathroom.

'Is Philippa okay?' I ask Ben as we put the drinks down.

'I . . .' He looks at Alice. 'I think she might be . . .'

'She's pissed off because I told her something about Ben and me.' Alice laughs. 'Jesus, Ben. You picked an uptight one this time. If you wanted to find someone totally different to me you sure succeeded.'

Ben laughs uncertainly. I can't believe that he is just sitting there, and I'm about to ask if he wants me to go and check on Philippa when Robbie stands up.

'I forgot the water,' he says and heads back to the bar.

And then I see why Ben is not in any hurry to chase after Philippa. As Robbie turns away, Alice puts her hand beneath the table. She puts it on Ben's thigh, *high* on his thigh, and then moves it so that her hand is directly over his crotch.

I stand up immediately. Alice is smiling at me, a

smile completely devoid of warmth, and I'm certain that she knows what I've just seen, and that she's glad.

'I'm just going to the bathroom.' I manoeuvre myself between the table and my chair so clumsily, that the chair tips backwards. 'Shit,' I say as I grab the back of the chair before it falls. '*Shit!*'

'Calm down, Katherine,' Alice says. 'What's the matter with you? You look like you've just seen a ghost.'

I pull myself up straight and glare down at her, and then I look at Ben, who at least has the decency to look embarrassed. 'I'm going to the bathroom,' I say as coldly and as calmly as I can. 'To see if Philippa is okay.'

Alice lifts her shoulders dismissively and I turn and head towards the bathroom. I wonder as I walk away if Robbie will return to the table and see what I've just seen, or if not see it, at least sense that something very odd is going on. I don't particularly want Robbie to see Alice's hand between Ben's legs, it pains me to imagine his hurt and embarrassment, and I don't want the evening to end in drama and tears and painful recriminations. But Alice is humiliating Robbie and he deserves better, and there's a definite part of me that wants Alice to be punished for it, a part of me that wants to see Robbie slap her face and dump her for good. And yet I still have a small and ridiculous (but persistent) hope that everything will miraculously turn out all right –

that Alice will wake up to herself, stop acting so crazy, apologise, so the three of us will be able to go home happy and laughing; return to normal.

But even if Robbie does see Alice touching Ben, it may not necessarily be the end of their relationship. After all, I've just learned that Alice had sex with someone else while they were on holiday and Robbie still wants to be with her. I've really no idea how much Robbie would put up with from Alice but I'm concerned, and quite sad, to think that my friendship with Alice may have changed irrevocably. She has been so unkind tonight, so deliberately cruel to both me and Robbie – and to Philippa – that I don't think I'll be able to trust her again. At least not so blindly, so faithfully. Right now, I'm not even sure that I like her.

In the bathroom one cubicle door is closed and I assume that Philippa is hiding inside.

'Philippa?' I tap gently on the door.

There's no answer, but I sense her become stiller, quieter.

'Philippa. It's me, Katherine. I just wanted to see if you were okay.'

'Katherine?' I see her shadow move beneath the door and then she unlocks and opens it. 'Thank goodness it's you,' she says. 'I thought you might be Alice.'

Her eyes are bloodshot and her cheeks have bright

red circles of colour on them. She looks as though she's been crying.

'Are you all right?' I say.

'Yes.' She puts her hand over her mouth and looks down. When she has composed herself she looks up again and smiles. 'I'm fine. Thanks.'

She goes to the sink and washes her hands, catches my eye in the mirror.

'So, what are they doing out there?' she asks.

'Oh.' I look away. 'Just talking, waiting for the food, you know.' I'm not sure what she's seen, don't know how upset she is.

She ignores my question. 'So Alice and Ben aren't screwing on the table yet?'

'What?' I say.

She laughs shortly, checks her face in the mirror, fixes her hair. 'I don't care if they are, you know. I couldn't care less. Ben's a creep. I hardly know him. This is only the second time we've been out together.'

'Really?' I stare at her. 'So he's not your boyfriend?'

'No way.' She shakes her head. 'God, no. Give me a little more credit than that.'

I am smiling now, with relief and amusement.

She grins back at me and then tips her head back and laughs delightedly at the ceiling. She laughs loudly and happily, and with relief, as if she's been holding it in, and I realise that she hasn't been in the cubicle crying at all. 'Alice had her hand on Ben's thigh. *He* thought I couldn't see. *She* knew I could. I can't tell you how truly *embarrassing* it was sitting there like that, playing her weird, psycho little game. Completely sur- real . . . I wish I'd said something. But I'm never quick enough, I can never think of something witty or intel- ligent to say when I'm in a situation like that. It takes a certain personality type, a certain sharpness that I just don't have.' She pauses for a moment, then looks at me more seriously. 'What is it with her? With Alice? I'm sorry, I know she's your friend, but why does she have her hand on the leg of some creepy guy who is out to dinner with another girl? And why on earth would she do something like that when she has someone as lovely as that Robbie guy with her? They are together, aren't they? It's hard to tell. Especially when she's so busy flirting with Ben. But he seems really nice. Robbie, I mean, not Ben. Ben's about as nice as a bathful of slimy toads.'

'Robbie *is* nice. He's lovely,' I say quickly. 'And I don't know. I don't know what's wrong with Alice to- night. But, honestly, she's not normally like this. She's not usually so horrible.' But as I say it I realise that my words feel hollow and untrue. I haven't seen Alice behave quite this badly before but, in some way, it seems that she's been getting progressively worse since I've known her. The more I see of her, the more I see that I don't like. I shrug. 'I'm sorry. She's been really unpleasant. There's no excuse.'

'Unpleasant?' Philippa stares at me incredulously. 'Unpleasant? Sorry, but that's not unpleasant. Unpleasant is a hot westerly wind, or someone in a bad mood. I wouldn't exactly use that word to describe your friend. A better word would be cruel. Or vicious. Or spiteful. Or all three.'

And though I'm starting to wonder if Philippa may not be right, I also feel a prick of indignation. Alice is my friend, after all, and it's not fair of Philippa to judge her so harshly, so quickly.

'She's not that bad,' I say. 'She's got some fantastic qualities. She can be incredibly generous and charming when she wants to. She can be a lot of fun.'

'So could Adolf Hitler,' she says. 'Look, I don't want to offend you. And I shouldn't say this stuff, I know. I get myself in trouble all the time for opening my mouth like this. You've heard of big foot? Well, I'm big mouth. I can't stop myself. Anyway. Your friend is a total bitch. And I don't think it's curable.'

'What?' I sound a lot more surprised and offended than I feel.

'Yep. And I absolutely know what I'm talking about. I'm studying psychology at university.' She shrugs. 'I'm practically a psychologist so I'm totally qualified to make a diagnosis – Alice is a bitch. In fact, I think she's probably got mental problems. And you seem not to have figured that out yet.'

I just stand there, silent, bewildered.

Philippa watches my face, then bursts out laughing. 'Okay. Sorry. That was just a bad joke. I mean, Alice is definitely a bitch and I *am* studying psychology, that's true, but I was just kidding about being qualified to diagnose it. I mean, anyone could see that she's not a good person. I was just trying to say it in a funny way. Cheer you up. You look so serious and upset.'

I turn away and occupy myself looking in the mirror, fixing my hair. I *am* upset, Philippa is right, but I don't want her to know how bad I feel, and I certainly don't want to cry in front of her. I should be angry, offended on Alice's behalf, but Alice has behaved so horribly to-night that I can hardly blame Philippa for thinking as she does.

'I doubt very much that you can have any kind of real understanding of a person after knowing them for just half an hour,' I say unconvincingly. 'She's just having a bad day.'

'I've known her for almost an hour and a half, actually.' She leans into the mirror right next to me, forcing me to meet her eye. 'And I don't know about you, but I've had lots of bad days and I've never behaved like that. And I'll bet you ten million bucks that you haven't either.'

I'm about to tell Philippa that she's being ridiculous, that Alice may be eccentric and a little self-centred, but she's not a terrible person, she isn't *sick*. And Robbie and I are not a pair of gullible idiots. But then we hear the creak of the toilet door as it swings open, and suddenly Alice is standing there in front of us.

'What are you two doing?' she says as she walks into a cubicle. She leaves the door open as she pulls her skirt up, lowers her underpants, sits on the toilet and starts to pee noisily. 'The food has started to arrive. And it's so divine that if you don't hurry it'll all be eaten before you even get back to the table.' She stands up and flushes, walks to the basin to wash her hands and looks first at Philippa and then me in the mirror. 'And guess what? We're all going back to my place after this. To make margaritas. And we're all gonna have one. Even you, Katherine. It's all been decided.'

We return to the table and eat our dinner, which is, as Alice said, delicious. Alice gives all her attention to Philippa and is suddenly interested in asking Philippa about herself. Philippa is polite, and answers Alice's questions as briefly as possible without elaborating or encouraging conversation, but she glances surreptitiously at me every now and again, a bemused look on her face.

Apart from the obvious coldness with which Philippa treats Ben, the dinner passes smoothly and without further incident and when we leave the restaurant and start walking up the road towards Alice's I'm surprised to find that my anxiety has dissipated. In fact I'm feeling quite relaxed, am almost enjoying myself. There are a lot of people on the streets, laughing and talking as they walk, and there's a contagious vibe of excitement. It's Friday night and everyone is buzzing with anticipation and enthusiasm, there are happy-looking people everywhere, funky clothes, noise and laughter. So Alice is a bit drunk and has been a bit of a bitch. So what? Worse things have happened. It's hardly the end of the world.

We stop at a bottle shop on the way and buy tequila for the margaritas. We buy handfuls of lemons from the small grocery shop on the corner of Alice's street. And when we get to Alice's we are all happily occupied; finding enough cocktail glasses, squeezing lemons, blending the bittersweet mixture. Alice puts on some music and we sing loudly as we work in her hot, crowded kitchen. And we're all suddenly enjoying ourselves, and each other's company, and for a while I forget about Alice's earlier behaviour, forget my fears that the night was going to end in disaster.

'Let's play a game,' Alice says when we've each got an enormous, icy cocktail in our hand. I don't intend to drink mine, but I'll sip on it just to keep Alice happy and tip it out when she's not looking. I'm going to remain stone-cold sober. Vigilant.

'Yes,' I agree and I look at Robbie and smile, and it's a smile that says, *Look, everything is going to be fine. We're all having a great time.*

And Robbie smiles back tentatively, still uncertain.

'Truth or dare.' Alice rubs her hands together excitedly and heads into the lounge room. 'Come on. I *love* this game. It's the best way to get to know people.'

We all follow her and sit cross-legged on the floor round her coffee table. Someone turns the music down.

'Me first?' Alice pokes her tongue out at Robbie. 'And you can ask me. Since you think you know me so well. You might find out something surprising.'

'Truth or dare?' Robbie says.

'Truth.'

'Okay, then.' Robbie takes a sip of his drink and looks thoughtful for a moment. Then he looks at Alice seriously. 'Do you ever regret things? Things that you've said or done?'

Alice stares at him for a moment. Then she rolls her eyes. 'God, Robbie. This is meant to be fun.' She sighs. 'Regret things . . . um, let me ponder on this for a moment.' She shakes her head firmly. 'Nope. I don't. I regret nothing. Regret is for the incompetent and the unconfident. And I am neither of those. Okay, thanks for that boring contribution, Robbie.' She looks round at everyone, smiling, 'Who should I pick next?' And then she looks pointedly at Ben. 'Young Ben. You might help me keep this game on track. Keep it dirty and fun the way it's meant to be. Truth or dare? And answer quickly before I fall asleep.'

'Truth.'

'Good. Just what I hoped you'd say. And I have a question all ready for you.' Alice raises her eyebrows and leans forwards. 'So, young Ben, where was the most interesting place you've ever had sex? And you have to answer, or I get to give you a dare. And it won't be nice.'

Ben laughs nervously and looks down at his drink. 'Um, well I guess it was once, well, it was a couple of years ago. When I first came to Australia. There was this very wild girl I met. And she wouldn't take no for an answer. No way. Not this girl. And my God, her body was awesome, so I wasn't about to say no myself. And anyway, this one night, we were at a friend's house and this girl, she drags me into the parents' bedroom. And, you know, we're making out on their bed and then the parents come in so we scuttle into the cupboard, this huge walk-in robe thing, and well, it's nice and dark in there and cosy, and so, you know, we just continue with what we were doing before.' He stops talking for a moment and looks at Alice and grins. Alice looks back at him, smiling, encouraging, and it's suddenly very obvious that the girl he's talking about is Alice. And Robbie is staring at Ben, his face devoid of expression, but I notice that his fist is clenched tightly in his lap. And again I feel that sense of panic, an overwhelming desire for everything to just stop. Rewind. Go back to the beginning. The night is going to end horribly after all. Robbie was right.

But Ben is oblivious, and I wonder if he has even realised that Alice and Robbie are an item. Alice has certainly done a good job of acting as if Robbie means nothing to her.

'But that's not it,' Ben continues. 'The really kinky bit was when—'

'Thanks, Ben,' Robbie interrupts, his voice loud and cold and sharp with sarcasm. 'Thanks for that. But I think we've all heard enough now. And thanks Alice for asking such an intelligent question. 'Cause that was so interesting, just *so* great to listen to. I didn't realise, but now I do, that seedy sex stories are what makes a game fun. Great. Thanks for that, Ben. I'll try to be as . . . well, as crass as you, when my turn comes.'

Ben blushes a deep red and sucks furiously on his cocktail and Philippa smothers a horrified, embarrassed laugh in her hand.

'My turn, my turn,' I say, falsely cheerful. I turn to Philippa expectantly, hoping that she'll help me try and smooth everything out. 'Philippa? Truth or dare?'

'Truth,' Philippa says obligingly. 'I love truths. Don't you? I think they're just hilarious. You can find out some brilliant secrets about people. And I really love hearing the questions people ask too. They often reveal a lot more about the person asking than the person being asked, don't you think?'

I smile at Philippa, grateful for her chatter. But it's hard to come up with a something to ask her, and I'm silent for a moment, thinking.

'Katherine,' Alice laughs. 'You haven't even got a question, have you? Let me have a go. Come on. One more. I'll ask you.'

'But you've already had a turn,' Robbie says. 'Let Katherine have her go.'

'We're not playing properly anyway. Really, Ben should be having a turn. So it doesn't matter, does it?' Alice says. And it's clear now, that she's drunk. She's speaking slowly, carefully, trying hard to enunciate each word, but the slur in her voice is obvious. 'And since when did you become such an annoying stickler for the rules, Robbie? Since when did you become such a boring bloody killjoy?'

'Killjoy?' Robbie laughs. 'There's not much joy to be killed here, Alice.'

Alice ignores him and looks at me.

'Truth or dare?' she asks.

And I hesitate while I decide. I have so many secrets, so many things I don't want to reveal, but this is only a game, only a bit of fun. And I know that Alice's dare won't be something easy or straightforward. 'Truth,' I say finally. 'I can imagine one of your dares, and I don't fancy running down Oxford Street naked tonight.'

'Truth,' Alice says, slowly, drawing out the vowel sound as if she's savouring the word. 'Are you sure? Are you sure you can be completely honest?'

'I think so. Try me.'

'Okay.' And then she looks at me curiously. 'So. Were you glad, deep down? Were you glad to be rid of her? Your perfect sister? Were you secretly glad when she was killed?'

And it's suddenly as if everything is coming to me in slow motion, through a hazy fog. I hear Robbie sigh with irritation and tell Alice to stop being a fool. I sense Philippa looking at me, wondering what is going on, if Alice can possibly be serious. I feel Philippa's hand on my arm, the concern in her touch.

But I can only look at Alice's eyes. They are cold, appraising, and her pupils so large that all I can see is black. Hard and unyielding. Deep. Ruthless. Black.

15

I wake early, when it's still dark. Sarah has left her own bed and hopped into mine while I've been asleep, and her warm little body is pressed close against me. Her head is on my pillow and I'm lying right near the edge, so that the entire other side, more than half the bed, is empty.

I slide out of bed slowly and smoothly so as not to wake her and grab my heavy woollen jumper from the chair where I tossed it the night before. It is cold and I head straight to the living area and turn on the gas heater. It fills the small room with a comforting golden glow and warms it immediately. I make a pot of tea and take it to the living room, where I sit in the corner of the sofa, my legs tucked beneath me.

I started waking early like this when Sarah was little and I've been unable to sleep late since. Sometimes I spend this time cleaning or getting ready for the day while Sarah is asleep – making her lunch, preparing her clothes – but usually I sit and sip tea, enjoy the time to myself. I don't think about anything in particular; I've become very good at not thinking. I avoid making futile plans for an uncertain future, and even more than that, I want to avoid remembering the past. So I go into an almost meditative state, my brain empty, my thoughts focused only on the taste of my tea, or on the regular in and out of my breath. And often, when Sarah wakes around seven and comes out, crumpled and warm and smelling of sleep, I'm surprised that two or more hours have passed so quickly.

But this morning I drink my tea and sit for less than an hour. I'm excited about the day ahead and can't wait for Sarah to see the snow, can't wait to hear her excited squeals of delight when she rides a toboggan, makes a snowman. I want her awake and enjoying the anticipation with me, so at six I get up and make Sarah's favourite breakfast, French toast with sliced banana and maple syrup and a large mug of hot chocolate. I place our plates and mugs on the table and go into the bedroom to wake her up.

'Are we going to the snow now, Mummy?' Sarah asks as soon as she opens her eyes. She sits up, immediately bright and alert. 'Is it time to go?'

'Not yet.' I sit on the bed and hug her. 'But I've made French toast, a big, enormous pile of it, and hot chocolate. I hope you're very hungry.'

'Yummy yummy.' She pushes the blankets from her legs, stands up and runs from the room, leaving me there, smiling, alone on the bed.

I follow her into the dining room and find her already kneeling on her chair, eating with gusto.

'Are you having some, Mummy?' she says, her mouth full. 'There's enough for you.'

'I should think so.' I sit opposite and take a piece of toast from the tray in the middle and put it on my plate. 'Actually, I think there might be enough for ten.'

'I don't think so.' Sarah shakes her head and looks serious. 'I'm very hungry. I need ten today. French toast is my most favouritest.'

And she does manage to eat an extraordinary amount – and gulp down her hot chocolate between mouthfuls. And as soon as she's finished she climbs down from her chair.

'I'm going to get ready now,' she says. 'I think we've got a very big day ahead of us.'

I laugh at the way she has appropriated one of my phrases, her attempt to be grown-up. 'We have too. A very big day. But we've still got lots of time. The sun is only just starting to come up.'

'I want to be ready first,' she says. 'I want to be ready before the sun.'

16

And I hear it again. The knocking, gentle but insistent. Whoever it is has been knocking for over ten minutes and I'm tired of trying to ignore it, sick of pretending that I'm not here.

I go to the door but don't open it.

'Go away,' I say. 'It's the middle of the night. Go *away*.'

'Katherine. It's me, Robbie.' And his voice is so familiar and comforting, and so filled with kindness that almost I start crying again. 'And Philippa's here too. Please let us come in.'

'Is Alice there?'

'No.'

I sigh and release the deadlock. I turn and walk away down the hall without greeting them, leaving them to push the door open themselves. I know they mean well, that they are concerned about me, but I'm exhausted with the events of the evening and with crying and want to be left alone. Not to sleep – sleep won't come – but to be miserable in private.

I head to the living room and sit on the sofa, where I've been curled up for the past hour.

Philippa and Robbie follow me and sit on the sofa opposite.

'Alice told us,' Robbie says gently. 'About your sister.'

I nod. If I talk I'll start crying again, so I remain silent.

'Would you prefer it if I left?' Philippa glances at Robbie and then at me. 'I just wanted to make sure you were okay. I just wanted to be sure that Robbie found you. But I don't want to intrude.'

I look at Philippa and shrug – she looks dreadful. Her skin is pale and she has deep shadows beneath her eyes, as if the events of the evening have left her shell-shocked.

'I'll stay, then, if you don't mind,' she sighs. 'I'm too tired to actually go anywhere right now.'

It makes no difference to me if she is there or not but I'm suddenly very glad that Vivien is away for the weekend, that she's not here to witness all this.

'Should I make tea?' Philippa says suddenly, looking pleased to have thought of something useful to do.

'I'd like some.' Robbie smiles at Philippa gratefully. 'Katherine?'

'Sure,' I say. 'But I—'

'She likes it made properly,' Robbie explains to Philippa. 'The pot and tea leaves are on the shelf above the kettle.'

'Are you okay?' Robbie puts his hand on my knee when Philippa has left the room.

I nod and attempt a smile. 'What a shitty night that was. I should have listened to you. I should have gone home early, like you said.' I lean forward and whisper. 'Philippa thinks Alice is a complete and utter bitch. She thinks she's got mental problems. Did she tell you that?'

'I don't blame her.' Robbie shrugs. 'She has been a total bitch tonight. And maybe she has got something wrong with her. Who knows? But what difference does it make anyway? Those kind of things can't actually be fixed. Maybe Alice is just a rotten person.'

He leans back and sighs, looks down at his knees and picks at a loose thread from his jeans. He looks tired, defeated, and very, very sad.

'What about you, Robbie? Are *you* okay?' I ask him. 'You don't look very good.'

'No. I'm not.' His eyes, which are already red, suddenly fill with tears and he shakes his head irritably as if to be rid of them. 'It was just a crappy night all round, wasn't it?' He laughs bitterly.

'Yes.' And there's nothing else to say.

Philippa returns and we sip on our tea, quietly,

without talking, each of us caught up in our own private thoughts, our own fatigue and misery.

By the time we've finished our tea it's 4 a.m. and I persuade Robbie and Philippa that they should get some sleep at my place. I find Robbie a blanket and pillow so that he can sleep on the sofa, and ask Philippa if she minds sharing my bed. The evening has been so emotionally draining and Philippa and I are both so exhausted that we are able to lie side by side, beneath the same blanket, with no awkwardness whatsoever. In fact I feel comforted by her presence. And before I close my eyes to sleep, Philippa smiles at me and takes my hand and squeezes.

'Sleep well,' she says.

'Thank you,' I say, closing my eyes. 'I think I will.'

When I wake, the sun is shining brightly into my room and Philippa is no longer beside me. But I can hear the soft hum of voices, hers and Robbie's, coming from another room and I'm glad that they're both still here, that I won't have to face the day alone. I close my eyes again.

The next time I wake the sun has moved from my window and I can tell by the quality of light that it is afternoon. I can no longer hear Robbie or Philippa, but I can hear the canned laughter and tinny music of the television. I get up and go to the living room.

Philippa is sitting on the sofa, watching an old black-and-white movie, and she looks up as I approach. 'Good morning! Or afternoon, actually. I've just been waiting here until you woke up. I watched this old movie, *All About Eve*. It was brilliant! I think you'd like it, you should get it on DVD. Robbie and I didn't know whether you'd want to be alone or not. And he had to go to work. But he said he'd come back later.' She stops talking for a moment to take a breath and smiles warmly. 'How *are* you?'

'I'm good.' I sit down on the sofa next to her. 'Thank you for staying.'

'Oh, it's nothing.' She picks up the remote control and mutes the noise of the television. 'Are you hungry?'

'Yes.' I nod. 'I am, actually.'

'Good. I bought the ingredients to make a salad. It's a hearty kind of salad, really a whole meal in itself, tomatoes and prosciutto and asparagus and boiled eggs and stuff, and I got some fresh bread too. It's totally delicious. My favourite salad in the world. Do you think you'd like some? Should I make it now?'

'Oh. Wow. Yes please. But only if you're sure you want to. You don't have to do all this. I'm really fine. Honestly. But, yes, if you want to, that would be awesome.'

'Excellent.' She jumps up. ''Cause I'm bloody starving.'

I offer to help prepare the food but Philippa refuses, says that she can't stand cooking with other people. So I perch on a stool in the kitchen and watch and when it's finished we take it out onto the verandah. And we eat quickly, both of us ravenous. We don't talk about Alice, thankfully, or Rachel, or the events of the night before, but Philippa is so naturally talkative that there is barely a moment's silence. Philippa is twenty-three and is doing a masters in psychology. She tells me about her degree, how fascinating it is to learn about the way people think, and how much we still don't understand about the human mind.

'I can't believe you're only seventeen,' she says. 'You seem much older, much more serious than most seventeen-year-olds.'

'Everyone says that.' I smile. 'I don't know whether to take it as a compliment or as an insult.'

She tells me about her little brother, Mick, and how he's the drummer in a band that's starting to gain some respect in the Sydney music scene.

'They're playing at the Basement on Friday night. They're so absolutely brilliant. Really talented. Do you want to come and see them? With me? I'd love it if you would. I love showing them off to people. They really *are* fantastic.'

But before I can answer, before I can even think about whether I'll possibly want to go out and see a band later in the week, there is a knock on the door.

'Robbie.' Philippa puts her fork down and looks inside. 'He said he'd come back.'

I go to the door. Just as I'm about to open it, just as I put my hand on the deadlock, the knocking comes again, louder and more insistent. And I suddenly know that it's not Robbie. He would never be so impatient.

But it's too late to hide, to pretend not to be home; I've released the bolt and the door is being pushed open. It's Alice.

She's holding an enormous bunch of red roses and wearing a clean white T-shirt and jeans. Her face is free of make-up and her hair is tied back from her face. Her eyes are red-rimmed, as if she's been crying, but apart from that she looks so young and fresh and innocent that it's hard to accept that she is the same Alice I was with last night. Seeing her now, like this, it's almost impossible to believe that she could be malicious, that she could be the cause of so much misery.

'I'm sorry, Katherine.' Her lip starts to quiver and her eyes fill with tears. 'I'm so, so sorry. I just don't know what got into me.'

She hands me the roses and I take them but I don't say a word.

'I just . . . sometimes I just . . . I dunno.' And she is sobbing now, her hands up to her face, her shoulders heaving, her voice thick and broken. 'Something comes over me and I lose . . . I just feel so – so *angry*. As if everyone is, I dunno, *judging* me or something. But I know it's crazy because I think they're judging me for what I'm *going* to do – what I know I'm going to do – before I've even done it . . . and then I feel I *have* to do it, to *test* them, to see if they really do care about me. And I know it's unfair, I know I can't really expect people to, you know, put up with this, but I can't . . . I mean, I know I'm going to do something, or say some-thing really horrible, but I can't, I can't stop, and then I want to. It's as if I have this self-destructive compulsion to lash out at people – at the people who love me.'

I feel the hard core of my anger start to dissolve. 'Come on.' I take her arm and pull her gently inside.

I get Alice a plate and she sits with Philippa and me on the verandah and we share our food. At first Philippa is wary and cold and watches Alice suspi-ciously. But Alice is her usual open, warm and engaging self and she apologises profusely for the night before. She laughs at herself and mocks her own behaviour so candidly and with such self-deprecating good humour – she is contrite and ashamed and amusing all at once – that it is impossible not to forgive her. And I can tell after a while that Philippa is thawing, that despite her mistrust, she is succumbing to Alice's charm. The three of us stay outside talking and laughing well after the food is finished and only move back inside when the sun disappears and the afternoon air is too cool to be comfortable.

'Let's get some movies. Order a pizza later,' Alice says.

'Oh. I don't know,' I say. 'Last night was such a late one. I need some sleep.'

'We won't stay late,' Alice says. 'And I just don't want this day to end yet. We're having too much fun. I don't want to go home and be alone tonight.' She goes to Philippa and takes hold of her arm with both hands. 'Please, Philippa? Let me prove that I'm not really that awful bitch you met last night. I'll go and get the movies. And some food. And you two don't have to do anything. Or spend a cent. It's my shout. Please?' She looks between us, imploring. 'For me? Please?'

Philippa looks at me. 'It's up to Katherine. It's her place. She's probably sick of us.'

'Sounds all right to me.' I shrug. 'I'm actually starting to feel hungry again, if that's believable. And vegging out in front of a movie sounds good.'

We find a menu for one of the local pizza restaurants and choose what we want. Both Philippa and I offer to go with Alice, to help her carry everything, to contribute some money, but she refuses our offers, insists that she wants it to be her treat entirely, and sets off on her own.

When she's gone, Philippa and I go the kitchen to wash up the lunch plates.

'She's not as crazy as you thought, is she?' I say.

Philippa has her hands in the dishwater, and she keeps her eyes down as she speaks. 'She can be very nice. Very likeable.'

'Yes.' I elbow her playfully. 'But you're not answering my question. I mentioned the word crazy.'

It makes me feel a little disloyal to be talking about Alice, whom I consider a very close friend, with someone I've only just met. But Philippa is so down-to-earth and honest and I can't help wondering what she thinks. I like her. She is obviously very smart, but she's also warm and kind and interestingly quirky, and I hope very much that we're going to be friends. Already I trust her judgement, and value her opinion.

Philippa sighs, takes her hands from the water, and wipes them off on her jeans. She looks at me and shrugs. 'I still think she might be a little crazy. You know, one of those super-extreme people. The kind of person my dad would call high-maintenance.'

'But that's a parent's perspective.' I laugh gently to soften the impact of what I'm about to say. 'And it's a bit cold, isn't it? A bit . . . well, she's a *person*. And she doesn't act like that all the time. I've never seen her like that before. And she's my friend. And in lots of ways she's an excellent friend. Honestly, you haven't seen how generous and kind she can be. So, should I really just dump her? Dump her and run because it's a hassle to have a friend like that? I think it's a bit . . . well, a bit *off* to treat people like that.'

'Oh.' Philippa stares at me and smiles. She looks both surprised and sad all at once. 'You're probably right. But that's a very nice way to look at it. I'm clearly not as nice as you because I probably would dump her. I'd probably dump her and run as fast as I could in the opposite direction.'

I'm mildly embarrassed by her penetrating gaze and busy myself putting plates and cups away. 'It's just that I know what it's like to feel . . . to feel people don't want to be with you because it's all just too hard. After Rachel was killed I got that feeling a *lot*. From all of my closest friends too. They were all concerned and kind and they tried so hard . . . but it was such a fun time for everyone else. It was the end of Year 10 and there were dances and parties and all that. All the other kids were just having a ball. No one wanted to sit with me in my room and cry. No one wanted me coming to their party, 'cause they'd have to worry about me, you know, look after me and try and make me happy. It was just such a drag. And I couldn't blame them. I knew that I was a downer. I knew nobody wanted to think about death and murder and tragedy . . . but I *had* to. It was my life.' I shrug, surprised by my own words. I haven't actually thought any of this through before, these ideas are more or less forming as I speak. But they feel real.

They feel *right*. 'I just think that if you're a true friend you have to take people as they are. The fun times and the boring times. The good and the bad.'

'I can see what you mean. I totally get it.' Philippa pulls the plug and starts to wipe round the sink. 'But I still don't think you should be friends with people who bring a lot of negative crap into your life. I wouldn't. No way. But that doesn't mean you should do what I would, does it? I mean, we're all different, aren't we? We all have to make our own way in this crazy world.' And I can tell that she's making an effort to keep her voice warm and non-confrontational. She wants us to be friends as much as I do.

Eventually Alice gets back and we sit round the kitchen table and enjoy the food. Robbie arrives when we're cleaning up, the three of us laughing and cheerful. At first he's a bit cold, aloof towards Alice, and a little disapproving towards Philippa and me. But we give him what's left of the pizza and continue talking and eventually he starts to thaw, to allow himself to be drawn into the conversation, to smile, even. And Alice is so gently solicitous, so loving and considerate towards him that I can see he's finding it impossible to maintain his anger.

We end up in the lounge room, the lights dim, the four of us quiet and relaxed with food and fatigue. Alice selects a DVD and goes to the machine to put it on. Before she presses play she turns to face us.

'I just want to say something first. Before we all fall asleep.' She smiles sheepishly. 'First up I want you all to know . . .' she looks pointedly at Philippa and then Robbie '. . . that nothing happened between Ben and me last night. He left not long after you all did. And that's the honest truth.' Robbie looks down at his lap and tries to suppress a smile but it's perfectly clear that Alice's announcement has made him very happy.

Alice continues. 'But most importantly, I was horrible last night and I want to apologise properly. To all three of you. Philippa, Robbie, but especially to you, Katherine.' She looks down at me, her eyes wide, beseeching. 'I had no business saying what I did last night. None at all. And I don't actually think it's true for a second. Just because I would have had horrid, evil thoughts like that if I were in your shoes, doesn't mean you ever would. I was, what do they call it, transferring? Yes. I was transferring myself onto you. Which is unfair and ridiculous and I'm so unbelievably sorry and you will never, ever know how much I hate myself for hurting you. You are always so good to me and I know I don't deserve your forgiveness, but if you're willing to give it to me I'll very happily and gratefully accept it.'

'Oh, for God's sake,' I say, hoping that the dim light will hide my blush. 'Sit down and be quiet.'

'I will,' she says, looking down at her feet. I hear a tremor in her voice and wonder if she's crying. 'But first I just wanted to say how much I treasure your friendship. You have no idea how important it is to me. How special you are. You have no idea.'

17

It was much darker inside the barn than out. There was no proper lighting, just strings of fairy lights hanging from the ceiling that had barely any effect on the thick darkness. It was hard to see and the tin walls of the enormous shed made the noise echo and vibrate – there was such a wild cacophony of music and laughter and shouting and people that walking inside was disorienting, even a little frightening. Rachel and I stayed close to each other, holding onto each other's arms.

Carly strode ahead, confident and sure, completely in her element. We followed her towards a big, old free-standing bath which was filled with ice and cans of beer and Coke. Carly lifted three cans of beer out and handed one each to Rachel and me.

'Whose is this?' I said.

Carly shook her head, indicating that she couldn't hear.

'Can we just help ourselves?' I shouted.

Carly shrugged, and looked round. 'I don't see anyone stopping us,' she shouted back, grinning. 'Let's go.'

Carly stepped straight into the crowd of people who were dancing in front of the stage and started stamping her feet, nodding her head, moving in time with the music. She lifted her can of beer in our direction, winked and took a large swig, then put her other arm up and waved us over.

Rachel looked at me questioningly but I shook my head. I didn't want to dance yet. It was quite possible that my boyfriend Will would be there and I wanted to search for him. But I reached over and took Rachel's beer so that her hands would be free and indicated, with a nod, that she should go.

Just as she did when she played the piano, Rachel lost herself when she danced. All her self-consciousness disappeared and she moved smoothly and rhythmically and in perfect unison with the music. She looked at me with an enormous happy grin on her face and I laughed. I was pleasantly tipsy with all the alcohol, giddy with the crowd and the music, and high on the contagious sense of excitement surrounding me. I was excited by the possibility that I might see Will. And I was quite sure that he'd be just as pleased to see me as I'd be to see him.

I leaned my back against the wall, sipped slowly

on my beer – which I didn't really like – and watched Rachel and Carly. I was just about to take a walk round the shed to see if I could find Will when he appeared right in front of me.

He was smiling his wonderful, snaggle-toothed grin, and shaking his head in faux disapproval at my being there. I smiled back, but neither of us said a word, just moved together until we were pressed against each other and I could smell his smell – spice and something chocolate-like and the faint tang of sweat – and his lips were against mine and our mouths were open and exploring hungrily.

We kissed and embraced and leaned back so that we could look at each other, laughed and pushed our bodies together again. We were both so delighted to find each other, both so excited by the atmosphere and our mutual desire that we couldn't stop smiling. Even as we kissed I could tell that Will's lips were curving upwards in a smile.

And as he pushed against me I could feel that he had an erection – and knowing that I did this to him so quickly, that he just had to see and touch me and his body would react like this, was exhilarating. And I felt a responding flutter in my groin and I knew that I wanted to go all the way with him. To make love. Not tonight, but soon. Very soon. And I pressed myself back against him in answer. A promise.

And because I was now with Will, the beer started to taste good, and I was suddenly very glad for the darkness – it was comforting and romantic. It made me feel cocooned and as if, despite the crowd, we were alone together.

18

It's the night after Alice's apology. I'm watching television, curled up on the sofa in my pyjamas, flicking through channels with the remote control, when there's a knock on the door.

I immediately think it might be Alice and wonder if I should hide, turn off the television and climb under the covers and pretend I'm not home. It's not that I'm still angry with her, I'm just tired and even the thought of her never-ending energy is exhausting. But I don't hide. I sigh, flick off the television and go to the door.

It's not Alice, it's Robbie, still in his work black and whites. He grins and holds up a tub of chocolate ice-cream, a box of drinking chocolate, and a packet of Tim Tams.

'I come bearing gifts,' he says. 'Chocolate, chocolate and more chocolate.' He waves the biscuits under my nose. 'Double coated.'

I laugh and hold the door open, stepping back so that he can enter.

'I wanted to talk.' Robbie hesitates in the doorway and looks at me apologetically. 'I hope you don't mind? We just didn't get any time alone yesterday. And there's so much to talk about. I mean, I really wanted to talk to you about your sister and all of that. And about Alice, of course.' He shakes his head and speaks in a rush. 'But I know you're probably exhausted and ready for bed, so if you're too tired to talk I thought I could just make you a hot chocolate and tuck you in, and leave you in peace and come back another time.' He looks at my pyjamas. 'You were just about to go to bed, weren't you? Sorry. I'll just—'

'Robbie,' I interrupt. 'Stop. Come in. I'm not that tired. I haven't suddenly turned into a fragile old woman. Anyway, I wanted to talk to you too.' I take the tub of ice-cream from his hands, turn and head down the hallway, 'And I want some of this. Right now.'

We go to the kitchen, scoop out two generous bowls' worth and take them to the lounge room.

The ice-cream is delicious – richly chocolate with a swirl of even richer chocolate sauce through it. I smear some on my lips deliberately and smile clownishly.

'This is yummo,' I say.

Robbie laughs. 'Very funny.' But the smile leaves his

face too quickly and he looks down at his bowl, pushing the spoon around without eating anything.

I lick my lips clean, wipe my mouth with the back of my hand. 'Are you okay?'

'Yeah.' He shrugs. 'I didn't come here to talk about me. Honestly.' He looks at me, frowns. 'What about you? Are *you* okay?'

'Yes.' I nod. 'I'm fine.'

'You never told me about your sister. You've always been so brave about it. And I'm always telling you all my problems. You must . . . I mean . . .' And he looks at me, hurt and angry all of a sudden, and slaps his hand on his leg. 'Why *didn't* you tell me?'

I put my bowl on the coffee table, crouch close in front of him and put my hands on his knees. 'I'm so sorry. I know I've hurt your feelings by not telling you. I know it must seem that I haven't trusted you enough or something, but it wasn't that. I promise.'

Robbie looks down at me, silent, waiting.

'When Rachel died there was a lot, no, a *huge* amount of media attention. I was stalked by the press, basically. Mum and Dad were too. And it was awful. And they said some really horrible, horrible stuff in the papers about our family and about me, stuff they made up or truths that they twisted into lies.' Just remembering that time makes me cry, and I wipe my eyes and sniff, try to stop the flood of tears.

Robbie sits beside me on the floor and puts his arm round me. 'It's okay.' He sounds shocked and I know that I've made him feel bad, that he will blame himself for my tears. 'You don't have to tell me. It doesn't matter. I didn't realise. God, Katherine, I'm a complete idiot and I just don't know how to keep my big fat foot out of my stupid mouth.'

This is such an absurdly inaccurate description of Robbie's character that it makes me laugh. I look at him and wipe my eyes. 'You haven't made me cry. I cry whenever I remember that time. And I remember it a lot. I just want to explain why I didn't tell you.'

'It's okay, it's fine; you don't have to.'

I push his arm from my shoulders, slide away and sit so that I'm facing him. 'But I want to and I'm going to. So just be quiet and listen. Please.'

He nods.

'My name isn't really Patterson,' I say. 'It's Boydell.'

Robbie's eyes widen with recognition. He's heard of us, of course, he remembers the Boydell sisters.

'See? You know of us. At least you know what the papers said about us.'

'I remember the name.' He shakes his head. 'I can't remember much else, oh, except that your sister was some kind of musical prodigy. That's right, isn't it?'

'Yes. Yes, she was.'

'Shit, Katherine.' He shakes his head. 'I can't believe

it. It's just so incredibly hard to fathom.'

'I know.'

'That was your sister? My God. What happened to her was so fucked up. Those psycho bastards that did it. It was unbelievable.'

'Yes. And the media kind of made us famous afterwards. Famous in a really bad way. A destructive, invasive way that made us all . . . that made us even unhappier . . . as if it wasn't already unbearable enough,' I say. 'And there were psychologists and all sorts of people making comments about us, about our family life. It was revolting. We just felt completely . . . invaded, violated.'

'Like what? What did they say?'

'All this really mean stuff. A lot of articles said that Mum and Dad were exploiting Rachel, pushing her too hard. And of course they were pushing her, to an extent. But in an encouraging way. Rachel was a genius, yes, but there's no way anybody gets to be that accomplished a musician without being ambitious, without working their guts out. And the papers were so happy to lap it up and take advantage of it while she was alive. I mean, there used to be all these self-congratulatory headlines about "our local prodigy" and stuff. They loved it all while she was alive. But then after she was murdered everything changed. It was like they turned on us, as if we were the enemy. We went from being the family Melbourne was proud of to being this bunch of pushy, horrible, selfish misfits that everyone loved to hate. They didn't exactly lie, but they made everything sound so bad. Like they'd say Rachel had to do three or four hours of piano a day – and she did, of course she did – but they made it sound as if Mum and Dad forced her into it. They just made it sound so ugly and horrible. And it was all wrong. Rachel loved the piano, she'd have played all day if she could. She *wanted* to work at it, she wanted to be the best in the world, she said that all the time. And Mum and Dad *were* ambitious for Rachel, that was true, but they loved her more than anything. They were good to her. They were good to both of us. We were a happy family,' I say, my voice shaky now. I sigh and put my head in my hands, try to stop myself from losing control. 'We were happy, all of us.'

'Of course you were.'

'So,' I say, taking a deep breath. 'That's why I changed my name and became Katherine Patterson instead of Katie Boydell. And that's why I moved to Sydney. And that's why Mum and Dad left too. I didn't tell you, I didn't really tell anyone except Alice, because I just didn't want to *be* Katie Boydell any more. I didn't want to be that girl. I didn't want you to know about me before you actually knew me. If that makes any sense at all?'

Robbie nods, puts his hand on mine and squeezes.

'But I wanted to tell you, Robbie. Really I did. Lots of times. Especially when you were telling me all about your mum, and you were being so truthful about it all and I really, really wanted to let you know that I understood how you felt.'

'I thought you seemed particularly clued in to it all. As if you'd thought it all through or something.' He smiles, teasing. 'I just thought you were super-intelligent, super-sensitive Katherine, but really it was just a case of been there, done that. A case of been there, done that even bigger and harder than anyone else.'

We finish our ice-cream, which has melted and become soft, and I tell Robbie about the night Rachel was murdered. And, just as I did when I told Alice, I sob and sob, and hit at the floor in angry frustration. Robbie hugs me and listens carefully and shakes his head in horrified disbelief. He brings me more ice-cream and holds my hand and asks me a thousand gentle questions. He cries with me and we dry one another's tears, laugh at our shared misery and snotty noses and red-rimmed eyes.

At midnight I tell Robbie that I'm exhausted and need to sleep. But when he offers to leave, I ask him to please stay. To sleep beside me. Not for sex but as a friend. Because I don't want to be alone, because I need comfort and closeness. And he says yes, that he'd love to, that he's glad I asked.

I give Robbie one of my spare toothbrushes and we brush our teeth side by side in the bathroom, taking turns to spit into the basin. Somehow, the fact that we've cried together and revealed so much of our inner selves has brought us immediately closer, made us more comfortable with each other. We lie side by side on our backs beneath the blankets. It's dark in my bedroom, and I listen to the sound of Robbie's breathing and enjoy the soothing warmth of his body beside me.

'I wouldn't normally sleep with another girl's boyfriend,' I say. 'Even though we're not actually doing anything. It's a bit weird, isn't it? But somehow, for some reason, all of those normal rules don't seem to apply to Alice.'

'That's because Alice doesn't follow any of those so-called normal rules herself. She doesn't respect any of those boundaries, so why should anyone else when it comes to her? It's the Alice phenomenon. Hang around her for long enough and you start behaving badly. I mean, come on.' He laughs. 'What about the other night with Ben and Philippa? And what Alice said to you about your sister, and the way she was flirting with Ben? She hardly treats anyone else with respect, does she? We're entitled to a bit of bad behaviour too, aren't we?'

'Yes. No. I don't know. Anyway,' I say, 'I'm not sure that we are behaving badly. By being here together tonight, that is. If we're not hurting anyone then it probably doesn't matter.' I shake my head in the dark. 'No. It can't matter. Because we're friends and we're looking after each other and we're not hurting Alice. Even if she knew, she probably wouldn't really care.'

'Alice would care all right. But not for any of the normal reasons. Not because she loves me so much that she can't bear the thought of me being close to someone else. She'd care because she's not involved. She'd care because she's not the puppet master in this situation.'

I don't respond because I don't like the implication that Alice has as much control over me as she does over Robbie. I can understand Robbie feeling that she controls him; after all, he's in love and he puts up with a lot of crap from her. He allows himself to be available to Alice whenever she wants him. But I'm just Alice's friend and my perception isn't distorted by lust, I'm not madly in love with her. But I don't want to point this out tonight. I don't want to say anything to add to Robbie's misery.

'Anyway,' he continues, 'you used the word boyfriend. You actually said that I was Alice's *boyfriend*.' He laughs, and it's a dry, bitter, unhappy sound. 'But I'm not really, am I? I'm just someone she uses when the mood takes her. I'm just a loyal puppy that she can use and abuse whenever and however she wants.'

'If that's how you feel, Robbie—'

'Yes,' he interrupts. 'Of course that's how I feel.' He

sounds angry and miserable. 'That's how it *is*. And I tell myself over and over that she's bad, that I have to stop seeing her. But then I hear her voice or see her face and I . . .' His voice cracks and he's quiet for a moment, breathing, bringing his emotions under control. He sighs shakily. 'You know what?' he whispers. 'You know something that's really weird about all this?'

'What?'

'My dad has been seeing someone. A woman he met at a party one night. Shit,' he says suddenly, 'you wouldn't believe it, but her name is Rachel.'

'What's so weird about that? It's a common name. I've met lots of Rachels since my sister died.'

'No, that's not the weird bit. I just remembered that out of the blue. But see, my dad's been happy since he met her. *Really* happy. Happy the way he was before Mum got sick.'

'But that's so great, Robbie. Have you met her? Is she nice?'

'No. I haven't met her. I don't *want* to meet her. I don't want to know about her.'

'Oh.' And I'm quiet for a minute. 'Do you feel he's betraying your mum or something?'

'Nope. Not at all. Mum's dead. She'd want Dad to be happy.'

'So?' I'm puzzled. 'Why aren't you happy for him, then? What's the problem?'

'I'm jealous.' His voice is full of self-loathing. 'I'm so pathetic that I'm jealous. I know I should be happy for him, he'd definitely be happy for me. But all I can think is, how come he gets to be in love and have this fantastic relationship while I'm having my heart torn to shreds by Alice. How come he gets to be so happy? He's an old man. I'm the one meant to be having the great love life. Not him. It's humiliating. I can't bear looking at him and the ridiculous lovesick look he has on his face.'

'Oh, Robbie.' I'm glad he can't see the smile on my face.

'See? I'm an evil bastard. I'm bad. I deserve everything I get from Alice.'

And I can't help it – I burst out laughing. Robbie is quiet and his silence, the feeling that I shouldn't be laughing, only makes me laugh harder. I try to stop, try to stifle my giggling, but then it doesn't matter because suddenly Robbie is laughing too. And we laugh so hard that the bed shakes and we kick the blankets off and roll around. We laugh until our stomachs hurt and it's hard to breathe and we are almost choking on our own mirth. When we stop my face is wet with tears.

'Anyway,' I whisper carefully, trying hard not to laugh again. 'If you're not bad, you can't be good.'

'What? You have to be bad to be good? That's stupid. It doesn't make any sense at all.'

'No.' I giggle quietly. 'It doesn't, does it? What I meant was that if you see the bad in yourself, and dislike it, and try to rid yourself of it, then that's good. Nobody's really good through and through. At least I don't think so. Trying to be good, or at least trying not to be bad, is probably as close as we can get.'

'Maybe you're right,' he says.

'Maybe I am.'

Now we are quiet, quiet and still. I hear Robbie's breathing become more regular. I close my eyes.

'You're nice, Katherine.' Robbie's voice is soft, drowsy.

'You're nice too, Robbie.'

'If only I'd met you before. Before I ever met Alice,' he says, taking my hand in the dark and squeezing it tight. 'We could have . . . we might have . . .' He doesn't finish the sentence.

'Yes,' I say sleepily, 'I know.'

19

'They're great, aren't they?' Philippa is staring up at her brother's band. She's beaming with pride, tapping her feet in time with the music.

'They're fantastic.' I nod and smile with as much enthusiasm as I can muster. And they are. They're all accomplished musicians and their repertoire is well rehearsed, smooth. It's the kind of folksy, easy-to-listen-to rock music I would usually enjoy from a live band, but I have a dreadful headache and I really want to be home, in bed. Philippa showed up at my place earlier in the evening to pick me up. She was so excited about the night ahead that I was unwilling to disappoint her. I hoped that my headache would eventually go away, but it has only got worse. And Philippa ensured that we got the table closest to the stage, and so the music is too loud, pounding, painful.

Philippa's brother, Mick, is playing the drums. He's very good-looking in a cool, withdrawn kind of way –

I haven't seen him smile once all night. He's pale, like Philippa, and has longish black hair that hangs over his eyes. And every so often I've caught him staring over at our table quizzically, wondering, no doubt, who the strange girl with Philippa is.

And though the music is good I'm glad when the band stops for a break. The sudden quiet makes my head feel marginally better. Mick talks to the other band members for a while, then he comes and stands beside our table.

'Hey, Pip,' he says, touching Philippa on the shoulder. He looks at me, his expression quite blank and unfriendly. I smile but he looks away, back towards Philippa.

'Hey.' Philippa takes his hand. 'This is Katherine. I told you about her, remember?'

'Yep.' Mick nods, still unsmiling, and looks at me for the briefest of moments. 'Hi.'

I'm not in the mood to put up with such indifference, and have no inclination to try and charm him. 'Hi,' I say, just as coldly and then I turn away, look round the bar.

'Katherine's got a headache,' Philippa says. I turn to her and frown, surprised. I haven't told her I have a headache so I'm not certain how she knows, and I'm also a little irritated that she thinks my lack of warmth needs explaining. It's her brother who's being rude. I'm only responding in kind. Philippa leans forward and puts her hand on mine. 'Mick can get rid of it.'

'Rid of what?'

'Your headache,' Mick says, looking at me. 'If you want me to.'

'What?' I shake my head, suddenly certain he means to offer me drugs. 'Oh, no thanks.' I lift my glass of lemonade. 'I've got to study tomorrow. HSC.'

'He doesn't mean pills, silly, if that's what you're thinking,' Philippa laughs, reading my mind. 'He can make it go away with massage. It really works. It's totally and absolutely amazing. Trust me. Give it a go.'

I picture this strangely unfriendly man massaging my shoulders, touching my skin, and almost laugh, the thought is so absurd. I shake my head. 'No. I'll be okay. Thanks anyway.'

But before I realise what's happening or have time to react, Mick is sitting in the chair opposite me and taking my right hand between his. He holds it still and with the fingers of his other hand he presses the soft, fleshy spot between my forefinger and thumb, moving in small, firm circles. He runs his thumb up over my wrist, then back down my palm and middle finger.

I'm about to laugh and pull my hand away, express my cynicism towards such methods, when Mick squeezes my hand even tighter and says, 'Not yet. Give it a chance to work.' And then he smiles.

His smile is the most transformative smile I've ever seen. It enlivens his entire face; what once seemed surly, dark and closed-up is now warm, open, kind. His grin is large, his teeth straight and white, and his eyes are deep-set and brown and framed by insanely long lashes. He is handsome. Incredibly so. And I'm suddenly quite certain that he's the most beautiful man I've ever seen.

Amazingly, the squeezing tension in my temples is easing off. It's as if with each little circle he presses into the skin of my hand he's drawing away the headache, erasing it. I watch his face as he concentrates on what he's doing. He's no longer looking at me, no longer smiling, but is staring at my hand with an intent expression on his face.

And then he pinches the skin between my thumb and forefinger so hard that it hurts. 'Ouch.' He releases my hand and I snatch it away. 'That hurt.'

He only looks at me quizzically, waiting.

'It's gone.' I put my hand to my temple and shake my head in disbelief. 'It's completely gone.'

'Wonderful, isn't it? I told you it would work. My clever little brother.' Philippa looks at Mick proudly but Mick keeps his eyes on me. He still doesn't smile, but I can now see that there is a definite warmth in his expression, a hint of amusement. He stares at me for so long that I begin to feel slightly embarrassed, feel my heart beating faster, the skin on my cheeks flush with colour.

'Yes. Yes, it is. Thank you.' I turn away from his gaze and look at Philippa. 'Let's have another drink,' I say, bringing my glass up to my lips and draining the remainder quickly. I stand up. 'Another one, Philippa? Do you want something, Mick?'

'No thanks.' Philippa shakes her head.

'I'll have a beer,' Mick says.

'Sure,' I say, and I head towards the bar.

'Wait,' he calls out. I turn back. He smiles at me and I'm glad I'm not standing too close, that there's no way he can hear the pounding of my heart, feel the slight tremble that has started in my hands. 'Just say it's for the band. It's free.'

'Okay,' I say.

'Wait,' he says again, and now he is laughing. 'I'll have a VB, if that's okay?'

'Yep. Fine,' I say. And then I go to the bar. Walking quickly. Eager to escape his scrutiny.

When I've ordered my lemonade and Mick's beer I glance back over my shoulder and watch him. He and Philippa are leaning close together, talking. He nods and gestures towards the stage, moves his arms energetically, in imitation of playing the drums. I'm relieved – they're clearly talking about music and are not sitting there wondering at my bizarre behaviour.

I know this feeling in my chest. I'm familiar with the butterflies in my stomach, the nervous thrill I feel when Mick looks at me. It's been a long time since I've felt anything close. Not since Will, since the night of Rachel's death, have I let myself think of a boy like this. And I can't help but be amazed at my physical response to this attraction: the pounding heart, the shaking hands, the heat in my face that betrays my feelings before I've even consciously acknowledged them. It's as if my body knows me better than I know myself.

I drink half of my lemonade straight down when it arrives. It's icy cold and hurts my throat but I'm thirsty. I take a deep breath, forcing myself to be calm, not to shake or blush or stammer. And then, as composed as I can be, I head back to the table.

'Talking music.' Philippa looks at me apologetically as I hand Mick his drink. 'Sorry.'

'That's okay.' I shake my head and sit down. 'I love talking music. My family . . . I mean, we always used to.' And I stop, at a sudden loss for words. Rachel's death, my history, is no longer a secret but it's almost impossible to bring up her death casually, to say, *Oh yes. My family used to talk about music a lot. Before my sister was murdered, that is. Her death ruined things for us – and we've barely talked about music since. But I'm familiar with the language, I share the love. Go ahead. Talk.*

Philippa notices my sudden discomfort and kindly

changes the subject. 'Oh my God,' she says loudly, putting her hand on Mick's arm. 'You'll never guess who I saw the other day!'

Mick looks at her, raises his eyebrows.

'Caroline,' she says. 'Caroline Handel. And, seriously, Mick, you wouldn't believe how much she's changed. If you saw her, you'd be absolutely amazed. She looks like a different person, all dressed up and smart. She's some kind of big-wig with some big company or other. The change in her is phenomenal.'

'Yeah?' He shrugs indifferently.

And though Philippa tries her hardest – and I assume it's for my sake – to get Mick talking about something else, he looks uninterested in Philippa's encounter with the girl called Caroline, and as soon as Philippa has finished her story he turns back to me.

'So your family used to talk music. Why *used to*? What changed?'

'Mick!' Philippa's voice is sharp. 'Don't be so rude. You can't ask questions like that.'

'What?' Mick looks baffled. 'Questions like what?' He looks at me and lifts his beer bottle. 'Was that a rude question?'

'No,' I say. 'Philippa, don't worry. It's okay.' And right then I make a decision. I'm going to tell them all about Rachel; it may not be the most appropriate place, or time, or circumstance – there is no right place to talk about death other than at a funeral — but it's a part of my history, an ongoing factor in my life that colours almost everything. If I don't talk about it, and in doing so somehow relegate it to its rightful place in the past, it will just sit there for ever, a shadow, haunting me.

'My sister was murdered,' I say.

Philippa nods.

'It might seem weird to tell you this now,' I talk quickly, lifting and placing my glass, making overlapping circles of water on the table. 'But it suddenly seems really important for me to say something, to tell people. You see, I've been trying to hide this from everyone for so long. Since I left Melbourne. And now that it's out, well, now that you know, I just feel that I have to tell people . . .' I look at Philippa and smile. 'My friends, that is. I feel that I have to tell my friends what happened. Because it's not just something that happened. It's kind of, and I don't want to sound all weird, but it was a very defining thing. It changed me. Completely.'

I look at Mick. 'And I understand if you don't want to hear this. But I'd like to tell Philippa. And you're welcome to stay and listen too.'

He nods, says nothing.

'We went to a party.' I put my glass down, place my hands in my lap, take a deep breath and begin.

And this time I don't cry or moan. A few tears wet my eyes but I brush them impatiently away. Rachel and Mick listen in silence, neither of them taking their eyes off me. And when I'm done Philippa stands up and comes round the table and hugs me tight.

'Thank you for telling us that,' she says.

I look at Mick. His eyes are wet with unshed tears. He looks at me and he smiles – a small half-smile, a smile of sympathy and sadness, a smile that shows he's confused and uncertain and has no idea what to say. It's the perfect response and I smile weakly back, grateful.

20

'Stop,' I said. 'Hold on. Not now, not here. I don't want it to be like this.'

'Okay.' Will rolled off me and sat up. He pulled my T-shirt down gently and sighed. 'Neither do I, Katie. Sorry.'

I sat up, put my arm round his neck and kissed him on the mouth. 'Don't be sorry. There's nothing to be sorry for.' I looked around us. We were outside, under a tree. The ground beneath us was hard and gnarly with old tree roots and pebbles and grit. I felt dirty and tired with the after-effects of too much alcohol. 'I'd really much rather lose my virginity in a bed. A nice, clean, soft bed. And I think I'd rather be sober.'

'Me too. Honest.' He smiled. 'You're driving me crazy but I'd rather it was nice. And I reckon it'd be a good thing if we were both sober enough to remember it later.'

'Shit. What time is it?' I took Will's wrist and turned

it so that I could see the face of his watch. But it was too dark to see it properly. 'Does this thing have a light?'

'Yep.' He lifted his wrist closer to his face and pressed a button. 'It's past eight. Almost eight-thirty.'

'Shit,' I said again. I stood up and brushed myself down. 'Shit. Shit. Shit. Shit. *Fuck!* It's late. We were only meant to stay for an hour. We're going to be in such trouble when we get home. Come on.' I took Will's hand and helped him up. 'I have to get Rachel. We have to go. Now.'

But we couldn't find her inside. We searched through the crowd who were dancing and she was nowhere to be found. We checked the groups huddled against the walls. We found Carly and asked if she'd seen her but Carly shook her head, shrugged and looked round the shed blankly. She was obviously drunk and was snuggling up to a boy I didn't recognise. Locating Rachel wasn't one of her priorities.

'Outside.' Will took my arm. 'Out the front. Near the cars, maybe.'

'Okay. I'll look out the front and you look out the back. It'll be quicker. I'll meet you back here.'

I was starting to worry. It was late and Mum and Dad would definitely be home by now. They'd be wondering where we were, they'd be getting anxious. We were going to be in for it. And if Rachel was drunk, if they were able to smell the alcohol on her, or otherwise tell that she'd been drinking, they'd be furious. We'd both be grounded for ever.

Because a lot of the kids at the party were seniors and were able to drive, there were plenty of cars parked at the front of the shed. They'd even lined them up in rows, so that the whole area resembled an organised car park.

I couldn't see or hear anyone when I first went out there, but then I heard male voices. Laughter. The clink of glass against glass. I headed towards the noise and came upon a small group of people gathered round a car. All the doors were open so that the interior light spilled out. Two boys were leaning against the car doors. One boy was sitting in the front seat. Another boy was in the back, with Rachel.

Rachel had a glass of beer in her hand which looked as if it was about to drop, she held it so loosely, her hand limp from the wrist down. She was lying back against the upholstery with her eyes half shut.

'Hello there,' the boy sitting in the driver's seat said as I approached. 'What can we do you for?'

I smiled. 'I've just come to get my sister.' I leaned into the car and put my hand on her knee. 'Rach. We've got to go. It's really late.'

'Katie.' Rachel opened her eyes and grinned. The movement made her beer slop out of her glass and down her leg. She didn't seem to notice. 'Katie, Katie.

I'm having such a lovely time. I've been telling them all about my . . . my . . . my . . . *watchamacallit?*' She giggled, mimicked playing the piano with her fingers on her leg. 'My . . . my . . . *music!* That's it! My music!' her voice was slurred, her gestures slow and exaggerated. 'They want to come to my recital. Can you believe it?'

I looked round at the boys. They were all dressed in the style of what the girls at our school called 'bogan' – flannel shirts worn open over tight singlet tops. The only one that met my eye was the one sitting in front, in the driver's seat. He was a lot older than the others, at least twenty, and was kind of handsome in a rugged way. A man, not a boy. I didn't believe for a minute that he or any of the others were interested in classical music.

'Great,' I said, taking Rachel's beer glass. 'And that's why we've got to go. There won't be any recital if we don't go now.'

I took Rachel's hand in mine and tried to pull her from the car. But it was awkward, she was a dead weight, unco-operative, and I felt that if I pulled any harder I'd make her fall from the car, and end up being forced to drag her.

'How are you gonna get her home?' The man from the front seat asked. He was looking at me quizzically, a cigarette between his lips.

'Walk. It's not far,' I lied.

The man laughed. 'I'm Grant. And yes it *is* bloody well far. Everywhere is far from here. At night. In the dark.' He nodded towards Rachel. 'When you're out of it.'

I shrugged. 'Rachel,' I said, loudly. 'Come *on*. We've got to go. It's getting late.'

She just giggled and slid sideways a little without making any real effort to move. She smiled dreamily and shut her eyes as if to sleep.

'Jesus,' I said, staring accusingly at Grant, although I knew if anyone was to blame it was me. I should never have brought her here in the first place. I should never have left her alone. 'How much beer has she had?'

Grant shook his head, and raised his eyebrows in an expression of innocence. 'I dunno. I haven't seen her have more than one glass. She's probably just not used to it. Sean?' He turned to face a very large sweaty-faced boy, who was sitting in the back on the other side of Rachel. 'Do you know how much she's had?'

'Nuh.' Sean laughed, an ugly wheezing sound that made his belly rise up, and spoke to Grant. He didn't bother to look my way. 'How the hell would I know? She was tanked up before she even got in the car.'

'What a nightmare.' I put my head in my hands. 'How am I going to get her home?'

I was talking to myself more than to anyone else, but Grant responded anyway. 'That's why I asked you, mate,' he said. 'We could drive you. We've got room for one more, ain't we, boys?'

'Oh no,' I said. 'Thanks anyway.'

'Suit yourself,' he said. 'But it's gonna take you at least an hour to get anywhere if you walk. And it's bloody dark out. And a cab'll cost you at least a hundred bucks.' He shrugged. 'I know what I'd be doin' if I was you.'

I stared at him as I thought. Walking home with Rachel right now was clearly out of the question and Will didn't have a car. I'd have to wait here until she sobered up – which could be hours – and Mum and Dad would start to panic. They'd probably even call the police. I couldn't just let them sit at home and worry, so I'd have to borrow someone's mobile phone and call them, let them know that we were safe. But they'd ask a lot of questions, they'd insist on coming out to collect us. And that was something I wanted to avoid. If they saw where we were, if they saw all the drunk kids, the state of the shed, all the alcohol and cigarettes and drugs, they'd be livid. And they'd probably do something devastating like try to break the party up, tell people to go home. They might even ring the police and get them to come and bust everyone.

It was inevitable that they'd discover we'd been drinking, but we were better off going home to face the music, better off avoiding the more dreadful fate of them coming here.

'Okay,' I said eventually. 'That'd be great. Thank you. I wouldn't ask but I don't know what else to do. Would you mind? We live in Toorak.'

'Toorak, eh?' Grant snorted. He threw his cigarette out the window, put a fresh one in his mouth, lit it and inhaled deeply. He let the smoke trickle out of his nose as he spoke, kept his eyes on the cigarette between his fingers. 'Toorak. Yeah. Nice place, that. Real nice place.' He looked at me and nodded. 'I don't think that should be a problem. Wouldn't mind a drive out that way. We were about to leave anyway. Weren't we, Sean?'

'Yeah.' Sean laughed again, a great dopey guffaw that made his belly shake. 'We were just about to fuck off from this shithole of a party.'

'Right,' I said. 'Okay. Can I just run back and tell my boyfriend?' I had a sudden idea. 'Maybe he could come with us? If you don't mind? You'd only have to take him to our place. He could make his own way from there.'

'Nope. Sorry. Can't do it, mate.' Grant shook his head. 'He won't fit in the car. There's me, Sean, Jerry and Chris. And you two girls. That's three in the front and three in the back. A full house.'

'Unless she wants us to leave her behind. Take her boyfriend and sister and leave her here,' Sean said, laughing, this time managing both to avoid my eye and talk about me as if I weren't present.

'Shut up, Sean. Fat fuck,' Grant said, his tone so curt and dismissive that I expected some kind of retaliation from Sean. But Sean smiled stupidly, put his hand on Grant's shoulder, and squeezed. It was an oddly affectionate gesture.

'Pass us a smoke, mate?' he said.

Grant threw a packet of cigarettes onto Sean's lap.

'I'll just go and tell him that we're going. I won't be long.' I put my hand on Rachel's leg and shook it. 'Rach? I'll be back in a minute. These boys are going to take us home. Okay? Rach?'

'Take us home?' She opened her eyes and stuck out her bottom lip in a pout. Her voice was even more slurred now and her eyes fluttered shut as she spoke. 'We have to go already? What a pity. I'm having such fun.'

'Okay?' I looked at Grant. 'I'll be back in a sec.'

'No worries.' He smiled, took another drag on his cigarette. 'We won't go anywhere without ya.'

I rushed back into the shed and found Will almost immediately. He was talking to a group of people near the back exit.

'No luck,' he said when he saw me. 'I was just asking these guys if they'd seen her.'

'It's okay,' I said. 'I've found her. She's really, really pissed. I have to get her home. We've got a lift.'

'A lift? Who with?'

'A guy called Grant. It's okay. Really. She's in their car and I can't get her out. She's too drunk to move.' I waved my hand impatiently and kissed him on the cheek. 'I have to go. I'm worried she'll spew or pass out or something.'

'I'll just come out with you.'

'No. No. It's okay. Don't bother.' I smiled and squeezed his hand, stood on tiptoes to kiss him on the lips. 'Stay here with your friends. Have another drink for me.'

I turned and ran quickly back to the car.

The boys were already inside, waiting, when I returned. I slid into the back, next to Rachel, and closed the door. Rachel's head was tipped back and her eyes were closed. Her mouth was open slightly. I reached up and pushed her lips back together, touched her cheek.

'Rach?' I said. 'We're going home now.' I reached over and clipped her seatbelt on.

Her eyes fluttered open for a moment and she attempted a smile. ''Kay,' she said.

'Have a beer?' Sean reached across Rachel's lap, an open can of VB in his hand. He kept his eyes down and avoided meeting mine.

'Oh, no thanks. I've had enough.'

'Shit,' he said, thrusting it closer. 'At least hold it, will ya? I opened it specially.'

I took the can and lifted it carefully to my mouth, let the cold liquid wet my lips without taking any into my mouth. I didn't want any more to drink. I was thirsty and tired and longed for a glass of water and the comfort of bed. 'Thanks.' I tried to smile at Sean but he'd already turned away.

'Thanks so much for this,' I said to Grant.

'That's okay. Um . . . I don't—'

'Oh my God. I'm so sorry. I've been so rude. I'm Katie. Katie Boydell.'

'Katie. Right. Good.'

He didn't introduce me to the other boys and for a moment I considered introducing myself, tapping them on the shoulder and saying hello, offering my hand. But the whole atmosphere was so awkward and they were making so little effort to be friendly themselves – their heads were set stiff and looking straight ahead – that I didn't bother.

Instead, I stared out the window, watched the landscape pass me by in a blur and said nothing. I thought about what I was going to say to Mum and Dad. I'd just have to tell the truth, be completely honest. They were going to realise immediately that Rachel was drunk, they'd probably even have to help me get her inside. They'd hear and see the car as soon as we pulled up – I could picture them rushing out – Mum's face creased initially in concern, changing quickly to her hard, set look of anger, her cold silence more condemning than any words; and Dad's disappointment, his head shaking in bewilderment. *But Katherine,* he'd say, *how could you? We trusted you.*

It was going to be dreadful, we were all going to have a miserable weekend, and Rachel and I would certainly both pay for our bad behaviour. And yet I didn't regret it. Even then, when all the fun was over and all we had left ahead were recriminations and lectures, I possessed a hard little nugget of joy inside that nothing and nobody could take from me. I loved Will. He loved me. And he was so wonderful, so gentle and kind. And I would hold this little piece of knowledge, the treasure of my love for him, and it would keep me warm and happy no matter what happened. When I was at home alone in my bedroom – grounded (as I knew I would be) – the thought of Will, the memory of the time we'd spent together tonight, the promise of what was to come, would be enough to make it bearable – worth it, even.

I was so busy thinking of Will, remembering his touch, and going over and over every single thing he'd said, that it took me a while to realise that the landscape outside my window was completely unfamiliar. I looked hard at the trees and buildings alongside the road, trying to place them, trying to recognise something. But it was no good. I had no idea where we were.

'Um, Grant?' I said. 'We live in Toorak, remember? I don't know if this is the best way.'

'*We live in Toorak, remember?*'

It took a moment for me to understand what Grant had said, to realise that he was imitating my voice, mocking me. Before I had time to wonder why he was suddenly being unkind, he laughed and said it again.

'*We live in Toorak, remember?*' His voice was ludicrously high-pitched, his vowels clipped and sharp. 'Lucky for some, eh? Some of us don't get to live in *Toorak.*' He laughed viciously. 'But someone's gotta live in the shitholes, eh? Someone's gotta live at the arse end of the universe out near the tip and the sewerage and the prison. Some of us get to smell the roses while the others get our faces rubbed in shit, eh? That's just how it is. Isn't that right, Sean? The way of the bloody world.'

Sean laughed, a short, nervous and very artificial laugh. I turned to look at him, to smile, but he refused to catch my eye. He stared straight ahead and lifted a can of beer to his lips. I realised, as I watched him, that he actually had a very attractive face beneath his fat – striking blue eyes, lovely skin. He'd be handsome if he lost some weight. And then I thought how odd it was that his hand was shaking – so much that he missed his mouth and dribbled beer down his chin. His forehead was wet with sweat and it struck me, suddenly, that he was scared. And for a moment I felt sorry for him and wondered what exactly he was scared of.

That's when I realised that Rachel and I were in danger.

Fear hit me immediately. My throat clenched up so tightly that it became hard to swallow. I felt a painful twisting in my gut, felt my hands start to tremble and my heart start to pound. The air of hostility from all of the boys in the car, the way they didn't look at me or acknowledge my presence, was suddenly so obvious that it was almost palpable. I wondered how I'd failed to notice it before. In my desperation to get Rachel home I'd been careless, stupid. I'd thought they were simply rude, but I now realised that their coldness was far more sinister.

They'd *known* this was going to happen. I didn't know what they had planned, or where they were taking us, but *they* did. They were all in on it. And they could do anything they wanted.

They've drugged Rachel, I thought. And as soon as it occurred to me, I knew that it was true. And they tried to drug me too. That's why they wanted me to drink some of their beer. *Rohypnol*. I'd heard of it, been warned about it by policemen at school. Always get your own drinks, they'd said. Never ever drink something that you're not 100 per cent certain of.

But Rachel was so trusting, so naïve. She would never have imagined.

They didn't want to look at me or talk to me in case they felt sympathy. It was clear that Grant was the ring-leader. He was relaxed and confident, humming as he drove, his arm resting on the window. The other boys all seemed nervous, stiff, but not Grant. Perhaps they knew that what they were doing was wrong. Perhaps they would take pity on us.

'Please. Could you just take us home? Please?' I said, trying to keep my voice steady.

'I *am* taking you home. Jesus. The ingratitude. We're just going to make a little detour first. Take care of some business.' He looked at me over his shoulder and smiled and winked in a cruel parody of reassurance.

Maybe Grant simply enjoyed scaring people and this drive was some kind of game. After he'd had his malicious fun maybe he planned to take us home or just abandon us somewhere – safe and untouched. That was the best that I could hope for, the best scenario I could imagine. But there were a lot of different pictures in my head, more chilling scenarios, alternatives that seemed more likely – rape, torture – and suddenly they were all so petrifyingly possible that I started to cry, with great, gulping sobs that made my body shudder and my breath come in noisy, rasping heaves. I put my hand to my mouth to try and quieten myself – I didn't want to irritate anyone, give them cause to dislike me – but Grant turned round and looked at me, shook his head and tutted as if he was disappointed.

'What's wrong, Princess?' he said. 'Things not going to plan? Daddy's little girl not getting everything her own way?'

'Sorry,' I muttered, quite irrationally, as I pressed harder against my mouth, and turned to look out the window at the unfamiliar landscape. 'Sorry.'

Grant laughed nastily and slapped his hand on the steering wheel. '*Sorry?*' He said it loudly, aggressively. 'What perfect manners she has!' He turned to look at me and sneered. 'Your mother would be proud.'

And as he turned back to the road he had to adjust his steering, the car had swerved onto the other side of the road, and for a moment the headlights of an oncoming car shone blindingly through the windscreen. As the car passed, its horn sounded long and loud.

'Fuck you!' Grant shouted, sticking his middle finger up to the blackness. 'Fuck you!'

And for a moment I wished that we'd crashed – the passengers in the front would have been most in danger – and then I considered the possibility of trying to distract Grant so that he *would* crash. In a head-on collision with another car, or a tree, Rachel and I would have a good chance of surviving. It might be a better alternative to being at the mercy of Grant, who was clearly sick in the head.

But, no, it was too difficult to pull off. Far too risky.

And if I failed, which was likely, things would only get worse for me and Rachel.

The only thing I could do was wait. Wait and see where they took us, what they had planned. Try and get away at the first opportunity. And this wouldn't have seemed so difficult, so terrifyingly impossible, if Rachel were awake. But she was deeply asleep, or unconscious, breathing slowly and heavily, and when I put my hand on her knee and squeezed her as hard as I could, pinching her skin, she didn't even stir.

21

Mick plays for another hour and I take the opportunity, while he's on stage, to watch him. I watch the way his shoulders move rhythmically as he plays, the obvious strength in his hands and wrists as he uses his drumsticks. Occasionally he catches me looking and smiles, but he's performing and it's perfectly normal that I should be looking at him, and I feel safe enough to grin back openly. As soon as the band has finished playing he comes and stands beside our table.

'What are you guys doing next?' he says.

'Going home,' Philippa says. 'To bed. Katherine's got to revise tomorrow.'

It's getting late and Philippa's right, I really should get home to bed, but I have no desire to go. 'Oh.' I shake my head. 'Don't worry about me. I'm fine. I feel so much better and I've got a second wind now, and anyway—'

'We should go out somewhere,' Mick interrupts, looking straight at me, and I can tell that he wants this night to continue just as much as I do. 'Get something to eat. I know some good places we can still get dinner.'

'Okay,' I say, enthusiastically. 'Sounds great. I'm starving.'

Philippa looks at her watch, and then back at me. She frowns. 'It's almost midnight. I thought you wanted an early night?'

'No.' I shake my head. 'Not really.'

'Sorry, but I'm totally and absolutely knackered.' Philippa hooks her bag over her shoulder. 'Let's do it next time. I really do have to get home to bed. I'm about to turn into a pumpkin. And that would scare you, believe me.'

She stands up, kisses her brother on the cheek and says goodnight. And she waits, clearly expecting me to get ready to leave with her, and there's an awkward moment where I don't know what to say, what to do, how to make it clear that I don't want to go. But Mick saves me from having to say anything at all.

'You and I could still go,' he says, speaking directly to me, his face all serious and unsmiling again. 'If you want to. I'll make sure you get home safe.'

'Okay, yes, good idea,' I say in a rush, suddenly nervous and awkward, afraid of what Philippa might think. I stand up and collect my bag. 'I'd love to.'

Philippa frowns, looking both puzzled and exasperated at once.

'What are you . . . ?' she says, and then her eyes widen and a slow, knowing grin spreads across her face. She stares at Mick and then at me and I can feel my cheeks burning red. She laughs suddenly, tipping her head back, 'I knew you'd like each other,' she says. 'I knew it.'

I hold my breath and wait for Mick to deny it, to laugh at the suggestion that he likes me, but he meets my eye and smiles shyly and I smile back and I know that it's true, and I know that with our smiles we are both saying a million unsayable things. For a moment the three of us just stand there, silent and grinning, awkward and happy all at once.

'Well, then,' Philippa says eventually, 'I'd better go.' She turns to Mick. 'Make sure she gets home safely. Or I'll kill you.'

'Shut up, Pip,' he says.

'You know he rides a motorbike?' she says to me, her eyebrows raised.

I didn't, but it doesn't surprise me. 'That's fine,' I say cheerfully, forcing the thought of my parents – the certain horror they would feel at the thought of me on the back of a motorbike – to the back of my mind. 'I like bikes,' I lie.

Philippa hugs Mick and then me, giving me an extra squeeze before she lets go. I take it as a sign that she approves of all this and I feel a rush of tenderness towards her. She's so generous and warm and open. Such a good friend.

'I've just got to help pack up a bit,' Mick says when she's gone. 'Won't take long. You want to wait here?'

I offer to go and help. He takes me to the stage and introduces me to the other band members and I spend the next ten minutes helping them clear up, bundling electrical cables and returning empty glasses to the bar. When we've finished and the stage is clear and the instruments are loaded into the lead singer's van, Mick goes backstage and returns with two bike helmets and a leather jacket.

He reaches out and takes my hand with his free one – grasps it tight, his palm big and firm and warm against mine. Then he smiles, wide and happy and natural, and I laugh.

'Let's go,' he says.

We walk without talking. I don't know where he's taking me and neither do I care. It's odd how comfortable I feel being alone with him, this man I've only just met, but it feels natural holding his hand. Right. Our hands fit together perfectly. There's something easy between us, something almost magical, and when I look into his eyes there's a feeling of something I can only describe as familiarity, a sense of safety. Like coming home.

'Here,' he says when we reach his bike. He puts both

helmets on the seat and holds out the jacket. 'You can wear this.'

The jacket's a little big, but it's soft and it smells good and wearing it makes me feel like a different girl altogether – someone wild and impetuous, someone brave. And when we've got our helmets on and I'm sitting on the bike behind Mick – my arms round his waist, the front of my body pressed tight against his back – and he takes off into the night, easy and quick through the streets, I believe I can really be that girl.

22

Grant pulled off the road into a bushy area.

'So,' he said, unclipping his belt and turning to face me, smiling. 'Here we are. Time for some fun, eh? You ready, Katie? Katie, Katie? Katie, me matie?'

I didn't respond, just looked back at him stonily. There was nothing I could say to him, and by now my fear was so great, and my hatred for Grant so enormous, that I was barely capable of speech. I was shaking – my arms, hands, legs and even my head. My teeth were chattering and I had to force my lips closed, bite my teeth together, to stop them from making a dreadful noise. And the effort of that gave me something to concentrate on, something to focus my energy on instead of screaming, jumping across the seat and attacking Grant, which was what all the adrenaline in my body was urging me to do – and which would, I was quite certain, only make things much worse.

And, despite my frequent poking and pinching,

Rachel hadn't moved, or blinked, or shown any other sign of being conscious since we left the party. In a way I envied her the oblivion.

'Come on.' Grant elbowed the boy sitting next to him, rolled his eyes in exasperation, then leaned over him and yelled at the boy sitting closest to the door. 'Get out then, would ya? You just going to sit there all night waiting for me to tell you what to do?'

'All right.' The boy opened the car door and slid out, the second boy following close behind.

Grant got out, slamming his door shut so hard that the car shook. And then Sean, so heavy and so nervous that I could hear the wheeze of his breath, got out, and slammed his door too. Rachel and I were alone in the car. Trapped, surrounded.

'Rach.' I put my hand on her knee and shook as hard as I could. 'Wake up. Rachel! Wake up.' I heard the hysteria in my voice. 'Please, Rach.' I spoke louder, not worrying if they heard me. '*Please.*'

The door next to me opened and I felt the rush of the cold night air. And then Grant leered in at me. 'She can't hear you, mate. You're wasting your time.' He looked at his bare wrist as if he were checking the time. 'Oh. Another hour at least, I'd say, before she even comes near to waking up.' Then he put his hand on my knee and squeezed gently in a falsely affection-ate gesture that made my skin crawl and repulsed me as much as if I'd been touched by a venomous spider. I wanted to scream and kick my legs and slap his face. But I bit my lip and looked down at my lap, forced my hands not to move.

'What do you want, Grant?' I said. My voice was quiet, even. 'What do you want from us?'

He looked thoughtful. He took a drag on his cigarette and blew smoke into my face. I turned away and coughed into my hand.

'Oh shit. Sorry, mate. Don't you smoke?'

'No.'

'Maybe you should take it up. I like a lady who smokes. It's sexy. Don't ya think? Kinda sophisticated.'

He took another drag of his cigarette and, again, blew the foul smoke from his lungs into my face.

I closed my eyes, held my breath. But then the butt of his cigarette was against my mouth, his fingers pushing it roughly between my lips. I turned away.

Suddenly, shockingly, my head snapped back and there was a searing pain in my scalp. He had pulled my hair, forced my head back, so that I was looking at him from an almost upside-down angle. 'Listen, bitch,' he said, his face so close to mine that I could feel the scratch of stubble on his cheeks. 'Don't fucking turn away from me, all right? I don't like it. *All right?*' He let go and I nodded. I started to cry.

'Oh,' he said, sighing. 'Not this again. Look.' He

opened the car door wider and perched on the seat next to me, one leg inside the car, one resting on the ground. 'Things'll just be a lot easier if you co-operate, okay? If you just do what I say, when I say it. Okey-dokey?'

His air of smug arrogance, possible only because he had the advantage of strength and numbers – the power of the bully – made me want to laugh at him, spit in his face. But my reluctance to be hurt again, my desire to stay alive and intact and as uninjured as possible, was stronger than my desire to strike out.

'Okay,' I said. 'Okay.'

'Good girl. Now have a bit of this smoke. It won't hurt you. Here.' He pressed the cigarette between my lips once again. 'Now suck.'

I breathed in, as shallowly as I could, drawing smoke into my mouth, and immediately started to cough and splutter. Grant laughed, shook his head as if amused by the antics of a child, and put the cigarette back between his own lips. He stood up.

'Come on,' he said. 'Time to get out now.'

'Where are we going?' I said, looking back at Rachel anxiously. 'And what about Rachel? I don't want to leave her alone.'

Grant peered back into the car and sighed, balancing the cigarette expertly in one corner of his mouth as he spoke. 'What did I say, Katie? You're not listening, mate. Do *what* I say, *when* I say it and everything will be fine.' And then he stopped, took the cigarette between his thumb and forefinger, turned it, and looked thoughtfully at the glowing red end of it.

I understood what he was going to do a moment before he did it. And then I was screaming, and the skin on my leg, just above my knee, was consumed with a hot, burning, pain. He held the tip of the cigarette deliberately against me and I screamed. And my arms moved involuntarily, pushing him away, slapping at him, hitting, striking out.

He grabbed my arms with both of his and held them down so hard that it hurt. He was so much stronger that I could neither resist nor pull away; I could barely even move my arms beneath his grip. 'Shut up,' he said, so viciously that spit collected between his lips and splashed my face. 'Don't ask questions. Don't ask any more fucking questions. Just fucking. Do. What. You're. Fucking. Told.'

And my fear and anger and hatred – for I hated him then, and if I could have killed him I would have, gladly – were so strong that I forgot the pain in my leg, could barely feel it. I wanted to scream at him, and I could feel my top lip curl with the force of my loathing, with the effort of not expressing it; *How dare you!* I wanted to say. *You stupid, dumb, ignorant, ugly fuck. How dare you! You're going to be sorry for this. You're going to pay.*

And if I get the opportunity, if you turn your back, if I get the chance, I'll kill you. I'll pound your head with a rock, pound and pound and pound until your brains are a liquid pulp. I'll smash you until there's nothing left of your stupid, cowardly face, nothing left of your pathetic, evil, sad little mind.

'Come on!' he screamed at me suddenly, making me jump and put my hands up to my face defensively. 'Get out of the fucking car! Now!'

I slid across the seat and got out.

Sean and the other boys were standing together not far from the car. I could hear them muttering and laughing. Their laughter sounded forced, unnatural. They were nervous, it was obvious, and their voices were full of an artificial bravado. The three of them held cigarettes which made arcs of glowing orange in the dark as they moved their arms, or lifted them to their mouths.

Grant held my forearm tightly and dragged me past the others.

It was dark and I stumbled occasionally; each time he pulled on my arm sharply and made a grunt of annoyance. I tried hard to walk evenly but I was so terrified that my legs were shaking, and my balance was off. It was an enormous effort not to fall to the ground and start screaming; instead I sobbed silently, tears running down my cheeks and splashing onto my collar.

And then there was a building in front of us. Some kind of small storage shed. I could see the ripples of its corrugated-iron walls in the glow from Grant's cigarette. Grant pulled on the door, which made a loud, creaking protest, and pushed me inside. And then there was the crack of a bolt and I was locked in.

It was black inside. It smelled of damp and dirt, a smell that reminded me of the cellar at my grandfather's, a place that had always frightened me. As I heard Grant walk away I fell to my knees and started to moan in terror.

'Oh God,' I whispered into the blackness. 'Please, please, don't leave me here. Please.'

My instinct was to scream – to scream and yell and bash and bang on the wall; to protest as loudly and as violently as I could. But I knew that it would do no good, that no one would hear me. I'd only make Grant angrier and provoke him into hurting me again. Or he might hurt Rachel. It took all my effort, all my energy and self-control, to muffle my sobs, be as quiet as I could.

I put my hands on the ground, and felt dirt, damp and cold and packed down hard. I crouched on all fours and let my head hang for a moment. I breathed in and out, in and out, and tried to calm myself. It would be so easy to let myself scream and shout, so easy, and in a way, such a relief, to let myself succumb to mindless hysteria. But I needed to keep my head, I needed to think. After all, I was still alive, Rachel was still alive, nothing irreversible had happened yet. And the best, no the *only* defence I had was my brain. Grant and his friends were stronger, but I had to believe that I was smarter and if I remained calm there was a chance I could outwit them and find a way to escape.

I ran my hands along the ground, trying to feel out the edges of the shed, to work out how big it was and get a sense of where the walls were. I wanted to see if there was any possible source of light, any place where I might escape.

I kept one hand against the wall and crawled along the floor. I went slowly, afraid, in the blackness, of crawling on something sharp, or of hitting my head. But it felt better to be moving, to be doing something. It felt much better to have a plan, however feeble and unlikely the plan might be.

The shed seemed larger inside than it had from out-side. As I turned a corner along the second wall my hands touched something. It was soft, and had an odd texture. I recoiled in horror and put my hands to my face to muffle a sob.

My first thought was that it was some kind of animal, but I heard and felt no movement, no sound of breath-ing. Slowly I reached out my hand to touch it again.

It was soft but coarse. Not an animal at all, but some

kind of sack. Hessian. Probably filled with seeds, or hay. I crawled further and discovered that there were piles and piles of these sacks stacked up against one entire wall.

I crawled round the rest of the shed and found no holes or gaps between the walls and the earth, no obvious way of escape. I sat back and tried to think, and as I looked round I noticed that my eyes had adjusted to the dark. Apart from the sacks the shed was completely empty. The only source of light came from the gaps round the doorway. But I knew the door was firmly locked, I'd heard Grant push several bolts when he left.

I could move the sacks. I knew the chance was slim, but there might be some kind of hole or way of escape behind them. Corrugated iron could be bent; all I needed was a small gap between the wall and the ground and I'd be able to squeeze out.

The sacks were heavy and hard to budge, but my fear and anger gave me a strength I wouldn't usually possess. I didn't care how much my arms hurt, or my back; the need to escape, to *live*, kept me moving. I didn't move the sacks far, I just piled them neatly, arranged just as they were, about a metre from the wall. As much as I wanted to shove them rapidly out of my way, toss them anywhere, I didn't want Grant to notice that they'd been moved when he returned.

And I was rewarded. When I finally began on the

last row, I saw a silvery reflection coming up from the ground. Light. I started moving much faster, suddenly more anxious and afraid than I'd been only moments before. I felt my stomach twist, and had a sudden overwhelming urge to go to the toilet. The possibility of escape only heightened my fear, made me conscious of how much danger I was in, how terrified I really was. But I squeezed my muscles together and held on, I didn't have time to stop.

When I'd moved all of the sacks far enough that I could get between them and the wall, I crouched down on my hands and knees and looked at the gap. The wall was very slightly bent up and outwards at the bottom and that left a space about ten centimetres high and almost a metre wide. I'd be able to squeeze beneath if I could bend it away just a little further, make the gap wide enough for my head and then my body to fit through.

I stood up, put my foot against the iron and pushed out as hard as I could. It didn't budge. I needed to be able to put the full weight of my body into it. I got on the ground, on my back, with my head against the sacks, and using my feet I pushed with all the strength I had. The iron bent up. A little.

Again, at the idea that I might escape, I felt hysteria rising in my throat. I stifled a sob, shook my head, and concentrated. I pushed again. I pushed so hard that it hurt. The wall bent up further.

The gap now looked big enough to fit through. I lay flat on my stomach and pushed my head through first, sideways, so that my cheek scraped along the earth and I felt the sharp point of pebbles against my skin. It was harder getting my shoulders through, but I pulled with my hands and pushed with my feet and forced myself to squeeze through. The rest of my body was easy and I pushed myself along the ground, not caring that the ragged edge of the iron was scraping my back, cutting through my clothes, bruising my skin, until I was free. I stood up.

And now that I was out, it was even harder to control my rising hysteria. I was free, at least for now, and I so desperately didn't want Grant to find me that I was momentarily paralysed by my own terror. But I forced myself to breathe, my legs to move, and I walked to the corner of the shed, and peeked round.

The car doors were open and enough light shone from the car to show that Rachel was on the ground beside it. She was on her back, her skirt gathered messily up round her waist. Grant knelt between her open legs. He was moving back and forth, thrusting into her. Rachel moaned softly each time. The other boys leaned against the car, watching.

The bastards were raping her. My baby sister.

I had to bend over double and clamp my hand over my mouth to stifle a scream. I wanted to run towards them, hit them, scratch them, kill and maim and injure. But I had to force myself to be still, to think. There was no way I could overpower them, no way I could hurt them.

An angry hatred so powerful that I could taste it, sharp and bitter, rose up in my throat. I crouched down in the dirt and picked up a rock, clenched it in my hand so tight that it dug into the surface of my skin. But I was glad for the hurt of it, glad of its sharpness.

I looked around desperately for something, anything, and I'm not sure what I was hoping to find, but through the trees in the distance I saw light.

I looked back towards Rachel, and just as I did Sean lifted his head. He seemed to look straight at me. I don't know whether he really saw me – I'll never know. It was dark where I was standing so perhaps he didn't, but I didn't wait around to find out. I panicked.

I turned and ran. Towards the light.

23

We ride down towards Circular Quay and then to the Rocks. Mick takes me to a pub where he says they serve good late-night food. We're both starving and we order huge meals – steak and chips and salad – and eat enthusiastically, grinning at each other across the table whenever our eyes meet.

When we've finished our dinner and our table is clear and we're each sipping on a Coke, Mick kisses me. It's surprising and unexpected and yet totally wonderful all at once. He stands up, leans across the table and puts his lips against mine. It's not a passionate kiss, his mouth remains closed, but it's tender and soft and lasts much longer than a brotherly peck. It's a kiss that makes everything more certain, a kiss that makes it clear that he's as attracted to me as I am to him.

'Why did you scowl when you first met me?' I ask. 'I thought you must hate me. I thought you were horrible, actually. Unfriendly and rude.'

'Because I felt weird. When I first saw you. As soon as I saw you, I knew something was going to happen between us. I knew it. Straight away.' He smiles – looks shy for the first time. 'You made me nervous.'

We're both jubilantly happy, both surprised at the unexpected delight of finding one another, and when we leave the pub and head back to his bike Mick asks me where I live.

'I don't want to go home,' I say.

'You don't?'

'No.'

We go to Mick's place. He shares a tiny flat with a student called Simon, who is out for the evening. We make tea and take our mugs to Mick's bedroom. His bed is a simple mattress on the floor – but the doona is pulled up tidily, the pillows arranged in a single pile at its head. Books are stacked against the wall beside his bed, a guitar leans against the wall.

We sit on his bed side by side, our backs against the pillows, legs crossed, knees touching. We talk about music, our favourite bands, our favourite songs. We drink three cups of tea each, and share a bar of chocolate from the near-empty fridge. At almost 3 a.m., Mick shuffles down the bed so that he rests on his side, facing me, his head on a pillow.

'Lie down,' he says. 'You must be getting tired.'

I wriggle lower so that we are next to each other, our faces close.

Mick touches my face with his fingertip, traces a line down my cheek, across my chin, down my neck.

'You're beautiful,' he says.

We kiss, pressing our bodies, our mouths, tight. And we fit together so well, so naturally, and soon we are breathless and tense with heat and need.

I pull away, suddenly full of a powerful and intrusive desire to talk, to tell my story. 'I haven't done this for . . . the last time I kissed a boy . . . the last time,' I pause, take a deep breath. 'He was called Will. William Holloway. It was the night Rachel was murdered.'

Mick is still. He nods, listens.

'We didn't do anything that night,' I say, and I remember Will's face, how much I had loved him, how painful and awkward it was when I saw him afterwards. 'We were going to, though. We had great plans for losing our virginity together. But everything just turned to shit after that night. We were really uncomfortable around each other. I think we were embarrassed. Which seems a ridiculous thing to feel when someone's been murdered. But we couldn't look at each other properly. He kept coming round to see me and he'd sit there, all stiff and unhappy, while I cried. Eventually I just told him I didn't want to see him any more. He was so relieved.' I laugh sadly. 'You should have seen his face. He was trying to pretend to be sad that we'd broken up. But he couldn't get out the door fast enough.'

'I guess it was a pretty heavy scene for a sixteen-year-old.'

'Totally,' I say. 'I didn't really blame him at all. I was relieved too. It was horrible having him feel so sorry for me. But he was too polite and kind to dump me.'

'And since then?'

'Nothing,' I say. 'Nobody.'

'I'm lucky, then.' He smiles, kisses my forehead. 'But we can slow down. There's no hurry. I can wait. I don't want to pressure you.'

But I know what I want, and the idea of waiting any longer is so frustrating it only makes me more certain. I shake my head and smile shyly. I take his hand and place his arm round me, move forward so that our bodies are close and tight and press my lips against his.

'Katherine,' he says, when we finish. We're breathing each other's air and are lying side by side, face to face.

'Mick,' I say.

'I love your name. It suits you perfectly. Katherine. Katherine. Katherine and Mick.'

And when he says my name like that, right next to

his, everything is different. I've never really liked being called Katherine – all this time I've missed being called Katie. I've missed being Katie.

But I'm no longer Katie, I'm Katherine – and tonight, for the first time ever, I don't want to be anyone else.

24

You run and you run and you run. You run faster, harder than you've ever run before. You trip and stumble, fall hard on your hands and knees, get up immediately, continue running.

'Please, please,' you sob. 'Help me. Please. Someone. Help.'

You are terrified that they are behind you, chasing you, getting closer with each step. Your own ragged breath is loud in your ears, deafening you can hear them behind you, and so you run faster. You don't turn round to check, you're too terrified to do anything but run. Despite the pain in your sides, your fatigue, the ache in your legs, you force yourself on, force yourself not to slow down, not to turn round, not to collapse in a hysterical heap on the ground.

And as you get closer to the light it becomes clear that it comes from a house, as you'd hoped. And as you get closer still you see that the windows are open to the night breeze, the front porch light is on, a car is parked in the driveway. Someone is home.

You run down the drive, fall onto the front porch, pick yourself up and run to the door. You pound and pound with your fists. You kick. You try to yell out.

After a moment the door is pulled open. A woman stands there; she looks angry at the rude intrusion. But as she takes in your appearance, your obvious fear, the urgency of the situation, her expression changes to one of alarm and concern. Her mouth drops open, she puts one hand on her chest, the other on your arm.

'What's wrong?' she says. 'What's happened?'

By the time the police arrive and organise a search, the boys have gone. They've left her there, on her back in the dirt like an animal. One of the policemen reassures you that she looks peaceful, the expression on her cold dead face one of serenity and calm. It's something, he says, something to hope that she didn't really know what was happening.

She didn't know that you left her there. Alone with them.

Part 2

25

Alice is already seated at a table in the corner of the cafe by the time I get there. She is sipping on a mug of coffee.

'Hey.' I sit opposite her. Smile.

Alice rolls her eyes. 'I've been trying to call you all weekend. Why don't you ever take your mobile with you?' She is irritable but she can't do anything to change my mood. Nothing can; I'm far too happy.

'What was it? What did you want?' I say pleasantly, ignoring her temper. I don't bother explaining what has happened, where I've been. I don't say a word about Mick. It's still so new, so lovely and I want to keep it to myself.

'I just wanted to tell you. I've got this new man.' She leans forward, her eyebrows raised, her anger of only a moment before apparently forgotten.

My immediate thought is of Robbie. How devastated he'll be.

'Oh.' I pick up the menu, stare blindly at the laminated cardboard. 'Is it serious?'

'*Is it serious?* God, you could sound a bit happier for me.'

I put the menu down and look at her. 'I'm sorry. But what about Robbie? Does he even know about this yet? He's going to be devastated. He really—'

'Robbie schmobbie,' she interrupts. 'It's not as if I ever promised him anything. Honest, Katherine. I never did. Never. In fact I made it perfectly clear that it wasn't serious between us. He just made us up in his head. Anyway, Robbie will just have to deal with it. He has no choice. He doesn't own me.'

'I guess not.' And I realise that this is probably the best outcome in the long term anyway. In a way I can only feel glad, for Robbie's sake. This will force him to face up to reality – Alice simply doesn't care about him. It's going to hurt but he needs to forget her and find someone else – someone who appreciates how fantastic he is.

'So?' I say. 'Who is he? What's he like?'

'He's gorgeous. He's wonderful, beautiful, sexy. I'm in absolute heaven. I think about him every minute of the day.'

I smile. I know exactly how she feels.

'What's his name?'

But Alice doesn't answer. Instead she lifts her cup to her mouth, peers at me over the rim. 'He's forty-eight.'

'Shit, Alice. That's ancient. Doesn't it bother him? That you're still at school?'

Alice smiles. 'Maybe he thinks I'm twenty-seven.'

'You're lying to him?'

She shrugs. 'Stretching the truth a bit.'

'But he's so *old*. Isn't that weird?'

'No. No, it's not. You'd be surprised. It's great. He's really smart, Katherine, and unbelievably knowledge-able. It's as if I've been looking for an older man all this time, you know; it's just a million times better. He's just so much more mature, so much more open and confident and independent. And he doesn't act like a lovesick puppy around me, which is such a relief.' She laughs. 'And he's just so good in bed, so experienced. He's just so fucking unbelievably *skilled*.'

I try hard to concentrate on the menu. I'm not even hungry – the excitement of being newly in love has ruined my appetite – but I don't want Alice to sense my disapproval, my judgement. Whenever I've been around her lately I've felt like an older sister, a disap-proving and cranky older sister.

I'm not even sure why Alice's new relationship should bother me. They're both adults, after all, and as long as nobody gets hurt the age difference shouldn't really matter. It's just that, with Alice, things are never as simple as they first seem.

'He's not married, is he?' I say, and I can't help it, I

sound suspicious.

'No, he isn't,' says Alice, offended. 'As if I'd do something like that!'

The waitress comes to the table and I order coffee and a sandwich. Alice just orders more coffee. I can see that she's itching to tell me more about her new man.

'You're not eating?' I ask.

'No. I've got no appetite.' She leans forward and puts her hand round mine, squeezes. 'I think I'm in love, Katherine. I've never felt like this. Never. I can't eat. I can't sleep. I'm overdosing on adrenaline. I have no idea how I'm going to get through the damn HSC like this. I can hardly even read a magazine, let alone Shakespeare. All I do is wait for him to call. It's as if I'm only half alive when I'm not with him, in some kind of weird limbo-land. You know, I honestly think he might be the true love of my life.'

And though I'm feeling almost exactly the same way about Mick, I'm surprised that I have no reciprocal urge to confide in Alice, no desire to tell her about all the glorious new feelings pulsing through my veins, or how much things have changed since I last saw her. In fact I'm shocked to realise that I want to keep the whole thing from her, keep it safe, hidden. Mine.

I smile and listen while she tells me everything – where they met, how they ended up together. But I tell her nothing about Mick. Nothing.

26

I have ten days of self-directed study before the HSC begins, and then ten days of actual exams before I am forever free of high school, and it feels as though those twenty days will be some of the longest days of my life. It isn't the anticipation of the exams that I find so unpleasant, or even the exams themselves, but my self-imposed separation from Mick. There's no way I can concentrate on schoolwork when we're together, and so we both agree that the best thing is not to see each other in person at all. Just for twenty days. It seems reasonable at the time. Easy, even. But not seeing him is harder than I expected and I miss him so much that I feel it like a physical pain.

I set myself up comfortably, all my books and papers around me, at my desk at home. Vivien is heading off on a month-long business trip round Europe soon. But she's home now, having a rare few weeks without any travel, and she takes care of all of the domestic stuff while I study. She cooks us delicious, healthy meals and insists on doing all the washing-up so I'm free to study without interruption. I finish each day at about five and go for a walk to clear my head, then I eat dinner and go back to my room for a few more hours' work.

I'm usually too tired and brain-dead to work much past nine and when I've showered and put my pyjamas on I hop into bed and call Mick on his mobile phone. I always feel slightly nervous before I call, afraid that I'll interrupt him, that he'll be annoyed or unfriendly or for some reason less than happy to hear from me. But every time I call he answers almost immediately with my name, *Katherine*, and he always sounds relieved, joyful, as if he has been looking forward to hearing my voice as much as I've been looking forward to hearing his.

He asks me each night what I've been working on, how I'm feeling, if I'm ready for the exams. He tells me about his day, how his band practice went. If he has a gig that night he always sounds a little more upbeat, distracted. My favourite nights are the nights when he is at home too, in bed, and we talk to each other for an hour or more. We talk until our voices grow soft and sleepy and his tender 'goodnight' is the last thing I hear before I close my eyes.

On the afternoon of my final exam, Ancient History,

he is there waiting for me when I walk out of the examination hall. I hadn't expected him to be there and I feel myself blush as I walk towards him. I feel silly in my school uniform, unattractive and girlish, and I'm acutely conscious that some of the other students are staring at us. But Mick smiles, grabs my hand, pulls me close and wraps his arms round me. And in Mick's arms I am suddenly indifferent to what other people think. I no longer give a stuff what I look like. He loves me and that is all that matters. We go straight back to Mick's place, to his bedroom, and when he wraps his arms round me and kisses me, I am overcome. Lost.

Several hours later when it has become dark and I've woken from a deep, contented sleep, Mick brings me a sandwich and a cup of tea and watches me as I eat. I'm hungry and eat quickly and when I've finished Mick lies down beside me and makes love to me again. And when we've finished, when we are lying side by side, face to face, I begin to cry.

'What is it?' Mick frowns, rests his head on his elbow. 'What's wrong?'

'This is too good. Too much. I'm too happy. It's scary.'

He laughs, kisses me. 'Don't be dumb. You're allowed to be happy, Katherine.'

'Am I? I'm not sure, sometimes I think . . .'

'No.' He shakes his head and kisses me again so that

I can't speak. His voice is urgent, almost panicked. 'Shhhh. Don't say anything. You'll bring bad luck. You're happy. I'm happy. It's not too good to be true, people are happy all the time. It's normal. It's good. Don't think about bad stuff. Just don't.'

'Okay,' I say. 'Okay.' And in the face of Mick's superstitiousness, his own obvious fear, I keep my concerns to myself and pretend to believe that I deserve happiness as much as anybody else.

I go home to sleep that night because Vivien is leaving for Europe and I want to have breakfast with her and say goodbye.

'Did you have fun last night?' she says the next morning, tucking in to the scrambled eggs I insisted on making.

'Yes. It was fantastic.' And there must be something in my voice, an extra note of happiness or excitement, because she looks at me quizzically, her eyebrows raised.

'That good, huh?'

'Yeah.' And I look down at my plate, hope my cheeks aren't as pink as they feel. 'Just so good to be finished. So good to be free.' I don't tell her about Mick. I can't. I'm afraid that talking about it too soon may jinx it, cause everything to unravel. And though I'm pretty sure she would never betray a confidence, I'm not ready for my parents to know.

'You're looking much happier lately,' she says as she hugs me goodbye. 'So much happier.'

'I guess I am,' I say.

Mick has a gig that night. His band is playing from ten until one at a pub nearby. We spend the day together at his place and he leaves for work at eight. I stay behind to have a shower and get dressed and wait for Philippa. She arrives at half-past nine, with Danni, a friend of hers from university. They've brought a bunch of flowers for me, a congratulatory gift for finishing the HSC.

'Well done,' Philippa says, leaning in to kiss me on the cheek, 'for making it through all those years of torture.'

'No more school,' I say. 'Ever. It's hard to believe.'

'So?' Danni asks. 'How do you think you went?'

'Okay, I guess.' I shrug. 'I'm just glad it's all over.'

'I'll bet Mick's glad too.' Philippa grins, elbowing me. 'He missed you desperately. He pined like a love-sick puppy.'

Though Mick has already told me how much he missed me, hearing it from Philippa makes it seem even more real, more precious.

The band is already playing when we get there and I sit at our table, a cold drink in my hands, and stare at Mick shamelessly. He is playing, concentrating, his face as intent and serious and closed-up as the first time I saw him. Danni and Philippa talk, try to involve me in the conversation, but I'm distracted, waiting for Mick to notice me. Danni and Philippa laugh. Philippa squeezes my leg. She is happy for me, happy for her brother.

Eventually he turns our way. He grins when he sees me, his enormous, transformative smile, and my heart pounds in my chest with grateful love. I want to rush on to the stage and kiss him, embrace him, hold him close. But it's almost as good watching him play, knowing that it's me he's thinking of, me who has made his face open up like that, me he will come to when he's finished.

As the band is playing the final song of the first set Mick keeps his eyes on mine, and as soon as it's over he rushes from the stage and comes to our table. He says hi to Philippa and Danni, reaches out for my hand, and drags me to the stage. He takes me to the back, where it's dark.

He pushes me against the wall, presses his body against mine, puts his hand on the side of my head, buries his fingers in my hair.

'You came,' he says.

'Yes,' I say, and my voice is feather-soft, breathless with love and lust and incredulous joy.

'I missed you.' And I hear it in his voice too, this mad happiness.

'Yes.' And there is little else to say, just yes. *Yes.*

And then his mouth is on mine, his tongue searching, his lips soft, the clean sweet smell of his breath now familiar. And I can feel him against me, his desire, and I want him too and I lean towards him, showing him that I feel the same. And yet I feel no great sense of urgency for the night to be over. I'm going to appreciate it, every moment, enjoy the anticipation, savour the fact that we will be together later. That there is better yet to come.

And then a familiar song comes on the jukebox.

'Rachel used to listen to this.' I move back and laugh, rock my body in time with the beat. It's an invigorating, happy song, impossible to ignore. 'She loved it. She always used to dance to it.'

Mick takes my hand in his. 'Come on, then.'

We go back onto the stage and jump down to the crowded dance floor. We dance, our hands clasped together tightly, moving in towards one another and away again. Our lips meet occasionally, and we taste each other, salty, sweet, our bodies pressed close. We separate and Mick twirls me round until I get dizzy and he has to hold me up while I laugh. We dance to song after song until we're both hot and sweaty and our palms are sticky. But we don't care, we don't want to let go. Neither of us can stop smiling.

The music is loud so I don't hear my mobile phone, but I feel the vibration against my hip. A message. I ignore it, plan to check it later, but a few minutes later it's buzzing again. I take the phone from my pocket, hold it up to show Mick. He kisses me. I go to the bathroom so that I'll be able to hear the messages.

It's Alice.

Katherine. Call me. She sounds as if she might be crying. *Where are you? I can never find you lately. Please call me. Please. I really need to see you.*

I call her mobile phone.

'Katherine. Thank God,' she answers.

'What's up? Are you okay?'

'No. Not really.'

'What's wrong? What's happened?'

'I'm bored. I've got nothing to do. My man is busy and can't see me tonight.'

I roll my eyes. Only Alice could make boredom seem so urgent. And though I really don't want to leave Mick, I say, 'Do you want me to come over? Bring you some chocolate?'

'I don't know what I want.' She sighs. 'Where are you? It sounds funny. There's an echo.'

'I'm out. At a pub. The William Hotel. I'm in the bathroom. The music's too loud to hear anything.'

'Oh.' She is quiet again. And then, 'Who are you with?'

'Philippa. And a girl called Danni. And Philippa's brother.' I avoid saying Mick's name. 'But I can leave.

I'll come over to your place. I'll bring something to help cheer you up.'

'No. No. I don't want to ruin your night. I'll come out. I'll meet you there.'

'But it's so noisy.' And as I'm speaking I realise how much I don't want her to come. I want to keep Mick and Philippa, my new friendship, my new love, away from Alice. I'm afraid she'll ruin everything, taint it somehow. 'We won't be able to talk.'

'Doesn't matter,' she says. 'I don't want to talk. I want to have some fun.'

I go back to the bar and sit at the table with Philippa and Danni. The band is back on stage and Mick winks at me from behind his drums as I take my seat. Philippa and Danni, who are listening to the music and tapping their feet, both smile at me. I smile back. But I feel different now, the sense of light elation has disappeared from my mood. The thought of Alice coming has made me feel tired, mildly anxious.

Alice is wearing the shortest dress I've ever seen. It's sequinned in silver and barely covers her underwear. She's wearing boots that come up to her knees. She looks fantastic, sexy, stunning, and I notice heads turn as she makes her way to our table.

She pulls a chair right up next to mine. She doesn't look at or acknowledge Philippa or Danni, but turns sideways so that she faces me.

'Hey,' she says, leaning close so that I can hear her. Her face is made-up and glossy, beautiful. 'This is a bit of a dive, isn't it? Let's go somewhere else. Just you and me.'

Before I have the chance to answer her, Philippa leans over the table and nudges Alice.

'Aren't you going to say hello?' She has to shout to be heard over the noise of the band.

'Hi, Philippa.'

'This is Danni,' Philippa says.

'Hi,' Danni shouts. 'God, I just love your dress! You look totally hot. And those boots! Where do you get your clothes?'

Danni's flattery obviously pleases Alice because her body language changes instantly and dramatically. She turns towards Danni and smiles. And as the two of them become engrossed in a conversation about clothes Alice clearly forgets her desire to leave. She drags her chair over closer to Danni's and leans in. Both of them are absorbed and animated. Philippa looks at me, rolls her eyes.

Alice and Danni spend the rest of the set talking closely. Philippa and I sit side by side and listen to the music, we don't talk, but we look at each other and smile every now and again. Philippa's smile is full of sisterly pride.

When the set is over, Mick rushes down to our table

again. He stands behind me, leans over and kisses my neck.

'I'm just getting a drink,' he says. 'Come with me?'

He takes my hand as I stand up and push back my chair. I notice Alice look up at us curiously. She stops talking and stares, her eyes wide, as I turn away.

When we return to the table Alice is leaning back in her chair, she has her arms folded across her chest. She is smiling.

'So? You and Mick?' She looks at me pointedly. 'Philippa has been kind enough to fill me in.'

I try to act as naturally as possible, although I know that Alice is probably upset and angry and offended that I've kept this from her. I feel the colour rising in my cheeks.

'Alice, this is Mick,' I say. 'Mick, Alice.'

Mick smiles. 'G'day.'

'You play the drums?' Alice asks.

'Yep.'

'I love the drums, just *love* them. But I can't actually comment on your performance. I didn't even notice you up there before. Sorry. But nobody told me you knew Katherine. I didn't even know you were Philippa's brother.'

Mick doesn't respond. Instead he looks at me, clearly wondering who this strange girl is, why she seems mildly hostile. He picks up his glass and takes a large gulp of his beer. He reaches out for my hand and stands, pulling me up with him. He drags me to the dance floor.

He pulls me closer, buries his face in my neck. We sway to the music, from side to side, our bodies in perfect rhythm. I breathe him in, let the smell of him, the feel of his body, the beat of the music, fill my senses.

We stay dancing until Mick has to go back on stage for the final set. When I return Alice has moved. She's sitting at a table behind us with two men. She is animated – talking and gesticulating energetically. Both of the men look charmed, captivated; they are both leaning towards her, both vying for her attention. I'm amazed at how easily she can forget about her boyfriend, the *true love of her life*, but I'm feeling far too happy to worry about Alice, and right now she just makes me smile. I try to catch her eye, but she doesn't look my way, doesn't notice me, she's so preoccupied with her new conquests.

At closing time we all leave together. Alice has linked arms with the men from the table. They're walking ahead of us. Her voice is loud, happy. She turns round and looks back at me.

'I'm going out with Simon and Felix,' she calls out in a sing-song voice, loud enough so that everyone around us can hear.

'Okay,' I laugh.

Alice and Felix and Simon head straight to the taxi rank and join the line of people waiting. Mick's bike is parked just a little further down the road and we have to pass straight by them to reach it.

'Oooh, look, a can-can line,' Alice says loudly, peering down the length of the queue. Some of the people waiting in line laugh. I hear someone else mutter a tired-sounding, 'Oh, for God's sake, shut up.'

And then she starts kicking her legs out and singing the melody of the can-can. The two men beside her support her weight as she kicks higher and higher. Each kick reveals more of the top of her shapely thighs, her underpants. 'Nah nah, na-na-na-na, nah nah, na-na-na-na, nah nah,' she sings, enjoying the attention, indifferent to the irritated and disapproving stares of some of the people waiting in line.

She drags them to the front of the line. When a taxi arrives, Alice and her two new friends hop into it.

'Bye-bye, everyone,' she calls out to the crowd as the taxi pulls away from the kerb. 'Have fun. Bye-bye.'

'Who *is* she?' Mick says, shaking his head, a bemused expression on his face.

'A friend of mine,' I say. And I wonder why I feel as if I'm lying.

27

'That was so fun, Mummy. So fun.' Sarah looks up at me. Her cheeks and her nose are red with cold, but her eyes are bright. 'Can I do it again? By myself this time?'

'Of course,' I say. And I watch her take the toboggan in one hand and trudge slowly back up to the top of the hill. It's not a very steep hill, but it's long enough to gain a bit of momentum on the way down, and go pretty fast. Sarah screamed all the way down the first time, and I was worried that she was scared, but as it turned out she was screaming with delight.

I'd forgotten how heavy and slow I feel when dressed for the snow. I don't enjoy the cold much, I've never particularly liked it. I prefer the weightlessness of summer, the feeling of freedom and joy and life it inspires in me. Winter makes me feel gloomy, it reminds me of death. But I don't want Sarah to be influenced by what I do and don't like. I want her have her own impressions, make her own choices – and through her enthusiasm I get to feel some of the magic and wonder of this icy, cold world.

On her fourth or fifth ride down the hill, just when the skin on my face is starting to sting, just when I'm starting to think that I may have to use the lure of a hot chocolate to persuade Sarah that we need to take a break inside, I see him.

Robbie.

He's standing at the bottom of the ski run. He's wearing the bright blue jacket that all the instructors wear and demonstrating a stopping move to several onlookers. He looks just the same, still just as handsome. He laughs, tipping his head back in a way that is immediately familiar.

He's standing so close I can see the clouds of freezing air coming from his mouth when he laughs. I can see the whiteness of his teeth, the veins on the back of his bare hands.

It's so shocking to see him that I can suddenly do nothing more than just stand there, motionless, my heart pounding in my chest, my eyes cast down, and try to gather some equilibrium. I don't know whether I should call out to him, wave to get his attention. I wonder for a moment if I should rush away and pretend I didn't see him, leave him in peace.

I decide just to continue with my day – not to make any special effort to approach him. If I bump into him again, I'll let him decide how to handle it. I stand up and call out to Sarah and she persuades me to take her for one more ride. And as I grab her hand and begin the climb back up to the top of the hill, I realise that Robbie has seen me. He is standing still, staring, his entire body rigid with the shock I too had felt only moments before.

28

'You can't go.' Mick takes hold of my hand, pulls me back down towards his bed.

I sit beside him on the mattress, lean down and kiss his lips, his stubbly cheek, his neck.

'I have to,' I say. 'It's Robbie's birthday. I promised to take him to dinner. And anyway, I have to go back to Vivien's and clean up a bit. The flat's a mess. I can't leave it like that. She'd kill me.'

'But she's in Europe, isn't she? How will she even know?'

'She won't. But I know and it makes me feel bad.'

'But what'll I do?' He pouts comically. 'Without you?'

'Sleep.' I laugh. 'You need to sleep.' Neither of us slept much the previous night and Mick has another gig later that night.

'But I can't. Not without you.'

'Of course you can. You *used* to sleep without me.

You've done so for most of your life, in fact.'

'Really? I can't remember. Anyway, that was before I knew the difference.' He pulls me down so that I'm lying on top of him, the doona a barrier between our bodies.

'Mick,' I say. 'Please. You don't know how hard it is to go. You're making it impossible. I'll meet you at the gig later. After dinner. I won't stay late.'

'Promise?'

'Promise.'

'Okay, then.'

'Okay.' But when I lean down to kiss him he wraps his arms round me, holds me so tight I can't move.

'It's true, you know, what I said. I don't know what I did before. Before you. I can't remember what I cared about or looked forward to. Whatever it was, it's gone now. All I care about now is you. It's mad, really, kinda stupid. But I've never felt like this about any girl before. Nothing like it.'

And my heart swells with gladness, with the thrill of hearing that all my crazy feelings are reciprocated. I bury my face in his chest, hiding the sudden tears that are pricking at my eyes.

'Me too,' I say. 'Me too.'

I go back home and get stuck into cleaning the flat. I work quickly, rushing from room to room, putting things away, dusting and vacuuming. It takes several hours and when I'm done I check the phone messages and find one from Vivien saying that she's arrived in Rome and is having a great time. There is also a message from my mother, just saying hello, and one from Robbie asking whether I still want to go out for dinner.

I call my parents first. I spoke to them very briefly the afternoon I finished my final exam and though they've already congratulated me, I know that they'll want more details, a longer conversation. I chat with Mum first and then Dad and it takes almost an hour to give them a complete rundown on the exams. They ask when I'll next get a chance to go and stay with them and I tell them soon. I don't mention Mick.

When I've finished talking to my parents, I call Robbie on his mobile.

'Of course we're still going out,' I say as soon as he answers. 'It's my birthday present to you, remember?'

'Okay.' He laughs. 'Cool. But it's probably just you and me. I haven't heard from Alice.'

'I get you all to myself, then. Lucky me.' I don't say it but I'm glad she's not coming. I couldn't stand to see Robbie and Alice together when I know that she's seeing somebody else. It would make me feel complicit in her deception – I'd feel cruel and dishonest, and the whole situation would be utterly humiliating for Robbie. I'm not entirely certain yet whether I'm going to tell him about Alice or not. I only know that I won't do it tonight. Not on his birthday.

'And my dad's organising a party on Saturday night. Can you come? You and Mick?'

'Of course. We might be late, though. Mick has a gig. But that'll be fun. You can meet each other.'

'Can't wait,' he says. But there's not much enthusiasm in his voice. He sounds flat. Unhappy. And I can only assume that his misery has something to do with Alice and I wish, yet again, that he would just forget about her, give himself a chance to meet someone else.

We agree to meet at the restaurant at seven and hang up. I choose the clothes I'm going to wear – jeans, boots, pink shirt – and go to the bathroom and run a hot, deep bath. I spend a long time in the water. I close my eyes and think about Mick and how lucky we are that we both like each other equally, how lucky we are that neither one of us is anything like Alice.

When I get to the restaurant, Robbie is already seated at a booth table and has an almost empty glass in front of him. He is busy reading the menu and is startled when I sit in front of him.

'Hi,' I say. 'You must've been early?'

'Yeah.' He smiles. 'Hungry. Couldn't wait.'

We talk briefly about what we've been doing – and I tell him about Mick, and my new friendship with Philippa, and how happy I am – and he smiles and looks genuinely pleased and says he's glad for me and that I deserve good things. And he's relaxed and cheerful and I think that maybe he's going to be okay about Alice after all, and that her new affair might turn out to be a good thing. Finally, he'll be forced to face the truth.

Robbie orders the food and when it arrives the portions are much larger than we expected. We struggle to get through it all, forcing ourselves to keep eating when we're full, giggling stupidly as Robbie puffs his cheeks full of air.

'This is ridiculous,' he says, shaking his head at the amount of food still left on the table. 'There's enough here for ten people.'

'I know.' I lift another slice of chicken with my fingers and put it in my mouth. 'God, Robbie. I'm totally stuffed but I can't stop. They'll have to come and take it away before I explode. I don't think I'll be able to move for another hour or so. You don't mind sitting here all night, do you?'

And I look up at Robbie, expecting him to laugh and continue on with the playful banter, but he is staring straight past me, at something or someone behind me – and there is no longer any hint of humour in his eyes; instead his face is stiff, contorted into an odd expression of confusion and fear.

I twist to look behind me and see nothing but tables full of unfamiliar faces. I turn back. 'What is it?' I lean forward and put my hand on his. 'Robbie? What's wrong?'

But he's beyond noticing me. He slides his hand out from under mine and stands up. He pushes his chair back clumsily, leans heavily on the table as if to gain strength, then starts walking towards whatever it is he has been looking at.

'Robbie? What are you . . . Robbie!' I stand up and follow him, feeling stupid and conspicuous in the crowded restaurant. I don't know what's going on, it's as if Robbie suddenly can't see or hear me, and I'm afraid that he may be having some kind of fit or seizure, some kind of mental collapse.

But then he stops right in front of an older man at the bar. And the man smiles happily, and reaches his arm out in welcome. Robbie's face remains cold, his body stiff, his manner strangely aggressive.

'What the fuck are you doing?' Robbie says viciously. 'What are you trying to do to me? What are you doing with her? Where is she? Where's she gone?'

The man's eyes widen with surprise. 'Where's who, Robs?' He says. 'What's wrong with you? What are you talking about?'

'I just saw you together, Dad!' Robbie shouts – and I look closer at the man and recognise the eyes, his jaw-line. 'You were kissing! I just saw her here. With you. I fucking well *saw* you together.'

'Robbie.' I put my hand on his arm, try to calm him. 'What . . . ?'

But he shakes me off and leans in closer to his father. 'I saw you with her. I *saw* you.' And though he is no longer shouting his voice is full of anger, and he is so distressed and agitated that he is shaking, almost crying.

But his father remains composed, and looks at Robbie kindly. 'Mate, calm down. She's just gone to the bathroom. You can meet her when she comes back. This doesn't have to be a problem. You're going to really like her.'

And I understand what has happened. Robbie has seen his father with a woman, his new girlfriend, for the first time. His anger is some kind of misplaced and inappropriate loyalty to his mother.

Robbie laughs bitterly – an unnatural and unhappy sound from somewhere deep in his throat – and gives his father a look of contempt. 'Meet her? What do you mean *meet* her? Is this meant to be some kind of twisted birthday present or something?'

I put my hand on Robbie's back. 'Come on, Robbie. Don't do this. Please. Why don't we just go back to our table? Leave your dad alone.' And Robbie's father smiles at me gratefully.

Then I see her. Alice. She is walking towards us from the bathroom. She is walking quickly, her head down, a small smile on her face, and for a brief, happily deluded moment I imagine that she's there for Robbie – that she's decided to turn up for his birthday after all. For a moment I'm even glad to see her, hoping that her presence may distract Robbie from this anger with his father.

But then Robbie and his dad turn and see her too.

'Aha,' says Robbie's father, his voice now full of a forced enthusiasm. 'Here's Rachel now. I'll introduce you.'

Rachel? I think, momentarily bewildered. *Rachel?* And though I'm barely able to put my thoughts together, or comprehend what is happening, my subconscious mind seems to connect the dots for me – and in an instant I know exactly what she's doing here, exactly who her mysterious older boyfriend is, and exactly what it is that Robbie has just seen.

At that moment Alice looks up. She stops walking and looks between Robbie and his father. The smile leaves her face and for the briefest time she looks shocked, scared, as if she might turn and run. But she hesitates for only a moment, and then she flicks her hair from her face, stretches her lips into something resembling a smile, and continues forward.

Robbie's father puts his hand on Alice's arm and pulls her in beside him. Alice's face is absolutely inscrutable – and though she'd looked shocked when she'd first seen us, she now looks perfectly comfortable, slightly amused even, as if this whole situation is just a game, and we are the toys.

'Robs, this is Rachel. Rachel, this is my son, Robbie.' Robbie's father tries to behave as if everything is normal, but I can see that he is both confused and upset by what must seem like some very strange behaviour from Robbie. He clearly has no idea who Alice really is.

Robbie doesn't say a word, and makes no physical acknowledgement of his father's words. He simply stares at Alice – his face so transformed by anger and hurt that it is barely recognisable.

'Oh, come on, Robbie,' Alice says. 'Don't look so serious. Where's your sense of humour?'

Robbie's father stares at Alice, and then Robbie, and back at Alice. The intimate tone of Alice's voice has clearly confused him. 'What? Do you two—'

He doesn't have time to finish the question. Robbie makes a horrible sobbing noise, turns and rushes away.

'Robbie! Wait!' I start to follow him, but quickly realise that he is going way too fast. And my bag is still at the table, and we haven't even paid for our meal. I watch him go and reluctantly turn round and head back towards Alice and Robbie's father. I don't want to stay here and face this horrendous situation. I would rather just get my bag and leave, head straight back home to Mick. I don't want to speak to Alice. I don't want to see her face, or hear her voice. I don't want to hear Robbie's father call her Rachel.

Robbie's father looks shocked. His face is pale, his eyes wide and damp.

'What was that about?' he says as I approach. 'Do you have any idea?'

I look at my feet, say nothing.

'I'm sorry.' He sighs, and I can hear the tremor in his voice. 'I've been extremely rude. We haven't even met. You must be Katherine. Robbie's told me all about you. I'm Greg. And this is Rachel.'

Greg and I shake hands but I refuse to look at or otherwise acknowledge Alice. And when she speaks I turn away.

'I think I should go,' she says.

'What an idiot I am,' says Greg. 'I thought this would be a nice way for you two to meet. I knew Robbie was coming here tonight. I didn't tell you. I didn't tell Robbie either. I thought it might be nice to just . . . I dunno, pretend to bump into each other or something, meet each other casually. I had no idea he'd react like that, he's usually such a great kid, it's just . . . I'm sorry, Rachel, I should have told you.'

'No. Please. Don't apologise,' she says, and her voice is different from usual. She sounds older, more restrained, and I'm amazed at how cleverly deceptive she is. But beneath the false maturity I can also hear the urgency and impatience in her voice. She can't wait to get out of here. She has created this mess and now she wants to escape and leave me here to clean it up. And I consider spitting out the truth before she has a chance to leave, forcing her to stay and confess and face the consequences, and leaving the two of them to sort it out together. *This isn't my problem*, I think. But I don't trust her to be honest or fair to Greg, and none of this is his fault. He has been lied to, manipulated. He deserves an explanation.

'I'll come with you,' he says.

'No, no,' she says. 'I'd rather just go, to be honest. Be alone for a while.'

And I have to turn away as they say goodbye to one another. I can't bear to watch Greg's innocent tenderness towards her, his apologetic manner. And hearing him call her Rachel makes me want to scream.

When she has gone, Greg and I sit opposite one another. I am quiet and stare down at my hands. I don't know how to begin, how to start breaking someone's heart.

'I can't believe it,' he says eventually. 'Just when things were starting to go so well. It was probably an idiotic thing to do, trying to engineer a meeting like that, but Robbie can't seriously expect that I'll never . . .' He stops talking and turns to look wistfully at the doorway that Alice has just escaped from. He sighs. 'I'll probably never see Rachel again. Not after that.'

I look up at him. 'Her name's not Rachel.' And though I'm feeling almost sick with nerves my voice is firm, stronger than I'd hoped.

'What?' He leans back in his seat, crosses his arms over his chest defensively. 'What did you say?'

And so I tell him as much as I can, as quickly and as coherently as I can. He doesn't believe me at first. He keeps shaking his head and saying, 'No way, it's just not possible,' but eventually he stops protesting and grows quieter, sadder.

'I knew about Alice, of course,' he says. 'But not much. Robbie never introduced us. Well, obviously. I always had the feeling it was a bit of an on-again, off-again thing. If only we'd met. This is all my fault. I should have insisted. If only I'd taken more interest. But I thought I was doing the right thing. Giving him his privacy.' He puts his head in his hands. 'This shouldn't have happened. This should never have happened.'

'It's not your fault. It's not. It's Alice. She does this.'

'But, why?' he says. 'Why?'

I am silent. I have no answers.

'She said that she was twenty-seven,' he says quietly, almost whispering. 'I believed her. She seemed so confident, so mature. I can't believe . . . Eighteen? Jesus. I believed her, I believed everything.' He raises his eyes to mine.

'I was starting to love her,' he says.

29

I don't tell Mick about Alice immediately, I don't want to contaminate my time with him by thinking or talking about her, so I wait until he has left for work the following evening before I call Robbie. That way there's no risk he'll overhear our conversation.

Greg answers the phone.

'He's gone, Katherine.' He sounds tired, defeated.

'Gone? Gone where?'

'To Europe. Switzerland. He just got on a plane this afternoon. He's going to try and get some work. Skiing. We have relatives there.'

'What about his party?' I ask stupidly, as if a party really matters. 'What about his job?'

'There won't be any party, sweetheart. And I'm pretty sure the restaurant will manage. They've got plenty of staff.'

Greg reassures me that Robbie will be okay, that he's strong, resourceful. He suggests that I give Robbie a bit of time to lick his wounds, to get over the humiliation of it all, and then email him. Before he hangs up he tells me not to worry, everything will be fine.

And although I'm still horrified by Alice's behaviour, and the memory of the previous night still makes my stomach churn, I can't help but be glad that Robbie has finally seen the truth. There's no way he could possibly accept Alice back now. And he's far away in Europe. Miles away. He's safe. Free.

I turn my mobile off and decide to leave it that way for a while so that Alice has no way of reaching me. I don't want to think about her, let alone talk to her. I don't want to hear her explanations, her excuses.

I leave my phone off for a week and the time passes in a relatively happy blur of late-night gigs and sleeping-in. But the thought of Alice is constantly at the back of my mind and, unpleasant though the idea is, I know I'll have to speak to her eventually. It would be easy just to avoid her until she gave up trying to contact me, easy to never speak to her again. But I have to say my piece, express my anger, defend Robbie. In any case I'm pretty sure that she'll be trying to contact me and that she'll keep on trying until she succeeds, and I'd rather just get it over with.

And so one afternoon when Mick has gone out to buy beer I find my mobile phone and turn it on.

I haven't had it on at all for the past week and haven't

checked for calls so when I turn it on there are fourteen voice messages and numerous texts. I don't bother listening to or reading them. I'm sure most of them are from Alice and that she's probably angry or upset because I haven't contacted her. But I'm not interested in what she has to say. I just want to call her one last time to let her know how disgusted I am. I punch in her number quickly, before I lose my nerve.

She answers almost immediately. 'It's the mysterious stranger. *Finally.* You know, I never had you pegged as the type of girl who'd dump a friend as soon as she gets a man. But you never can tell with the quiet types.' She laughs. 'That's what they say, isn't it?'

I roll my eyes. Only Alice would have the nerve to twist the situation in such a way, when she is guilty of so much damage herself.

'I'm sorry, Alice. But I've been a bit upset. With you. I haven't known what to say.'

'Upset?' She sounds irritated, scornful. 'For God's sake. This isn't about Robbie and his dad, is it?'

'I spoke to Greg that night,' I say. 'After you left.'

'Of course. I knew you would.'

'Yes. I did.'

'You did. Yes. Great. We've certainly got that established. So what, anyway? What did you want to say?'

I don't know whether she is being deliberately obtuse, but I feel slightly ridiculous, suddenly uncertain of my own righteousness. 'It was an unbelievably cruel thing to do, Alice.'

'Jesus, Katherine, I had no idea you two would be there, all right? None at all. That was all Greg's brilliant plan,' she says. Her voice is impatient, abrupt, as if she is bored with the topic already and resents having to explain herself. 'How was I supposed to know what Greg was thinking?'

'It's not about the dinner, Alice. Don't be ridiculous. I can't believe you think that's some kind of justifica tion. The whole relationship with Greg was cruel. Not just that night, not just the fact that you got caught. I can't believe you did it. I can't actually believe that you would be such a bitch – to Robbie, who has only ever been good to you.'

She is silent for a moment. She sighs. 'Okay. Fair enough. I see your point. Lecture over now?'

'No, not really, but there's no point continuing, is there? You just don't care. But this is all really horrible, Alice. Really upsetting.'

Alice laughs. It's a nasty, cold, humourless sound. 'I don't get it,' she says eventually. 'I don't actually understand what this has got to do with you. Why on earth should my relationship with Greg, or my relationship with Robbie, for that matter, upset *you*?'

And for the briefest moment I'm taken in by her, confused into thinking I've overreacted, that I should be minding my own business. But no, I think, it's reasonable to not tolerate such appalling behaviour from your friends.

'Because what you did was deliberately cruel, Alice. Destructive and awful. Robbie is devastated. He's gone to Europe. Did you know that? All because of you. And you've wrecked his relationship with his father,' I say. 'Robbie is one of my best friends. I'm amazed that you think I shouldn't be upset.'

'Oh, piss off. I haven't *wrecked* their relationship. They'll work it out. Neither of them knew about it so they didn't actually *do* anything to each other anyway. It'll probably bring them closer in the long run. And some time in Europe will do Robbie some good. He really needs to get his head sorted. He's got a lot of anger, that boy. And he's ridiculously possessive. And, anyway, they should both be glad to be rid of me, especially if I'm as bad a person as you seem to think.'

'Whatever happens between Robbie and his dad, it doesn't change what you did. It was just wrong, Alice, totally evil. And why did you tell Greg your name was Rachel? Why that name? I have a hard time believing that was just a coincidence.'

'I don't like this lecturing tone you've taken. You're not my mother, you're not better than me, I don't need your good opinion.' Her voice is suddenly low and cold and serious, a noticeable contrast to the lazy, indifferent way she was speaking only moments before. 'I seriously don't want to talk about this any more, Katherine. It's getting boring. Very boring. Do you want to go out on Friday night or not? Let me know. I'm organising a table at Giovanni's.'

'No,' I say, and though I'm outraged and shocked by her lack of remorse, her brazen audacity, my voice sounds surprisingly normal. 'No thanks.'

'Are you free on Saturday night, then?'

'No. Yes. I mean, no, Alice, I don't want to go out with you. I'm angry. I'm shocked. Don't you get how serious this all is? I'm really upset, really disgusted. Please stop asking me out.'

'Disgusted? You're disgusted?'

'Yes. I am, to be honest. I'm disgusted and ashamed.'

'Oh.' She laughs. 'You're ashamed too? You're ashamed for me?'

'*Of* you. Yes.' My voice is small.

'Don't you think you have enough to be ashamed of, Katherine? All by yourself?' And I know exactly what she's going to say before she says it. But I don't hang up, I leave the phone pressed hard against my ear and listen, compelled to hear the words. 'I may have done some bad stuff but at least I've never left my sister alone to get raped. Have I, huh? At least I'm not the gutless wimp who ran away and let her baby sister get murdered.'

30

Later that night, Mick and Philippa and I order pizza for dinner. Just as we're sitting down at the table to eat, Philippa asks if I've seen Alice recently.

'No. But I spoke to her on the phone today.'

'And?'

So I tell them, while we're eating, about what she did to Robbie and Greg, about my telephone conversation with her earlier in the day.

'You're kidding.' Mick puts his slice of pizza down, wipes his hands on his jeans. 'That's obscene. Unbelievable. What kind of person would do something like that?'

'A sick one,' Philippa says. 'A very confused, very unhappy one.'

'And what about this Robbie guy? Why was he with her? Is he crazy too?'

'Not at all,' Philippa says.

'Robbie's lovely,' I say. 'One of the nicest people you

could ever meet. A real gentleman. A great friend.'

'Then why—'

'Because he fell in love with her,' I interrupt. 'And you just wouldn't understand how charming she could be unless you got to know her.' I speak deliberately, wanting Mick to understand, not to think me foolish or judge Robbie harshly. 'I was really happy when she became friends with me. I was flattered. I mean, she's such good fun, people just want to be around her. She could be friends with anyone. And since Rachel died I'd been on my own for so long. I was lonely, I guess. Alice was like a breath of fresh air. She was fun. Being with her was awesome.'

Mick and Philippa are both looking at me sympathetically and I realise, too late, that I've gone off-track. I've started justifying my own friendship with Alice instead of Robbie's. But it's all the same really. Me, Robbie – we were both bewitched.

'Why didn't you tell me?' Mick looks hurt. 'When you found out about all this? Why didn't you say anything?'

'I don't know,' I shrug. 'I just didn't want to think about it. We've been so happy. I didn't want to spoil it.'

'It couldn't have spoiled anything. I don't even know them.' Mick is frowning. He looks quite upset, offended that I've kept this from him, and I'm about to explain when Philippa interjects.

'Don't be a sook.' She elbows him playfully. 'She's telling you now, isn't she? And you're right, you don't know them, so shut up.' But then she looks at me and speaks in a mock angry voice. 'But *I* know them. Why didn't you tell me? That was absolutely not fair. I'm totally and permanently offended. You denied me the opportunity to say I told you so.'

'I did, didn't I?' I smile. 'But, hey, you can still say it. You were right. I was wrong.'

'Right about what?' Mick looks confused.

'Right about Alice,' I say. 'Your clever sister warned me about her months ago. She told me she was a mental case.'

'Anyway, I *have* met her,' Mick says. 'She's that chick from the William Hotel, isn't she? The short dress?'

'The gorgeous one,' Philippa says. 'Yes. The one in the short dress that all the men couldn't stop staring at.'

'Not so gorgeous.' Mick makes a face, shakes his head and, childishly, I'm glad. 'Not to me. Too loud, too up herself. Not my type at all.'

'So. Anyway.' Philippa rolls her eyes at Mick and turns to me. 'I hope you told her that you don't want to play any more? I hope you told her to go away and leave you alone for ever.'

'I did,' I say. 'Well, I tried to. She's good at ignoring what she doesn't want to hear.'

'At least you told her,' Philippa says, smiling. 'Finally you've come to your senses. Seen things my way. I have to admit that I'm absolutely, totally glad. She doesn't deserve to be your friend. And I won't say anything about poor old Robbie. But I hope you're not sorry? You don't think you'll miss her, do you?'

'No.' I cover my eyes with my hands. 'All that drama. I couldn't bear any more of it. She's just so bloody exhausting. It sounds mean, but I'd be happy to never see her again in my life. I don't want to know about her, don't want to see her, talk to her. I've turned my mobile phone off and I'm leaving it that way for a while.'

'Seems she was pretty vicious on the phone,' Mick says. 'She sounds like bad news all round.'

'She is.' Philippa nods, reaches for another slice of pizza. 'Bad news. Exactly.' And then she looks at my plate, at my barely touched slice of pizza. 'You're not eating. Don't you like it?'

'Yeah, I do,' I say, but talking about Alice has made me feel weird – and the pizza isn't helping, it's too oily, too spicy. 'I feel horrible. Thinking about what Alice did to Robbie just makes me sick. You should have seen Robbie's face. It was all just so unbelievable.' I slide my still-full plate across the table. 'I think I just need some water.'

'I'll get it.' Mick jumps up, frowns down at me. 'Don't let her make you feel bad. She's not worth it.

Forget about her. You don't owe her anything.'

Philippa watches Mick as he goes to the kitchen. She turns to me and smiles, whispers. 'He really loves you.'

'I know,' I say and I smile back, but I suddenly feel so tired and queasy that I have to fight back an overwhelming urge to lay my head down on the table and close my eyes.

'He's never been like this around a girl before. Never. He's usually quite indifferent. Always polite, but indifferent, if that makes any sense. And, if it's okay to say about my own brother, he's always been a bit of a heartbreaker. Always had plenty of girls interested.'

I'm genuinely fascinated by what Philippa is saying – there's really no subject that could interest me more right now – but I'm having a hard time concentrating.

'I bet,' I say. I can feel the bile rising in my throat.

'Are you all right?' Philippa says. 'You're white as a ghost.'

'No.' And suddenly I have to stand up and leave the table. I rush to the bathroom and make it to the toilet just in time to throw up what little I've eaten of the pizza.

31

The band has no gig booked for five days and Mick and I spend the week together. Mick practises a new drum solo and we go shopping for food, but the rest of the time we stay holed up at his place. We talk – Mick tells me all about his childhood, about his dreams for the future, about his love of music. I tell him about my childhood, about life before Rachel died, about life after. We are both intensely curious about one another, and though I barely move from Mick's room, there is not one moment during that entire five days when I am bored or restless or wish I was somewhere else.

On Mick's last day off we call Philippa and arrange to meet her at a nearby cafe for breakfast. She is already sitting at a table when we arrive. She's wearing a yellow dress and has her hair pulled back in a ponytail. She looks pretty and fresh and I imagine that in my crumpled T-shirt and jeans I look scruffy in comparison.

She is cheerful and talkative and her desire to talk,

her energy, makes me realise that I feel quite unwell, and that I've been feeling like this for several days. I normally find Philippa's fast-paced conversation delightful, but today, listening to her rush of news and responding with the requisite level of interest and enthusiasm saps all my energy. Secretly I long to return to Mick's and go straight back to sleep.

When our food arrives – we've ordered French toast and coffee – I feel a familiar rush of saliva in my mouth, the taste of bile at the back of my throat.

'Oh God.' I stand up, clamp my hand over my lips. 'Sorry, guys.' I hurry to the bathroom, lean over the toilet bowl and retch. But I haven't eaten and there is nothing but a thin stream of bile.

'Katherine. Are you all right?' Philippa's voice is right behind me. I feel her hand on my back. 'You poor thing.'

I stand, go to the basin and rinse my mouth, wash my face. I look at myself in the mirror and am shocked at how pale and drawn I look beside Philippa, and I wonder, for a moment, if I've got some kind of terminal disease. Perhaps it's my fate to die young, just like Rachel.

'You were sick the other day too,' Philippa says. 'Is it food poisoning? Some kind of virus?'

'Dunno.' I shrug, scoop water into my mouth and swallow, hope I can keep it down.

'You should really go to the doctor.'

I nod.

'Maybe it's morning sickness.' She laughs. 'Maybe you're pregnant.'

Pregnant. Though she is only joking, as soon as Philippa mentions it I'm suddenly quite certain that is exactly what is wrong with me. It would explain a lot – the nausea that comes and goes, the paralysing tiredness, my sore, swollen breasts. And try as I might, I can't remember when I last had a period.

'Oh shit,' I say.

'Oh shit, what?' We look at each other in the mirror, Philippa's eyes become wide as she takes in the look on my face. 'What? Oh my God. Pregnant? Are you serious? Really? Could you be?'

'Fuck. *Fuck.*' I shake my head. 'I don't know. But I—'

'When was your last period?'

'That's the thing. I can't remember. Oh my God, Philippa, I can't even remember having a period at all. Not since I've been with Mick. I'd remember, wouldn't I? I mean, I'd remember because he would have noticed. We wouldn't have been able to . . .' I try to think. But I'm certain that I haven't had a period in months. It would have been awkward in bed with Mick, I would have had to explain when he tried to make love to me – and I would remember. 'How did I fail to notice? How could I be so hopeless?'

Philippa pulls me towards her, wraps her arms round me. 'Don't worry. It'll be okay. Anyway, maybe you're *not* pregnant, maybe it's just a false alarm. Stress can totally make you miss a period. I've read that. Somewhere.'

'But I haven't been particularly stressed.'

'But what about Alice? The HSC?'

'Oh God, I wish. But I don't think so. I've been happy, Philippa, not stressed,' I say. And suddenly it occurs to me how many strange changes have taken place with my body lately, how odd I've felt. 'That's why my bras are all suddenly too small. Even my jeans are getting tight.'

'Maybe you're just putting on weight?'

'No.' I shake my head. 'What am I going to do? Oh Philippa, poor Mick, what's he going to think?'

'Poor *Mick*? Don't be stupid. He's not a child. He knows about the birds and the bees. Poor *you*, you're the one with watermelon breasts.' Her eyes grow wide as she looks at my chest. She puts her hand over her mouth to cover her grin. 'They have become pretty enormous, actually. Now that I've noticed.'

I look down, cup a breast in each of my hands and lift them. They're heavy, full, tender. 'Jesus. Haven't they? Why on earth didn't I realise?'

'Too busy bonking your brains out?'

'Obviously.'

I lean over the sink. Stare at myself in the mirror. My skin is pale but apart from that I don't look any different. There is nothing different about the overall shape of my face, my eyes. It seems impossible that I could have a new life growing within me without it showing in my face, without me even knowing. Without me giving my consent.

'A baby,' I say, shaking my head. 'Philippa. It's just too . . . how could . . . I'm not even eighteen.'

She nods, looks solemn. 'You're still a teenager,' she says, as though it were a revelation.

'What will I do?'

'I don't know.' She shrugs, purses her lips. 'I don't know, Katherine.'

I look down at my belly, spread my fingers over it. It's so hard to fathom. A new life. Inside me.

Suddenly animated, Philippa grabs my arm, talks in an excited rush. 'Do you think you might keep it? If you are? It'd be pretty cool in lots of ways, if you think about it. It'd be so, so, *so* cute, and so totally beautiful and bright. And Mick would be an awesome dad. And I'd be an aunty. I'd babysit for you. Honest. I'd do heaps, I'd help you as much as I could. I'd be the absolute best aunty in the universe. You'd still be able to go to uni. Mum and Dad would help, they love little babies. And your mum and dad too, they'd help, wouldn't they?'

The thought of my parents makes me groan. I cover my face with my hands. 'Philippa! Stop. *Please*. Don't talk like that. I'm not even sure yet. And I have to tell Mick first. I can't make decisions like this now.'

'No. Of course not. Sorry.' She is quiet for a minute and then says, 'Let's go and buy a test. There's a chemist on the way back to Mick's place.'

I nod and turn away from her towards the sink. Philippa's right, of course, I should buy a test on the way home, find out as soon as possible, talk to Mick. But this is something I want to do alone. Not in company, not with an audience. I keep my eyes on my hands as I wash them and wonder how I can tell her that I don't want her with me without hurting her feelings. But when I sigh and look up, it's as if she's read my mind.

'Look,' she says. 'Why don't you head on back to Mick's first? Get a test on the way. I'll keep Mick here for a bit longer and we'll finish our breakfast. You can do the test and when he comes home you can talk to him about it. If you need to.' She smiles. 'I won't come. I don't think you need me there.'

'Okay.' I smile gratefully. 'That'd be good. Thanks.'

'But you will let me know, won't you?' she says. 'Soon?'

We return to the table and tell Mick that I'm feeling sick and am going to head home. He jumps up, concerned, and says that he'll come with me. But Philippa and I persuade him to stay and finish his breakfast.

'It's only a three-minute walk,' I laugh. 'Silly. I'll be okay on my own.'

He looks worried as I wave to him from the cafe door. I smile as reassuringly as I can and start walking. It's good to be outside in the fresh air, out of the stuffy, confined atmosphere of the cafe, which smells too strongly of coffee and bacon. Normally these are smells that make me hungry, but today they are only overwhelming, nauseating.

I've little doubt that I'm pregnant. Everything adds up – the nausea, the weird tiredness I've been feeling, the swelling of my breasts. And though we've been pretty careful, using condoms most of the time, we have been slack once or twice and thought we'd be safe if Mick didn't finish inside me. Clearly, we were wrong.

I go into the chemist and search the aisles for a test. I've never had to buy one before and am not quite sure where they're kept or what to look for, so I wander blindly for a moment until a girl approaches and asks if she can help.

'Yes. Um, pregnancy tests?'

A part of me expects her to be shocked, to give me a lecture on safe sex and contraception, but she doesn't hesitate, or make any visible reaction to my request. 'Sure,' she says. 'They're over here.' And she's politely neutral as she explains the differences between the tests and takes me to the checkout where she places the packet in a brown paper bag. But I can't help but wonder what she's thinking. We're about the same age and I imagine that she's feeling glad not to be me, glad not to have this problem, smug and superior and safe in her sensible white uniform.

I'm about to step outside when someone taps me on the shoulder.

'Tut tut, Katherine,' a voice comes loudly from behind me and I feel the colour drain from my face as she steps in front of me and I realise who it is. 'What on earth would Helen think?' Alice says.

I clutch my package close to my chest defensively. I feel strangely intimidated, scared even, and I have to fight a sudden urge to run. There is no warmth in her expression and it's hard to believe, facing her like this, that we were ever friends.

Alice eyes the package and nods towards it. 'Been a naughty girl, have we?'

I'm about to speak – to deny, explain, justify – but decide against it. I owe Alice nothing. My personal life is no longer any of her business. I shrug and go to step past her, but before I get anywhere she has put her hand on my shoulder and is leaning in, her face uncomfortably close to mine.

'Don't think you're going to get away with it,' she

says, her voice a vicious, low hum. 'I know people like you think that people like me are dispensable. I know that. But you're not going to get rid of me that easily.'

'*Rid* of you?' I attempt a laugh, but the sound is hollow, unconvincing. 'Is this some kind of threat? Are you actually following me?'

She only smiles.

'Leave me alone, Alice,' I say, forcing myself to look her in the eye. 'Leave me alone or I'll—'

'What?' She lifts her eyebrows in an exaggerated expression of surprise. 'You'll call the police? Huh? Is that it? Is that what you'll do?'

'Well, yes, I will. If you're going to behave like a lunatic, then I'm going to treat you like one.'

'Oh, yes, of course you will. But I already know that. You see, I *know* you. I know you better than you think. But I haven't actually done anything, really, have I? There's nothing to tell the police, is there? You can't shift the blame this time.' And she smiles sweetly, tips her head to the side, and makes her voice falsely innocent. 'And we're friends, anyway, aren't we? Friends for ever?'

I shake my head and step past her. 'Go away, Alice,' I say. 'Just go away. I don't have any idea what you're talking about. You need some kind of help. You need to see someone. You're sick.'

'Maybe I am,' she says, laughing, as I walk quickly

away. 'Or maybe it's you, Katherine. Did you ever consider that? Maybe it's you.'

I march ahead and will myself not to look back, not until I'm about to turn the corner into Mick's street. Then I stop and look behind me. I don't see her at first and I start to panic, afraid that she is hiding, following me, but then I spot her. She is still down near the front of the chemist's. She is talking to a tall, good-looking man – flirting, no doubt – and seems completely preoccupied.

It's probably a ridiculous precaution but I don't want her to know where I'm staying and so I turn into the street and run as quickly as I can up the road towards Mick's flat. I press the key in the lock, my hands shaking, and slam the door behind me. Once inside I'm immediately calmed – it is all so familiar and ordinary, shabby and comfortable and safely contained – and I can't help but giggle at the sense of hysteria I'd had only moments before. It reminds me of when I was a child and I was scared of being alone in the dark. I'd always run, panicked and terrified, back to wherever my parents were – the light, the warmth, the safety of company – and been immediately comforted. Like the dark, Alice can't really hurt me. Not if I don't let her. She may be full of shadow and mystery and hidden depths, but she has no real power. Not really.

I go to the bathroom and stand in front of the

mirror. I'm breathing quickly from the run, and my face is pale. I look dreadful. My stomach is knotted with anxiety and it takes me a moment to remember that I have something bigger than Alice to worry about. Something real. Something serious. Something that may affect me and Mick for the rest of our lives. And it has nothing whatsoever to do with Alice.

I open the package and pee on the test stick as instructed on the box. I place the test on the bathroom counter without looking at it. I go to the lounge room and pace the floor, back and forth, back and forth, until I think enough time has passed. I return to the bathroom and pick up the plastic white stick. There are two very clear and parallel pink lines.

I check the instructions again. Two lines is a positive result. I'm pregnant.

I toss the test away from me – as if it is burning hot, or dangerous – and watch it clatter onto the floor. It lands face up, the two pink lines strong and definite, taunting me. Although I'd been quite certain that it would be positive, the reality of the test is terrifying, unbelievable. I can feel my heart pounding quickly in my chest, the taste of shock and fear in my mouth. Suddenly I cannot move, can no longer stand, and I collapse down onto the floor and sit, knees drawn up, my head pressed down on top of them. I sit there, motionless, my head full of visions of a ruined future, until I hear Mick's key in the lock, his footsteps, his voice calling my name. And soon he's in the bathroom with his arms round me, asking me if I'm all right.

I don't look up, or say a word – it would be too much to speak, too hard to look Mick in the eye right now – but I reach out and point towards the test stick.

'What?' he says. I hear him picking it up. And then he is back, sitting in front of me.

'You're pregnant?' He sounds surprised and shocked, but not as devastated as I'd imagined. Not angry.

I look up. Nod.

'Wow.' He rubs his face. I can hear the scrape of stubble beneath his fingers. 'I don't know what to say.'

'No.'

He is quiet for a moment, staring at the test. He looks at me. 'So, um, is this a bad thing?'

'Yes. Of course it is. I'm pregnant, Mick. I'm seventeen.' And now I sit up properly, cross my legs and face him, so that our knees are touching. 'I'm seventeen Mick. *Seventeen.*'

He puts his hand on my knee and speaks carefully, as if he's afraid to upset me. 'Okay. It's a bit of a shock. But it's not the end of the world. I mean, we can do something about it. If you want to. There are ways to—'

'Abortion. I know. Just say the damn word. I'm not stupid.'

'Okay. Abortion. We can do that. If you want to.'

I nod, shrug, look helplessly round the room at the wall tiles, at the shower curtain, everywhere but at his earnest, sweet face.

'But you don't have to,' he says, and he leans forward so that I'm forced to look at him. 'You don't have to abort it, Katherine. I'm not saying you have to.'

'What's the alternative, Mick? Having a baby? At seventeen? Are you joking?'

'It's not as if this has never happened before. It's not totally unheard-of or impossible, you know.'

'I know it's not impossible, I'm not a complete idiot. I'm pregnant, Mick, not suddenly brain-dead.'

He sighs. 'Stop being so angry. I'm not your enemy.'

'Sorry.' I reach out, take his hand. 'I'm just . . . I can't believe we let this happen.'

'I can't believe it either.'

'Shit.' I squeeze his hand. Hard. 'Girls like me don't have babies, Mick. Girls like me go to university, have careers. My parents would absolutely die. They'd totally freak.'

'You could still go to university. People do it. They do it all the time. It's not like you'd be a single mother.' He squeezes my hand back, even harder, and smiles. 'Look, just forget about your parents for a minute. Just forget about what other people might think. You can't decide based on other people. That's dumb.'

And he's right. A lot of my horror at the idea of this

272

pregnancy is based on what other people might think. My parents, my schoolfriends, my teachers. I picture myself with an enormous belly and then a screeching baby – people staring, whispering, feeling sorry for me. It's hard, with all that imagined disapproval going through my head, to know what I really think, what I might really want.

'I'm going to make some tea,' Mick says, and he stands, pulls me to my feet. 'Why don't you go back to bed for a while?'

I do as he suggests and somehow, despite all the turmoil going through my head, manage to fall into a deep sleep. When I wake Mick is sitting beside me on the bed, flipping through a music magazine.

'Hi.'

'Hi.'

'Feeling any better?' He puts his hand on my forehead and I laugh.

'I don't have a temperature, idiot.'

'I know. I know. But didn't your mum always do that when your were sick? And didn't it make you feel good? As if you had something seriously wrong and might get a whole week off school or something?'

'But I'm not sick. I'm pregnant.'

'True. But you're sad.'

I sit up. 'Am I?'

'I don't know. Are you?'

'I don't know. Are *you*?'

He laughs. 'I am if you are. I'm not if you're not.'

'I'm not sure. For some reason it doesn't seem so bad any more.' I shrug, smile shyly. 'Maybe I'm still dreaming or something.'

He pinches my arm. 'Can you feel that?'

'Ow! Yes.'

'Not dreaming, then.'

'But seriously,' I say, 'what do you think? Is it such a bad thing? Being pregnant?'

'Jesus, Katherine. I don't know. Maybe it's not the end of the world.' He smiles – gently, tentatively, slowly – all the while looking at me, searching my face. 'But it's certainly a *big* thing.'

'It is.' And I don't know why a few hours' sleep has changed my perspective so much but all of a sudden this pregnancy has gone from being a shocking disaster into something that I might actually want to go through with. I laugh – a sudden bubble of hopeful excitement rising in my belly, my throat. 'It's bloody huge.'

'My God. A baby.'

'Yes,' I say. 'A baby.'

'*Our* baby.'

'Yes.'

'We couldn't possibly kill something we've made together. It's our baby. Ours. A bit of you and a bit of me,' he says.

'No.'

'I mean, unless you really want to. But you don't want to? Abort it? Do you?'

'No. No, I don't.' I allow myself to smile, to hope. 'I think I might want it. I think I might actually want to keep it.'

We spend the rest of the day in a semi-hysterical state of shock. We tell Philippa the next morning and she is so excited, so enthusiastic and full of ideas and plans for the future, that she makes us both laugh in shy delight. The nausea hasn't gone away, but now that I know what is causing it, it's far easier to cope with. And now that I know that I'm not actually sick, the overwhelming exhaustion, my ability to sleep at any time, seems only a mild and even strangely pleasant symptom of the fact that my body is busy making another human being.

We go to the library and borrow a pile of different books on pregnancy. The books contain glossy pictures of embryos at various different stages of development. We try to work out exactly how old our baby is in weeks, and try to match it with the corresponding picture. It's amazing to think that it has probably already got arms and legs, eyes, a mouth, a nose. A heartbeat.

Mick thinks that we should find our own flat, move in together. 'This is it,' he says. 'I've been dreaming about a girl like you my whole life. I don't need more time, I don't need to know you better. I just need to be with you.' And when I wonder aloud if it isn't too big a commitment, if we aren't rushing things, he laughs and shakes his head. 'We're having a baby, Katherine. There's no bigger commitment than that. It's too late to take things slowly now. It's too late for us to do things the sensible way.' And then he hugs me, kisses me. 'Don't worry. Everything's going to be fine. Don't worry.'

He whispers to me in the middle of the night. 'Let's get married. Down at the registry office. Tomorrow.'

I laugh and say, 'No way, I'm only seventeen, don't be crazy,' but I'm secretly thrilled at his romantic ideas, that he's just as in love as I am. That he would even consider marrying me.

But renting a flat together isn't such an insane idea. In fact it makes a lot of sense. There's no way Mick could move into Vivien's, and his flat is far too small. And we could hardly expect his flatmate to put up with a baby.

Early the following morning I wake early, before Mick. I get up and make a pot of tea. I take the tea and the previous day's newspaper paper back to Mick's room. I get back into bed, open the paper and start looking through the rentals.

'This might be cool,' I say after a while. 'One bedroom, timber floorboards, new kitchen. Not too far from Bondi beach. Three-fifty a week.'

Mick opens his eyes, and smiles slowly as he realises what I've just said.

'Read it again,' he says. 'Didn't hear you properly.'

'One bedroom, timber floorboards, new kitchen,' I say, but almost immediately my enthusiasm is tempered by less pleasant thoughts. I sigh. 'I'm going to have to call my parents. They're going to want to meet you. We can't really organise this until I tell them about you. They pay my rent, pay for my car, they give me an allowance, they totally support me.'

'Of course.' Mick sits up, puts his hand on my leg. 'But we'll be okay. Even if they don't want to pay for us to live together. We'll manage somehow. I'll get a day job.'

'You won't have to do that. They're not like that. They wouldn't cut me off or anything. They'd do anything for me.'

'That's understandable.'

'But, you know, there is something that they won't accept. Never. Not in a million years.'

'What?'

'Your bike. They'd absolutely spew if they had any idea I'd even *been* on it.'

'Yeah.' He shrugs. 'My parents hate it too. They're dangerous things.'

'So why do you ride it, if you think it's so dangerous?'

'It's fun.' He grins. 'It's fast. You can't spend your life being scared of everything.'

'I'm not scared of everything,' I say, suddenly annoyed. 'That's not fair, and anyway, I've been on the stupid thing lots of times. And I—'

'I didn't say you were scared of everything,' he interrupts. 'I wasn't even talking about you. I meant "you" in the general sense, as in everybody.' He frowns and his voice is short, unfriendly. 'Don't worry, I was planning to sell it anyway.'

'Good. So you should. We've got my car,' I say. And I'm equally abrupt. 'It's not worth dying for a bit of fun. And what's the big deal, anyway? You make it sound as if it's some big sacrifice to get rid of it.'

'It *is* a sacrifice. It's my bike. I love it.'

I look at him, incredulous. 'You *love* it?'

'Yeah.'

'It's an inanimate object. You can't love a thing, a stupid chunk of metal.'

'Well, I do. It makes me sad to sell it. I'll miss having it.'

I toss the paper aside and stand up, putting my hands on my hips. 'You'll miss having it?' I say, on the verge of tears now. I know I'm being irrational, overreacting, but I can't help myself. 'It makes you sad to sell it?' I point furiously at my still-flat belly. 'What about me? What about all the sacrifices *I'm* going to have to make? What about all the things I'm going to be sad about?'

But he doesn't rise to the bait, he doesn't fight me. Instead he reaches out his hand. 'Come back to bed.'

'No.'

'Please?'

'No.'

'I hate the bike,' he says. 'It's ugly and it's red and I hate red. You're much prettier. And you smell better.'

I try to remain angry, to keep a serious expression on my face, but can't stop myself from laughing. 'You're an idiot,' I say, and I climb back into bed, beneath the covers, and pull in close to him. 'I like the bike as well. I don't know why I'm being a bitch. I'll be sad when it's gone too.'

'I know.'

'But if Mum and Dad knew about it—'

'I know. Don't worry. I like you more than the bike. A tiny bit, anyway.'

'You're just going to have to meet them,' I say. 'Soon.'

'Yep. And you're going to have to meet my parents too. It'll all be official.'

'I know.' I sigh, bury my face against his chest. 'Doesn't it make you a bit nervous? That they'll think we're being crazy? Having a baby? Looking for flats already? Moving in together?'

'I'm sure they'll think we're crazy. At first, anyway. We'll just have to prove them wrong. And when my parents get to know you, they'll love you.'

'And mine will love you,' I say.

But I wish I could feel as certain as I sound. I don't really think Mum and Dad are going to be happy about the situation at all. I can imagine their faces when I tell them – Mum's quiet disapproval, Dad's shock. They won't say much, or show any anger, they would never shout at me or yell, but I'm sure they'll consider it a tragedy, some kind of disaster, and the pained looks on their faces will be a million times harder to bear than any display of anger. I'd rather listen to them scream and shout.

Not only am I worried about their reaction to the pregnancy but I also feel a renewed sense of guilt about Rachel. My life is unfolding, continuing, taking shape in new and unexpected ways. As my counsellor would have said – approvingly – I'm *moving on*. Rachel's death is no longer so pivotal, it no longer defines me, and I can see now that it's inevitable that the longer I live, the more that happens to me, the less significant her life and death will be. I will forget. I will no longer miss her every moment of every day. It feels, somehow, like a betrayal, just another example of me running away and leaving her behind.

And this is something that must hurt my parents

as well. Each time something big happens in my life, from finishing the HSC to falling in love to falling pregnant, it can only serve as a cruel reminder of all that Rachel will never have, never do.

I close my eyes and try not to think – about Rachel or my parents. I snuggle close to Mick, breathe in the now-familiar scent of his skin. And though I've only been awake for an hour I'm tired and I let myself fall back into a sweet, oblivious sleep.

32

'It's pretty good,' I say, looking round the sun-drenched living room once again. 'A bit small, but it's so nice and sunny. Mick will like it, don't you think?'

The flat is small but bright. The floor is timber, the walls whitewashed. There is one tiny bedroom with an even tinier room connected to it, advertised as a study, which would be perfect for a baby. There is a living room with the smallest kitchen I've ever seen tucked against one wall. It's really little more than a sink and an oven and a cupboard. But the whole place is clean and cheerful. Philippa stands beside me, puts her arm round my shoulders.

'He'll love it,' she says. 'Because you'll be here with him.'

'Do you think it's too tiny?'

'It's cosy.'

'We'll all fit, won't we? Me and Mick and the baby?'

'Of course you will. How much room could a baby need?'

'Should I put an application in?'

'Definitely. And ask if you can come back and look again tomorrow. With Mick. I'm sure he'll love it, though, don't worry.' And she strolls round the small room, smiling. 'I can just see you here. Your little family. It's going to be brilliant. Just like a fairy tale. You're going to live happily ever after. A princess in her castle.'

'A very teeny-tiny castle. A shoebox castle,' I laugh. But I like Philippa's picture of my future. I like it that she is optimistic and believes that we can be happy.

I fill in the application forms and give them to the letting agent and then Philippa and I walk down the communal stairs and onto the street.

'Let's get some lunch,' she says. 'Are you hungry?'

'Yep. I'm always hungry. It's just that a lot of the things I usually love make me feel like throwing up.'

And it is while Philippa and I are discussing what might appeal for lunch that I see Alice. She's on the other side of the road but I can't hide, or try to slip unnoticed into the nearest shop, because she's already seen us. She's standing still, staring, an odd smile on her face. My heart begins to pound. This is no coincidence. She is following me.

'What? What is it?' Philippa turns to see what I'm looking at. 'Oh, shit. Alice.'

Alice waves. 'Katherine! Wait! Hold on a minute.' And before we have the chance to get away she is crossing the road, walking quickly towards us.

'How are you? How did your little test go? Get the result you were expecting?' She directs her conversation towards me, avoids looking at Philippa.

And I know I should move, just walk away, but I stand there as though paralysed.

'I bet Helen's overjoyed at becoming a grandmother.' She folds her arms across her chest and looks at me nastily. 'Oh, but you probably haven't even told her yet, have you? Huh? You like your dirty little secrets, don't you, Katherine? Miss Goody Two Shoes?' she says, 'Oh, and by the way, I'm *great*, thanks, just fantastic, thanks for your concern.' She smiles – a hasty, unnatural stretching of the lips – then just as suddenly frowns. 'Although, I have to admit, I'm a little disappointed too, you know, upset with someone I thought of as a friend.'

'We're in a hurry, Alice,' Philippa says. 'We've got to get going.'

Alice ignores her. 'Although I shouldn't really be surprised at all. Knowing what I do, you know? A leopard doesn't change its spots. A coward is a coward is a coward. Wouldn't you agree, Katherine?' And she laughs, spitefully, tipping her head back. Abruptly she stops, stares at me closely. 'But you're more than just a coward, aren't you, Katherine? You ran away and left your sister to get murdered. And, come to think of it, she probably got murdered *because* you ran away. Have you ever considered that? Those boys were probably just going to rape you. Both of you. They probably freaked out when they found out that you were gone. Freaked out and killed poor little Rachel. So you're more than just a coward, Katherine, aren't you? You're more like an accomplice or something. I mean, it's kind of your fault that your sister died, isn't it? You saved your own skin, though. At Rachel's expense. You saved your own precious skin.'

'Shut *up*, Alice,' Philippa interrupts, her voice low and cold and serious. She takes hold of the top of my arm and pulls me close. 'Shut the fuck up you stupid dumb cunt or I'll hit you so hard you won't wake up for a week.'

I'm so surprised by Philippa's words, her unexpected aggression, that I can only stand there, mouth open, and watch.

'Oh. Right.' Alice looks Philippa up and down, sneers. But the haughty confidence has gone, and there's a new edge of uncertainty in her voice. 'So. That's the kind of person you like to hang around with now, Katherine? Trash? Well, that makes sense. Like attracts like, after all.'

Philippa puts her arm round my shoulders and

guides me so that we turn away from Alice. We start walking quickly away from her.

'Goodbye, ladies,' Alice calls out from behind us, her voice falsely gracious. 'It was just *lovely* bumping into you. See you soon, I hope.'

'I can't believe you said that,' I say. And I shake my head, both in horror at Alice and a kind of surprised glee at Philippa's unexpected bravery.

'I know. I couldn't help it, she made me so mad.' She sighs. 'My mother would be ashamed.'

'I thought it was wonderful. It was like Queen Elizabeth suddenly threatening to punch Saddam Hussein on the nose. It was great.'

Philippa turns to look behind her. 'We can slow down. She's going the other way. She's so awful, Katherine. She's quite psycho, really. It's a bit scary.'

'I know. Do you think she's stalking me? I keep seeing her when I least expect it. It can't be a coincidence.'

'I wouldn't put it past her. I guess she can't stand that you don't want to be her friend any more. She can't accept it. She's hurt, probably, or her massive ego is damaged.' Philippa stops walking, turns to face me. 'But you don't take it to heart, do you? What she says? All that vicious stuff about Rachel? You know that what she says is just crap.'

'It's hard to ignore,' I say. I look down at the pavement, speak quietly. 'Because she's right. I *did* leave

Rachel. I *did* run away. And that was something that the defence even pointed out in court. They said that the boys had never intended to kill anyone. That it just happened because they freaked out. They panicked when I disappeared.'

'So what? Of course they would say that. They weren't going to admit that the boys planned to kill Rachel all along. That was just their only chance at a defence. Doesn't mean it's true.'

I turn to look behind me and watch Alice striding off in the opposite direction. 'But how come she knows to say that? How come she always comes up with the most hurtful thing to say? How can someone so self-obsessed have such good insight?'

'Because she's so totally rotten inside. She's an expert bitch. She's got her finger right on the pulse of what is most ugly in the world. And anyway, she's probably been looking you up on the net. Doing her research. Finding the best way to hurt you. It wouldn't surprise me.'

'Yeah. Maybe. But it doesn't change the fact that she could be right. I did run away.' I stare at her hard. 'I ran away, Philippa.'

'Of course you did.' She stares back. 'What else could you have done?'

'I could have looked after her better. I could have made sure she didn't get so drunk that she couldn't walk. I could have bloody well made sure she went home instead of going to that party.'

'You could have. But you didn't. And—'

'Exactly. I didn't,' I interrupt. 'But I should have. I should've done a lot of things. And you know what? There's more. Something I've never admitted to anyone.'

'What?'

'I was pissed off with Rachel that night. I was so mad that she came to that party. I didn't want her there. I was furious. They were my friends and she didn't even like parties.' And I surprise myself by bursting into noisy tears. 'She shouldn't have been there!'

Philippa takes my arm and leads me across the road to a small park where we sit, side by side on a bench. I hide my face in my hands and cry. Philippa stays beside me, puts her arm round my shoulders, and waits.

'Sorry,' I say, when I've calmed down enough to speak. 'I just keep on crying lately. It's pathetic.'

'Don't say that. It's not pathetic to cry.'

'No. Probably not,' I say. 'Perhaps it's my hormones. It's just that this never goes away. All this stuff with Rachel. Am I supposed to feel bad for ever? My whole life? Is that my punishment just for being alive?'

'Of course not.' She shakes her head. 'But what do you feel bad about? Maybe you should tell me. Explain it to me. I mean, I know generally, of course, obviously, but maybe you should try and be a bit specific. Maybe you should try and put it into words, get it off your chest.'

And despite my serious doubts about the value of talking, I have a sudden urge to spit it all out, to confess my darkest thoughts.

'I was so angry with Rachel for coming to that party,' I say. 'She wasn't meant to like parties, she never did before. Normally you couldn't have paid her to go to a party. But it was like she was suddenly changing. Bit by bit. Getting more sociable. Opening up. And I didn't like it. She was meant to be the shy girl. The good girl. The genius. I was the party girl, not her. I was the popular one . . . I felt like she was going to take that away from me. She was just so talented, so perfect. If she'd started being sociable she would have . . . I don't know, she would have had everything. Everyone would have loved her even more. I would have been invisible.' My voice is small, full of shame. 'I hated her for that.'

Philippa is quiet for a minute, thoughtful, and I wonder if my confession has disgusted her.

'When Mick was little,' she says eventually. 'He was absolutely and totally hopeless at school. He was behind in everything. Reading. Maths. Everything. He had to have tutors and stuff just to avoid repeating. I was the brainy one and I used to pretend to feel sorry for him. But secretly I loved it. I loved being so much smarter than him because better at everything else. He was good at sport and he was funny and good-looking and he had so many friends. And I was, like, this total nerd, with disgusting ugly red hair and freckles, which he totally missed out on, which is so not fair, but hey . . .' She looks down at my belly. 'He's from the same gene pool as me, so you'd better watch out for your kid. Anyway, to get back to my point, when Mick was in Year 11 he suddenly started to change. He got all serious about schoolwork and started studying and stuff. And then he zoomed straight up to the top classes, came first in just about everything.' She shakes her head. 'I was so pissed off. So ridiculously jealous . . . and I wasn't even in school any more. I couldn't *stand* it. Although I've got to say,' and now she smiles, 'he never made school captain like I did.'

I laugh.

'The thing is, though,' she continues. 'That now I'm really happy that he's smart. I'd hate it if he didn't like books and reading and thinking about stuff. It would suck if he was a moron. We would have nothing in common. It would be a tragedy.'

'A terrible tragedy,' I agree.

'See? Now I've made everything better with my pointless ramblings, haven't I? You'll probably never cry again.' Philippa squeezes me closer, speaks more seriously. 'So you weren't the perfect sister. So what?

You didn't kill anyone. What happened wasn't your fault. And you did exactly what anyone with half a brain would have done in your situation. Listen, how do you think your mum and dad would feel if you'd both been killed? Both their daughters dead? Would that have been better? Because that's what would've happened if you hadn't run away, if you'd tried to fight. You would only have made things worse.'

'Maybe,' I say. 'Maybe not. We'll never know, will we? But I'm the one who took her to the party. And maybe if I'd just stayed where I was, in that shed, they would have raped Rachel and left. Maybe if I hadn't run away they wouldn't have killed her. Maybe she'd still be alive.'

'But if you want to think like that, if you want to blame yourself for running away or for taking Rachel to the party, then what about your parents? They'd have to blame themselves for not being home. They'd have to blame themselves for leaving you in charge in the first place. And what about that boy, your boyfriend, the one who let you get in the car? He'd have to blame himself too. The blame could just spread around to everyone . . . like a poison. And, yeah, maybe everyone who was involved *does* feel some regret, wonder if things would be different if only they'd done this, or that. But a bad decision doesn't make you a murderer. You were a sixteen-year-old girl and you went to a party. You broke a rule. So what? You didn't do anything that every other sixteen-year-old in the world hasn't done. You couldn't possibly have known what was going to happen. You have to stop thinking like that. It's crazy. The only people who are responsible for killing Rachel are those boys. You were a victim, Katherine. You and Rachel, and your parents, you were all victims. You were put into a terrifying, unexpected situation and you did the best thing you could think of at the time.'

I nod agreeably and smile and let Philippa think that she has made me feel better, that she's said something I haven't heard before. The trouble with words is that no matter how much sense they make in theory they can't change what you feel inside. And what I'm starting to understand is that there is no real end to this, there can be no complete absolution. Rachel's death and my own part in it is something I'm going to have to live with. The best I can hope for is that I can learn to forgive myself for being a less than perfect sister.

33

When I get home later that afternoon, Mick is already there, waiting for me. He swings the door open almost before I get the chance to knock – all happy and smiling – and puts his arms round me as soon as I step inside. 'We just got a phone call.' He laughs. 'We got the flat. We can move in next week.'

He takes my hand and drags me to the kitchen, pulls out a stool and hands me a glass of freshly squeezed orange juice. He's been preparing food. Sliced vegetables are piled together on a plate – capsicum, mushroom, beans – and the tiny kitchen, which is normally in a state of messy chaos, is clean.

'I thought we'd celebrate with something healthy. A stir-fry.'

'Sounds great.'

'It could be a disaster, but I'm trying. Hey, Philippa said that you bumped into Alice?' He looks at me with concern. 'Are you okay?'

'Yeah,' I say. 'I'm all right.' I sit down heavily on the stool and rest my elbows on the benchtop.

'Philippa said that Alice said some pretty vicious things. She said you were upset.'

'I was, I guess. But it wasn't really what Alice said. Not really. I just . . . well, she hasn't said anything I haven't thought myself a million times before. So I suppose it wasn't really Alice that upset me.'

'What do you mean?'

'Well, of course she's a bitch and everything. And she's deliberately trying to be cruel, I know that. And her nastiness is scary, the way she wants to hurt me so much. But what she said was already going round my head anyway. It's been there all the time. I did run away from Rachel, and I did leave her there to get murdered.' I lift my hand and raise the volume of my voice when I see that Mick is about to object. 'It's all true. They're indisputable facts. And I did take her to the party and let her drink. I *was* responsible. Irresponsible. And those thoughts were already there. Inside me. A part of me. Alice didn't put them there. In fact it feels like Alice is the only person who has been completely honest. The only person who has dared to say this stuff that everyone must have thought at some stage.'

'But you couldn't—'

'Please, Mick,' I interrupt. 'Just listen. I'm not finished.'

'Okay,' he says. 'Go on.'

'Sorry. It's just that I've realised something today. Something good, I think.'

He nods.

'I used to think that there would eventually come a time when everything would feel better. Like some kind of magic. I thought I'd just wake up and not feel sad any more. Not feel guilty any more. Just like, *wham!* and I'd be over it. And I've been waiting for that day. I've been thinking to myself that as soon as that day came I would feel better and then I would start getting on with my life properly, fully enjoying it again.' I laugh, a little embarrassed by the emotion in my voice. 'But what I finally realised today is that it's not going to be like that. This is going to stay with me. For ever. And that's okay. It's fine. I can accept it.'

'That's great, Katherine, but don't you think—'

I don't get to hear what he's about to say because suddenly there's a very noisy knocking on the door.

'Jesus.' Mick looks at me and shakes his head. 'Who the—'

'Katherine! Katherine! Are you in there?' A man is shouting desperately through the door, pounding so hard that the walls are shaking. 'Katherine! Open up!'

'Oh my God.' I sit up straight, feel the colour drain from my face. 'I think that's my dad.'

'What? Why?'

'I don't know,' I say, and I stand up and rush to the

door, pulling it open just as my father starts shouting my name once again.

Mum and Dad are standing side by side on the front porch. They look surprised when they see me, as if they hadn't really expected to. They look at one another and then back at me. They look strangely upright and tense.

'Dad! Mum! What's wrong? What are you doing here?'

'Oh, Katherine.' Mum rushes forwards and pulls me in towards her chest. 'Are you okay? Are you all right?'

'Yes.' I squeeze her against me and then push away. 'I'm fine. Everything's great. But why are you here? What's going on?'

And then Dad has his hand beneath my chin, he lifts my face and stares intently into my eyes. 'You're sure everything's okay?' He says. 'You're sure?'

I step away from him and frown. 'What's *wrong*?' I say, looking between them. 'You're scaring me. What are you *doing* here?'

In the next instant Mick is beside me, one hand in mine, the other stretched out in welcome to my parents. 'Hi. I'm Mick. Do you want to come inside?'

Dad ignores Mick's outstretched hand and stares, his eyes moving from Mick's face down to his feet and up again, in an obvious and rudely appraising way that I've never seen him use before.

Mum steps forward and smiles – but it's a forced, unnatural smile that goes nowhere near her eyes – and shakes Mick's hand. 'Mick. I'm Helen. This is my husband, Richard. And yes, we would like to come in. Thank you.'

Mick and I step aside to let Mum and Dad through the door. We follow them and Mick glances at me quizzically behind their backs. But I can only shrug. I'm just as puzzled by their presence, by their weird behaviour, as he is.

We go to the kitchen, which is light and bright and clean and full of the preparations for our dinner. I notice Mum and Dad glance at each other. They look almost as confused as I feel.

Mum turns to face us.

'We may as well be frank,' she says. 'Alice called us.'

'Oh,' I say, and the feeling of foreboding her name invokes makes me feel instantly tired. 'Why? What did she want?'

'She was worried about you, darling,' Mum begins, but Dad interrupts, his voice gruff.

'She said that you were taking drugs. She said that you were living with some . . .' he nods towards Mick, 'well, in Alice's words, "feral, motorbike-riding, drug-pushing musician".' And then he looks at me, and he looks so small and sad and afraid that I can hardly bear it. 'She also said that you were pregnant.'

I could easily defend myself. After all, I'm not taking drugs and Mick is not feral. There's enough evidence here – clean flat, wholesome food, our glasses of *orange juice*, for God's sake – to prove that it's not true. But the whole pregnancy thing sticks in my throat, renders me mute and ashamed.

'Alice is a liar,' Mick says, and I look up at him gratefully. He's so full of decency and common sense and honesty. They will have to see that. 'Katherine doesn't take drugs. That's ridiculous.' He stares straight into my dad's face and his expression is completely open and his eyes don't waver. 'And neither do I.'

Nobody speaks for a moment, but Mum and Dad look at each other and it's obvious by the expressions on their faces that they are relieved. They want to believe what Mick is saying, that much is clear.

'But why on earth would Alice say such things?' Mum asks, and already I can hear the lighter tone of her voice, the hope.

'Because she has problems,' Mick says. 'Serious mental problems.'

'Really?' Dad is looking at me, his eyebrows raised. All the tension that made his face so stiff and unfriendly and intimidating just moments before has disappeared. 'Katherine? Really? Can you promise me? You're not taking drugs?'

'No, Dad.' I shake my head, smile. 'Of course not. I

promise. I can't believe you even thought that was true for a minute.'

'We hadn't heard from you,' Mum says. 'You weren't answering the phone at Viv's and we couldn't get through to your mobile. We left several messages, darling. At least ten. We just . . . well, we were actually starting to get worried before Alice called.'

'Oh God. Sorry, Mum. My phone is switched off. I just had it off because I wanted to avoid talking to Alice. I had no idea she'd call you. Make up such big lies. This is all so crazy. I'm so sorry. It's my fault. I should have called, I should've let you know where I was.'

'Doesn't matter now.' Mum shakes her head, and before she has the chance to blink them away I see the tears in her eyes. 'As long as you're okay, I don't really care.'

And then, almost simultaneously, Mum and Dad both step forward and embrace me. They kiss my head, my cheek, and laugh with relief and happiness. When they have pulled away and composed themselves, the three of us stand there, looking slightly embarrassed, until Mick pulls seats from beneath the table, tells us all to sit down, pours fresh glasses of orange juice.

'I feel silly now,' Mum says, reaching over and putting her hand on mine. She looks at Mick. 'You must think we're dreadful, turning up like that. With all those insane accusations.'

'No. Just freaked out. As most parents would be.' He shakes his head, looks at my mother, and smiles his wonderful smile – and I can see by her response that she is charmed.

'I guess so.' And then she looks at me and laughs, squeezes my hand before letting go. 'I'm so glad that you're okay, darling. We were so worried. So afraid. You have no idea.'

And the next hour, though beginning in such bizarre circumstances, has a strangely happy, almost celebratory feel. Mick insists that Mum and Dad stay for dinner. The four of us sit round the table together and eat Mick's stir-fry and Dad tells us about the phone call with Alice. And though I find it hard to believe that she would have the nerve to tell such lies, and slightly alarming that she feels so spiteful towards me, I feel quite benevolent towards her. Her actions have only brought my parents closer, and though I've never doubted their love for me, I'm moved by their obvious concern, their panic. I feel loved. Cherished.

But my parents don't ask whether I'm pregnant – either they're assuming that everything Alice has said is a lie, or they're too afraid to ask – and neither Mick nor or I mentions it. As we eat and talk and laugh I keep thinking of different ways to let them know – *Oh, Mum and Dad, by the way, Alice wasn't lying about everything. I really am pregnant! Aren't you thrilled, you're going to be grandparents!* – but it's such an impossibly enormous thing to drop into the conversation, so heavy and serious and permanent, that I say nothing. Every time Mick speaks I imagine that he's going to tell them and the pace of my heart quickens, but he doesn't, and our dinner passes in conversation about Alice. And music. And how and when Mick and I met.

When we've finished eating, Mick insists on washing up. He looks at me pointedly when my parents' backs are turned and indicates with his hands that I should take them into the living room. I know what he's doing. He's trying to give me some privacy so that I can tell them about the pregnancy.

But when I ask them if they want to come and sit with me for a while – ostensibly so that I can show them some photos from the last few weeks of school – Dad refuses. He'd like to stay and help Mick clean up, he says. Mum shrugs and smiles and takes my hand in hers.

'Let him do it,' she whispers. 'He probably wants to get to know your young man.'

And though I've rehearsed numerous different ways of saying it gently, tactfully, in the end I just blurt it out as soon as we are out of sight of my father and Mick.

'Alice was right about one thing. I *am* pregnant.'

'What? What did you say?' Mum stops walking,

turns to look at me. She is frowning. 'I beg your pardon?'

'I'm pregnant.'

'Pregnant? Oh my goodness. Well, so that much was true.' She turns away, but not before I see the tell-tale wetness of her eyes, the quiver of her chin.

'Please, Mum. Please. I know you're disappointed. I know this isn't what you expected, or hoped for me. I know that. It wasn't what I wanted either. But I promise you, Mum, we'll be okay. I promise. Don't worry, Mick's fantastic. He's not about to run away or anything. We'll make it be okay. We will. It'll be okay. I can still go to uni. I'll still get an education, I promise. It'll be okay, Mum. Everything will be fine.'

'Pregnant?' She says the word again, as if she's having difficulty understanding. She walks over to the couch and sits down heavily. 'Pregnant.'

I sit beside her. I keep my eyes down, look at my hands, pick nervously at the fabric of my jeans. 'You're disappointed in me, aren't you?'

'No,' she says. 'No.'

'You're ashamed.'

'No,' she says, 'I'm not.' And now her voice is firm, indignant. 'Katie. You don't understand. I'm not disappointed, that's not it. Not at all. And, darling, the word ashamed isn't even part of my vocabulary. It's a bit shocking, of course, that you're actually pregnant, and it's a little hard to absorb. But for God's sake, Katherine, a few short hours ago we were worried that you were taking drugs. We seriously thought we might lose you.' She sighs, shakes her head. 'I've had a daughter die. I'm beyond such . . . I don't even *think* like that any more.'

I look at her. I'm confused. I have no idea what she's thinking, no idea what to say.

'Katie. Sweetheart.' She smiles. 'I probably shouldn't say this, or even think like this, I'm sure it's not in the handbook of good parenting, but you have to understand that it's very hard for me to see this as a catastrophe.'

'Oh,' I say. 'So, what *do* you think?'

And she puts a finger to her lips, stares wide-eyed up at the ceiling for a moment, then looks back down at me and grins. It's a gleeful, impish, guilty-looking grin. 'I think I feel quite excited, really; if I'm honest, quite thrilled.'

I must look as shocked as I feel because she laughs, shuffles closer to me on the couch and puts her arm round me.

She speaks quietly, intensely. 'Perhaps it's wrong of me, or selfish even, but all I can think is how wonderful this is. You're adding to our family, you're creating a new person for us all to love. You're creating life, darling, you're . . . you're *living* life. I think it's wonderful, actually.

303

I'll get a new grandchild, a new person to love . . . and just explain why should I ever think that was bad? And I think your young man is heavenly, really, an absolute gentleman. And so good to talk to, so intelligent.' And then she takes a handkerchief from her pocket and wipes at her eyes, blows her nose. 'I remember perfectly when I was first pregnant with you. All that wonderful innocent hope, all that excitement.'

'So you're seriously not disappointed? You're not upset?'

'No. No I'm not.'

'You don't think we're mad to keep it when we barely know each other?'

'Maybe. I can't possibly say. But I think you've got as much chance as anyone else of staying together. Some people get married after knowing each other for years and still end up divorced. There are no guarantees in life.'

'But I'm so young.' And I'm not sure why, but suddenly I'm expressing all the doubts and fears that I've barely let myself think. I want more of my mother's reassurance, it feels so good to hear her say such positive things. I can't get enough. I want her to tell me everything will be okay. 'Nobody my age has babies. Nobody.'

'I didn't think you were so concerned with what other people did or didn't do.'

'I'm not. I don't mean it that way. It's just . . .'

'I know what you mean, darling. Yes, it's a huge thing; yes, it'll mean you lose a lot of the freedoms that other people your age have. And that will be harder than you can imagine. But it will open another world to you as well. It will add a magical, wonderful, life-changing dimension to your life. Motherhood does that.' She puts her hand on my cheek. 'And your father and I will be here to help you. As much as we can. It would be our privilege.'

'I'm just so glad you're not angry or upset.'

'Not upset. Goodness me, no.' Again, she grins. 'I feel ridiculously excited. Excited for you and Mick. Excited for your father and me. And nervous. And thrilled. And I want to be the one to tell your father. Can I?'

'Of course.'

I'm unused to seeing her like this – so open and generous with her emotions – and my surprise must register on my face.

'What is it, darling?' she says. 'What's wrong? You look funny.'

'Sorry. It's just . . . you just seem so different. Really happy. You and Dad. It's great, of course. I'm just . . . I guess I'm not used to it any more.'

'I know, darling.' And then she puts her hand on my head, pulls me towards her so that my cheek rests against her chest. As she talks I can feel the comforting rumble of her voice, the regular rhythm of her heart-beat. 'I know. We haven't been fair, have we? And, you know what? Your silly little friend actually did us all a big favour. We were so worried, Dad and I, when she called and said those stupid things about you. We were so scared, so afraid of losing you. And then when we discovered that you were okay,' she takes a deep breath, sighs, 'it was like being given a second chance. And I know, darling, I *know* how you've felt about Rachel. I know that you feel guilty for that day, that you feel guilty that you're still alive when Rachel's dead. And I hope you can forgive me for never mentioning it, for never making it clear that I think you have absolutely nothing to feel guilty about, that you absolutely *must* get on with your life. There has to be some kind of end, some kind of . . . oh, I don't know . . . what's that awful word people like to use these days?'

I lean back and look at her. 'Closure?'

'Yes. That's it. Closure. There must be some closure. For you, at least, my darling. She was your sister, not your daughter. It's not right that you should suffer for ever. It's not right that this should ruin your life.'

'But—' I want to tell her about my new insights, explain why I don't need her to say this.

'No,' she interrupts, putting her hand beneath my chin and looking at me tenderly. 'I've been unfair. I've known that you've been suffering and I've been too caught up in my own pain to have the energy to do anything about it. I've known for a long time that I could help you feel better if I could just bring myself to say a few simple things. And I didn't. And I'm deeply ashamed of myself. But I can say it now, my darling.' She clears her throat and continues. 'Your father and I don't blame you for what happened to Rachel. We never, ever did. If anything, we blame ourselves. And don't, for a second, imagine that we wished it had happened to you instead of her. We loved you both equally. We always did.'

I nod but cannot speak. I'm afraid that I'll burst into tears. Sob like a baby.

'And outrageous as it may be to ask, I have a couple of favours I need from you,' she says.

'Of course, Mum, anything.'

'First of all, I need you to forgive me for my selfishness. For not being a proper mother for the last few years, for even letting you entertain the thought that your father and I might blame you in any way. Because we absolutely do not. We never did.'

And then I do start to cry. I can't help it. Everything I believed with such certainty only moments before seems suddenly very distant and unimportant. Knowing that she doesn't blame me provides immediate and glorious relief and gives me more joy than I could have thought possible. I hold my mother and sob in great heaving breaths against her chest. She hugs me tight but keeps on talking.

'And the second thing I need you to do is live your life. Live the best and happiest life you can. And you must never, never, *ever* feel guilty about being happy. Don't you dare. And if you can't do it for yourself, then do it for us. For me and your father. Because if you're not happy, my darling, if you don't live your life, then we've lost everything. We've lost both of you.'

I don't find out what my father thinks of the fact that I'm pregnant. Mum wants to tell him later, when they're alone together – give him the chance to digest it in private for a while. She thinks he'll be shocked and upset at first. 'Completely normal for a father,' she says. 'You'll always be his innocent baby girl, after all. But he'll come round, he'll get used to the idea, and he'll be as excited as I am, eventually.'

And as I knew we would, we get a lecture on the evils of the motorbike from my father before he leaves. He's relieved when we tell him that it's for sale, and he makes me promise never to ride on it again, and makes Mick promise to ride carefully, if he has to ride at all.

When they've gone, Mick and I turn the lights out and go to bed. Mick is particularly tender and gentle, he tells me he loves me again and again, and we move close together, my head on his chest.

'I know you must be sick of talking about Alice,' he says. 'But are you okay? You're not freaking out about her?'

'No,' I say. 'I'm too happy to even think about her.' And although it was far from Alice's intention, I'm feeling quite thrilled about the evening with my parents. Mum hasn't been so openly emotional in years and it was wonderful to have her be so effusive and warm, an unexpected delight to have her reassurance – not only about the baby, but about Rachel as well. 'I mean, Alice is clearly a nutter,' I continue, 'and I'm glad we're not friends any more. But she's only really hurting herself. She's making a big fool of herself. I feel sorry for her.'

'Yeah.' Mick yawns. 'Me too. She must be a real sad case. Desperate.'

'Yep. And anyway, what can she do? When we move she won't even know where we are. And I'm going to change my mobile number. She won't be able to call me. What can she possibly do to me now?'

'Nothing,' he says. And he leans over and turns the bedside lamp off, kisses my lips in the dark. 'You're completely safe. She can't do anything to hurt you.'

34

The next day Mick receives a book-sized parcel. It's delivered while he's out at band practice and when he gets home in the late evening I show it to him. He doesn't immediately rip it open like I would, just looks at it without interest, puts it on the coffee table.

'You should open it,' I say, picking it back up. 'It might be something exciting. A present.'

'Who from? It's not my birthday for ages.'

'Oh, come on. I don't know how you can stand it. Not knowing what's inside. Hurry up, I've been waiting all day.' I push the package into his hands. 'Open it.'

Mick shrugs, turns it over. It is wrapped in plain brown paper, with no return address. 'It's going to be really boring, I can tell. A booklet from the tax department or something. Unless . . .' he says, suddenly grinning, 'unless you sent it. You did, didn't you? That's why you've been waiting, why you're being so impatient.'

'No,' I say. 'I didn't. I promise.'

Clearly, he doesn't believe me. He shakes his head and continues smiling as he opens the package. Inside is what looks like a photo album. There is a black-and-white picture on the front cover, some writing. Mick holds it away from me.

'"Know who you're with?"' he reads aloud, and he's still smiling but sounds puzzled. He turns the pages, holding it high so that I can't see inside.

'Mick.' I laugh. 'I didn't send it. It's not from me. I don't know who—' But I stop when I see his expression. His smile has become a frown, all the colour has drained from his face. 'What?' I say. 'Mick? What is it? What?'

'Jesus Christ,' he says. And suddenly I know who the parcel is from.

'Let me see,' I say, reaching my arm out. 'I want to see it.'

'No. You don't need to. Don't. Please. Just don't.'

'Don't be stupid, Mick. Let me see the bloody thing.' My voice is sharper than I intended. 'Sorry,' I say. 'Please. Just let me see it. It won't help to hide it from me.'

He hands it over reluctantly. 'Katherine,' he says, shaking his head. 'It's crap. Just . . . She's insane. Don't let it—'

'Okay,' I say. 'Okay. I know. I know all that.'

The front page is covered by an old newspaper picture. It's a photo of me and Rachel – a family portrait that somehow got into the hands of the press after Rachel died. We are at the beach, standing side by side, our smiles enormous, our hair windblown and damp. We have our arms round one another. We look so happy, so innocent . . .

The picture has been torn in half in a deliberately jagged way and stuck down over the front of the album. Above the picture, letters – a random mix of upper and lower case – have been cut out from a newspaper and pasted together to form the phrase 'Do yoU reallY KnoW wHo yOu'RE wItH?'

The next page is covered with a random selection of editorial excerpts from the time shortly after Rachel was killed. And though they are all clearly from different articles, Alice has cut and pasted them together to form one long and rambling piece. She has also constructed her own disturbing headline.

wRonG peOple CoNVIcted? tHe gUILty
PaRTy goEs freE?

But who is really responsible here? Surely, in these so-called enlightened times, we can't expect a group of disadvantaged and undereducated youths to take sole responsibility for a crime that highlights all that is lacking within the typical 21st-century individual's sorry notion of what constitutes a sufficient duty of care towards those younger than us?

Grant Frazer was abused as a child. He was beaten black and blue by his alcoholic father on a regular basis and denied love by his drug-addicted mother. It's not surprising that he grew up with no social conscience.

The Boydell sisters had a life of wealth and privilege. Their home is enormous and yet quietly elegant, their garden a child's fairyland complete with secret courtyards, tennis court and swimming pool.

An expensive education didn't prevent Katie Boydell taking her fourteen-year-old sister to an illegal and unsupervised party and allowing her to drink herself under the table.

Who is really responsible here? Who is really to blame?

And after so long I'm surprised to notice that these words still have the power to sting. I still feel the overwhelming desire to scream out in protest, to defend myself, to explain and justify.

The following pages are filled with photos and articles from different newspapers – they are chopped out and cut up and placed randomly all over the page and there seems to be little order to their placement. It is the large letters pasted over the top of the pictures and articles that are most striking – 'COWARD, KILLER, SIBLING RIVALRY, BETRAYAL,

313

IRRESPONSIBLE, JEALOUSY'.

The second-last page has a colour photo of me on it. It's a real photo, and very recent – the only one not taken from a newspaper. I have my head tossed back in laughter. I look ecstatically happy.

'KatHeriNE PatTerSon NoW. LiFe wiThout Her sisTEr', reads the newsprint that runs across it.

The final page reads simply – 'kAtherInE paTteRsOn / KAtiE bOydeLL – viCtIm or MuRderER?'

'Bugger this.' Mick snatches the album from my hands, slams it shut and tosses it violently across the room so that it crashes into the wall, drops to the floor. 'Stop looking at it. It's sick.'

I say nothing. I can't speak. I can taste the bile rising in my throat. I turn away and go to our bed, lie down on my side, curl up into a foetal position.

Mick follows and sits beside me. He puts his hand on my shoulder. 'Maybe we should call the police,' he says gently. 'She's going too far. This is some kind of harassment.'

'No.'

'But we have to get her to stop.'

'I don't want the police involved.' I'm afraid to bring it all to the surface again, to have the past dredged up like a stinking corpse, the police useless and bumbling, the press like vultures tearing at the putrid flesh. 'They won't do anything. They can't.'

He lies down next to me and puts his arm round me.

Eventually we fall asleep, our arms wrapped tight round each other. When I get up in the morning, the album is gone.

35

Over the next few days, while Mick is working, I spend a few hours each evening getting ready to move. I go back to Vivien's place and pack my things. I'm no longer as tired as I have been and I enjoy organising my stuff, dreaming about my new life with Mick. The fact that my parents so obviously like him, and that Mum was surprisingly happy about the baby, has dispelled most of the doubts I had. We're doing the right thing. We love each other. It's going to be wonderful.

I let Vivien know via email that I'll be moving out. I promise to collect her mail and keep an eye on things until she returns. I end the note with an apology for the short notice. She writes back:

Don't apologise! I KNEW there was a reason you were looking so happy and I think it's absolutely marvellous that you've met someone who makes you feel that way. Can't wait to see you (and meet your Mick!!) when I get back home.

Take care. Lots of love,

Aunty Viv xxx

It takes three evenings of work to finish packing my things at Vivien's and to clean all trace of myself from her apartment. I want to leave it spotless, sparkling, as a thanks to Vivien for letting me live there. I finish at ten-thirty on the Friday night, and wonder if I've still got enough time to go and see the end of Mick's gig. He was going to call me when he finished, get a lift with the lead singer up to Vivien's and give me a hand if I was still working. But he hasn't called and I assume that there has been a good crowd and he's still playing. I decide to go and pick him up, surprise him.

It's raining out and the road is wet and dark so I drive slowly and don't arrive until eleven. The pub is quiet, almost empty, the equipment all packed up.

Mick's not waiting in the bar so I go backstage. I hear his voice and head towards a lighted doorway. I stop and take a step back when I see her in the room. Alice is leaning against a table, her long legs crossed out in front of her. 'Oh, for God's sake,' she is saying, her voice slurred and slow with alcohol. 'How can it hurt? Who can it hurt? How will anyone even know?'

Mick has his back to her. He is rolling electrical cables together. He shakes his head.

'You're insane. I'm not having this conversation. Go away.'

'Oh. Come *on*.' She laughs, flicks her hair back provocatively. It's a wasted gesture, Mick is not even

317

looking at her. 'Free sex. That's what I'm offering. Unconditional great sex. Why would you say no? What kind of man are you?'

Mick laughs shortly. 'I think the question is, what kind of person are you? What kind of friend?' And then he turns to face her. Sees me. Stops. 'Katherine.'

Alice turns my way. For the slightest moment she looks alarmed, but she recovers immediately, smiles, puts her arm out. 'Katherine!'

I stay in the doorway and stare at Alice. 'What are you doing here?'

'Oh, I saw an ad in the paper and I thought I should be supportive, come down and listen to my friend play.' She reaches her arm out towards Mick, smiles. 'I thought you'd be here, actually, Katherine. I was hoping we could catch up. You've been very difficult to find lately.'

For a moment I consider confronting her, asking why she is so hell-bent on hurting me, but I quickly decide against it. There's no point. I don't want to hear her explanation – there is no rational or forgivable excuse for what she's done – and I don't want to listen to one of her insincere apologies. I just want to get out of here.

'Are you ready to go?' I look at Mick.

'Yep.' He stops rolling the leads up and kicks them into a rough pile. He is usually meticulously tidy, but he's clearly as desperate to get away from Alice as I am.

'Goody.' Alice claps her hands together, stands up, staggers a little. 'Where are we going?'

'I don't know where you're going.' Mick's voice is icy. He puts his arm round my shoulders. 'We're going home.'

'I'll come with you, then. In fact, that might be fun. The three of us.' She stays close behind us as we leave the bar, walk up the street to where the car is parked. 'Three is better than two. Don't you think, Katherine? Huh?'

When we reach the car Mick opens the passenger door for me, but before I get in I turn to Alice. 'Go home. Go *away*. And from now on just leave me alone. Stay out of my life. You're sick. I feel sorry for you. You really need to get some help.'

She shakes her head, sneers, her top lip curling in an expression of disgust. '*I'm* sick? *Me?* That's weird. I thought you were the one with the problem, Katie. I thought it was you, you who left your sister—'

'Katherine!' Mick's voice is firm. He's already in the driver's seat, has already started the engine. 'Just get in. Get in and shut the door.'

And so I do. Mick locks the doors, puts the blinker on, checks the driving mirror for an opportunity to pull out. Alice keeps her eyes locked on mine through the windscreen and I find it impossible to drag my gaze from hers, to look away. And just as Mick pulls away from the kerb, Alice smiles – a cold and empty stretching of the lips – and steps forward, straight off the gutter.

I scream out, 'Mick! Stop! Wait!' But it's too late and there's a dreadful, sickening thud as Alice falls.

'Fuck! Jesus. *Fuck!*' Mick slams on the brakes and is out of the car in an instant.

I cannot move, cannot bear to look. My heart is thudding, thudding and I stare blankly through the windscreen at the oncoming traffic. *It's over*, I think. *She's got what she wanted. Ruined everything. It's over. It's over.*

'Alice!' I hear Mick shouting, can hear the panic in his voice. 'Are you okay? Are you hurt? Alice!'

And then I hear it; the high-pitched hysterical sound of her laughter.

36

I'm unpacking boxes in our new kitchen when it happens. I stand up and feel a small gush of liquid between my legs. I don't know what it is at first and wonder for a moment if I've wet myself. I rush into the bathroom and pull my pants down. Blood.

I do the best I can to dry myself with toilet paper and go straight to Mick. He's unpacking books into our makeshift bookshelves, humming, nodding his head in time with his own tune. He smiles as I approach.

'I'm bleeding.'

'What?' He jumps up. 'Shit. Is that bad? That's bad, isn't it?'

'I don't know. I think so.'

'Let's go to the hospital.'

I wrap an old towel round my waist, Mick grabs the keys and we walk carefully down to the car.

The accident and emergency department is busy and the nurse informs us that we will have a long wait before we can see a doctor.

'But she could be losing the baby,' Mick says. 'She needs to see someone now.'

'Sorry. We have a triage system. And I'm afraid that at this early stage, if you are having a miscarriage, there's really nothing we can do anyway. All we'll be doing is monitoring.' She smiles kindly. 'But that may not be the case. A lot of women bleed during pregnancy and then go on to have perfectly healthy babies. Take a seat and try not to worry.'

Mick and I shuffle over to the chairs. There are no two seats together but a lone woman notices that we are a couple and moves over so that we can sit next to each other. Mick thanks her, and though she catches my eye and smiles sympathetically, I look away. I don't want sympathy or kindness from strangers. If I'm going to have to grieve, I want to do it privately. The room is crowded and everyone present would have heard our conversation with the nurse. With the towel round my waist I feel exposed and conspicuous.

I sit down and close my eyes, rest my head on Mick's shoulder.

A nurse calls my name forty minutes later. She asks Mick to wait but when I burst into tears and clutch his arm she lets him come through with me. She leads us to a bed and asks me to sit down.

'How much blood was there?'

'I'm not sure. It seemed a lot.'

'A padful, do you think? More?'

'Maybe. Yes. Just a padful.'

She writes on a piece of paper. 'Are you still bleeding? Now?'

'I don't think so. I'm not sure. I can't feel anything.'

'Good. If you can't feel it, you're probably not.'

She writes more notes and then takes my blood pressure and my temperature.

'That's all good. The doctor won't be long. Just lie down. Rest.'

She drapes a blanket over my legs and pulls the curtains closed as she leaves.

Mick sits on the chair beside my bed and takes my hand.

'I shouldn't have let you unpack, should I?' he says. He looks forlorn.

'No. That's not it. I didn't even lift anything heavy. Pregnant women aren't meant to be treated like invalids.' I squeeze his hand. 'Anyway. Let's not assume the worst. Not yet.'

'Sorry. No. Of course not. It's just that I really want it to be okay. I don't want . . .'

'Neither do I.' I bite my lip, try not to cry.

And then the curtain opens and a tall, thin woman comes in. She has wiry red hair and reminds me vaguely of Philippa, which, irrationally, makes me feel immediately more comfortable. She is pushing a large machine. She notices me staring at it.

'Ultrasound.' She stands beside the bed, pats my leg. 'I'm Dr King. Let's try and have a little look at this baby, shall we?'

I'm terrified as she moves the probe round my belly. I stare at the screen which shows a collection of cloudy grey blobs and shadows I can make no sense of.

'Aha.' Dr King holds the probe still, points to the screen, smiles. 'Heartbeat. See? Nice and strong. And the baby's size is absolutely perfect for its gestational age.'

I see the pulsing of my baby's heart and I hear myself make an odd, strangled noise, part laugh, part sob.

Mick squeezes my hand. 'Wow.'

The doctor says she thinks everything is okay – it was probably just a one-off, unexplained bleed. Just one of those strange things, she says. She tells Mick to take me home and look after me for a few days, to bring me back immediately if it happens again. 'Try not to worry, I don't think it was anything too serious,' she says. 'But take it easy for a few days,' she concludes with a smile, 'just to be safe.'

I spend the next three days in bed. Mick goes to the library and gets me a pile of books on pregnancy and I read them from cover to cover. Fortunately, the weather is perfect for it – stormy and cold – and I feel safe and cosy and perfectly content lying beneath the covers of our bed. Mick practises on his digital drums with the sound turned so low that I can barely hear them, and brings me breakfast and lunch and dinner in bed. When I get sick of reading he drags the television in and we watch daytime soaps together and laugh at the absurd plots, the wooden acting. There is no more blood.

On the fourth morning I wake feeling fantastic and more energetic than I have in weeks. I leave Mick asleep in bed, get up and make myself a cup of tea. Downstairs there is a small communal garden shared by the four flats in our block. I take my tea outside and sit on the steps that lead down to the garden.

Though it's still early the sun is warm and the sky is enormous and high and a magnificent deep blue – a sky that I always think of as particularly Australian, a sky that I've never seen in Greece or Indonesia or Europe, or in any of the other countries we used to travel to before Rachel was killed – and I'm suddenly filled with a sense of happiness so great, and a feeling of such immense gratitude to be alive, that I smile. A huge, spontaneous, unseen grin. The wooden steps are warm beneath my feet, the tea is sweet and delicious, the sun presses gently on my skin, kissing me awake.

In the past I spent too long stopping myself from feeling this kind of happiness, the simple, sensual plea-

sure of being alive. I thought of it as unfair to Rachel –
a selfish indulgence, a kind of betrayal – as she'll never
enjoy such moments again. But I think of what Mum
said, how important it is that I live my life, that I let
myself enjoy it, and it suddenly occurs to me with an
overwhelming certainty that Rachel would want me
to be happy. She'd never, ever begrudge me a full and
happy life. And I'm suddenly very conscious of the fact
that I can choose how I feel, and that choosing to be
miserable means choosing to let the men who murdered Rachel destroy my life almost as surely as they
destroyed hers.

'I'm happy, Rachel.' I say it out loud as a kind of
prayer. 'Truly happy.'

But the sunshine doesn't last long and by mid-
morning the storm clouds have gathered again and the
sky is dark. I spend another day indoors, reading, while
Mick goes out to band practice. By the time he gets
home at six I am restless and bored and desperate for
his company.

I rush to the door and embrace him as soon as I hear
his key in the lock.

He laughs, but doesn't hug me in return. He is
hiding something behind his back. 'Surprise!' he says.
And he hands me a large white envelope.

There is a thick wad of hundred-dollar notes inside.
I look at him curiously. 'What?'

'Sold. One bike. Three thousand big ones.'

'Oh, Mick.' I wrap my arms round him. 'Are you sad?'

'Are you insane?' He squeezes me tight, kisses my neck. 'Your dad totally freaked me out. Convinced me I'd be killed instantly if I ever touched the damn thing again. I don't want to die. And, hey, today we're rich, let's celebrate, get takeaway for dinner.'

'No. No. Let's go out. I'm going mental cooped up here.'

'But do you think it'll be okay? Do you think we should?'

'It'll be fine.' I quickly pull my clothes off and head towards the shower. 'The doctor said I should take it easy for a few days. She didn't say I should stay in bed for the next six months. I haven't moved. I'll go mad if I don't get out of here soon.'

'We'll drive down, then.'

'Don't be ridiculous. We'll never be able to park.'

'True.' He sighs. 'But are you sure you'll be okay? I could go down and get us some takeaway.'

'I'll be fine. We'll walk slowly.' I laugh. 'Like old people.'

It isn't far to the restaurant and we take the path beside the beach. It's not raining but there are dark storm clouds in the sky and the beach is wild, the waves rough and foamy. It's a spectacular sight and we take our time, arms linked, strolling leisurely. We're both enjoying being out of the flat, taking in the fresh air, the beauty of the view.

And we take our time over the meal. Mick talks about the band, about composing music. We imagine a future tour of the world – money, fame, thousands of screaming fans. I laugh and tell him that I'll be fighting the girls off him.

'I'll be the witchy, jealous, fat wife at home. With six kids.'

'Yes,' he teases. 'I can imagine you like that.'

We contemplate taking a taxi home because it looks as though it might rain but decide against it. It's nice outside, and it's only a short walk. And a little rain can't hurt us.

37

You hear footsteps behind you – the sharp *click click click* of heels on concrete – but think nothing of it. As the footsteps grow louder, closer, you and he move to the side, make way for the woman to pass you by. She does, but then she stops, turns round, puts her hands on her hips. It's getting dark out, so it takes a moment before you realise who it is.

She tilts her head to the side, smiles. 'Katherine,' she says. And you can hear it in the way she speaks, slowly, carefully – she's drunk. She leans forward. 'I knew I'd find you here. I knew if I waited long enough that I'd bump into you and the little drummer boy.'

He pulls you away, holding your hand tightly. You keep on walking.

'It's such a beautiful, wild night to be out and about, isn't it?' She follows close behind, talking in an artificially friendly voice. 'I'm so glad I bumped into you. Well, both of you, actually. We've just got so much to talk about.'

You walk faster, don't turn round. Don't answer.

'Oh come on, you two. Don't you want to chat?'

He squeezes your hand. You keep walking.

'Okay, then. Maybe you don't want to talk. I can understand that. But I want to talk. In fact I need to talk. There's a lot that's been unsaid, Katherine, a lot you don't know about that night.' She laughs viciously. 'And I know you know which night I'm talking about. That night.'

You stop walking.

She laughs behind you. 'Oh, that got your attention, didn't it? Can't run away for ever and ever, can you, Katie? Got to face up to the truth sometime.'

You turn to face her. 'What are you talking about? What are you on about now?'

She puts her hands on her hips, looks you up and down. 'What's it like to have the perfect life, Katherine? The perfect family? Must be nice to be so spoiled, to be oblivious to the suffering of others?'

'The perfect family? Oblivious to suffering?' you say, incredulous. 'Are you joking, Alice? My little sister was murdered. My family is far from happy, far from perfect.'

'But your parents love you, don't they?' she sneers. 'I know they do. I've met them. You're their little princess. They worship the very air you breathe. That's why

330

you're so smug. That's why you don't care.'

'Why I don't care about what? You're insane, Alice. You talk in riddles.'

'You don't care about people like us.'

'People like us?' I look round her deliberately. 'Who's us, Alice? Who are you talking about?'

'Me and my brother. That's who I'm talking about. Me and my little brother.'

You shake your head in confusion. 'What on earth . . .'

'Everything's easy for people like you, Katherine. Your parents love you. The world loves you. You've never had to prove anything to anyone. And if your sister gets murdered, then of course everyone takes your side, everyone just accepts that you were innocent, that it wasn't your fault.'

'But it wasn't my fault.' And despite the hysteria that is rising in you, the feeling of anger that makes you want to scream and lash out at her, your voice sounds calm, almost normal. 'How dare you even say that? And you're wrong, anyway. People were horrible when Rachel was killed. It was horrible. I've told you that.'

'Horrible? What a pathetic little word. I don't think it could've been as horrible as you say. You weren't thrown in jail, were you? You weren't accused of murder, were you?'

He pulls at your arm and tells you to drop it, walk away, but you're too angry, too involved now to leave.

You push his hand away and stay where you are.

'Of course I wasn't!' And despite all the doubts that still haunt you, all the mistakes you made the night of Rachel's murder, you are suddenly filled with a burning fury – against Alice, against the press, against the murderers themselves – and the rage is obvious in your voice. 'I didn't do anything!'

'Oh. But you did, really, didn't you?' And now she is smiling, her voice falsely intimate. 'I guess on the surface it might look as though you were innocent. To someone who didn't know any better. But you and I know better, don't we?'

'No, Alice. No. We don't.' And you understand deep down that this conversation is pointless, but you feel compelled to defend yourself, to fight. 'You're wrong. What you're saying is disgusting. It's unfair. Untrue. I just got frightened. I saw a light and I ran for help. I was terrified. I had no choice.'

'Oh but you did have a choice, Katherine. You had lots of choices that night. And you made the wrong one every time. Every. Single. Time.'

'No.' You shake your head, try not to cry. 'No. You're wrong.'

She leans in close. Speaks quietly. 'You didn't have to run, Katherine.'

'I did,' you say. 'I had no choice.'

'No.' She straightens up, crosses her arms over her

chest, speaks with authority. 'You left them with no choice when you ran away. You forced them into doing something they didn't want to do.'

'Why are you saying this?' And now you are shouting. You grab her arm and hold it tight. 'Why? Why do you say I had all the choices? They took us against our will. They were the only ones with any choice. Not me. Not my sister. We were victims. Why do you want to defend such animals?'

'Animals?' She shakes her head. 'You see how you refer to them, Katherine? Hardly fair, is it? You don't even know them.'

'I know what they did.' You almost spit the words out. 'They killed my sister. I hope they rot in hell.'

Again her face changes and suddenly she is crying, her voice high and shaky. 'Nobody loved him. Nobody. Not our real mother. Not the bitches who separated us. Nobody. Don't you think that hurt him? Don't you think it might screw you up if your own mother doesn't want you? Don't you think he could have been excused for messing up, for being confused?'

'Alice.' You keep hold of her arm. You want her to look at you, to calm down, to stop talking such rubbish. Her behaviour is frightening, irrational, insane. You wonder if you should get her to a doctor. 'I don't know what you're talking about. You're not making any sense.'

She pulls away and stares at you. Her expression is full of loathing.

'My little brother's not an animal,' she says. 'But you put him in jail.'

'What are you—'

'You put him in jail,' she says it again, enunciating each word slowly and precisely. Then she smiles – a cold and venomous smile that chills your heart. 'How can I make it any clearer? My little brother, Sean. You put him in jail for murder.'

And suddenly you understand. You understand everything. Her friendship with you. Her spitefulness. It was this all along. Her brother. Your sister. This.

Sean Enright. The boy in the back of the car. The overweight boy with the nice face. He'd been so nervous; had seemed so frightened . . .

You remember thinking at the trial how incapable of murder he'd seemed. But still. Whichever of the four had finally ended Rachel's life, all were equally guilty. The judge had said so. At the very least Sean had stood and watched while Grant Frazer had raped and then murdered your sister. Deliberately and without mercy. He could have tried to stop him, but he didn't. He made his choice.

You stand there, as still and as mute as a pole, and stare at her. And you have the conflicting urge to both hit her and apologise all at once. She stares back at you, smiling triumphantly, gloating, and you are about to throw out your arm, slap her face, but he is pulling at you, urging you to move.

'Katherine. Come on. Let's go.' He puts his arm round your shoulders and forces you to turn away, to continue, to head for home. It has started to rain and water is splashing your face, your hair. You will be drenched by the time you arrive.

She follows behind you. 'Good idea, Mick. It's getting very wet, isn't it? We should all head up to your place. Discuss this some more.'

He stops walking. You can feel his fury in the way he grips your shoulder, hear it in the tone of his voice. 'Go away, Alice. Get the hell away from us. Leave us alone or I'll call the police. I'm serious. Go. Now.'

'The police? What good could they do? They never did my little brother any good.' She turns her head to the side, pouts. 'Oh, but they like people like you, don't they? Privileged middle-class arseholes like you two. They always take your side, don't they?'

And she continues ranting about the police as you turn away and continue walking until suddenly her voice changes tone.

'Aww, let's not fight. Hey, I know what. Why don't we all get naked and go skinny-dipping? Get to know each other a bit more intimately.'

And then she is running, in front of you, down the

grassy slope and onto the beach. She bends over, pulls her shoes off and tosses them on the sand. She lets her cardigan fall, lifts her dress over her head in one swift movement.

'Come on, Katherine!' she shouts, her hair blowing wildly over her face. 'Don't be a chicken-shit all your life. Now's your chance to show some courage. Come on!'

She runs straight into the water; runs through the crashing waves until she is thigh-deep, and then she dives under, disappears.

He looks at you. His face is full of fear. 'Fuck,' he says. And then he is gone, running down the slope towards the beach. You follow.

You stand on the beach together and scream her name. 'Alice! Alice!'

'Alice! Where are you? Alice!'

You both rush along the edges of the water, shoes and all, both shouting as loud as you can, hands cupped round your mouths.

'She's going to fucking drown. Alice!' he screams.

And then you hear it. 'Help!' It's so faint, coming from so far away. It's so windy down here near the water, so cold, so wet, the waves so relentlessly pounding. But you hear it again. 'Help!'

'This way. Alice! Alice! I think I see her.'

You know what you've got to do. You know, from

experience, what is right. This time you won't be a coward. You won't run away, you won't make the same mistake again. This time you'll show some courage. You pull your shoes off, toss them aside, start heading deeper into the water, towards the voice.

'Katherine!' He pulls you back, screams at you. 'What the fuck are you doing?'

'She's going to drown,' you say. 'She's going to drown.'

He drags you up and out of the water, pushes you down so that you are sitting on the sand. 'Wait there!' he shouts. 'Wait!' And then he is pulling his T-shirt over his head, his shoes off, his socks, stumbling as he rushes to the water.

'No,' you say. 'No. Wait.' But it's too late, he's running and before you even have the chance to tell him to take his jeans off, he is gone.

You get up and follow him, but it's so dark and the water's so noisy that he is lost immediately. You head straight into the water, walking slowly, shouting his name over and over, because you don't know where he is, how to find him. You walk until the water is tugging at your thighs, the current so strong you can feel it pulling, forcing you off your feet. You let it drag you down, feel yourself surrender to the black, black depths. And it is in your face, your nose, your mouth – and inside your head you scream his name over and over, but it is no good, you cannot find him, he cannot be found.

And then someone is dragging you, hurting you, pulling at your hair. There are lights and voices. Screams.

There is air.

You spend the night in hospital. Your chest is tight, your throat and your eyes are burning, raw.

'You'll be fine,' they say. 'In no time at all. One hundred per cent.'

But when you call his name, they turn away. 'You were very brave,' is their answer.

You will not be fine. Everything will not be okay.

You put your hand on his cheek and pull it immediately away.

The skin of the dead no longer feels like skin. It doesn't feel like anything human at all. It's too cold and hard and lifeless. He is gone – this stiff, unmoving grey thing on the bed just an empty container, a shell – and you have no desire to kiss those purple lips, or caress that icy cheek. There is nothing for you in this bleak hospital room but a cold and empty nothingness that has no answers, can give no peace, will provide no comfort to the living.

38

Mum and Dad and Mick's parents pack up the flat together. I stay at Mum and Dad's place, in bed, buried beneath the blankets. It's impossible that I should have to help pack away our life together, our future, our dreams, and nobody expects me to. They do it so efficiently that they have everything finished in less than a day. When they return home, Mum comes up to my room and sits on my bed.

'We've got Mick's drum kit. And his records. His parents thought you might like to keep them.'

I can't bear to think of Mick's silent drums, his unplayed music, but I nod my thanks and turn away, clasp my hand over my mouth.

Mum puts her hand on my blanket, over my thigh, and runs it up and down my leg soothingly as she talks. 'And we told them about the baby, of course.'

'Oh,' I say, and I try to be polite, to show some interest, but I just want her to go away and leave me in peace. Let me howl in private. It seems odd that just a few days ago I cared so very much what everyone would think about the baby. It now seems completely irrelevant – the baby itself an impossibility.

'They were quite shocked, of course, naturally, at first. But I think that they were pleased, in the end. It's Mick's baby, of course, and that's something. Some consolation,' she says. And I nod, waiting for her to go, but she doesn't move, and I can tell by the pressure of her hand, by the way she sighs, that there is something she wants to say. I turn to look at her, attempt a smile.

'They wanted me to tell you how much they appreciated what you did,' she says. 'Trying to help him, risking your life.'

I turn away.

'You did everything you could.'

But it wasn't enough, I think, not nearly enough.

I meet them for the first time at Mick's funeral. Mick's father looks like Philippa, his mother uncannily like Mick, and she pulls me close to her and hugs me tight. And I cling to her and breathe her in and eventually have to be forced to let her go.

I spend the next six months living like a robot. I do all the right things – I eat well and get plenty of exercise walking around the neighbourhood – but I feel disconnected from what is happening, uninterested in the baby. Mick's parents visit a few times, and Philippa, and it is only when I'm with them, when I feel some connection to Mick, that I feel anything close to being alive. The rest of the time I feel like some kind of zombie. The walking dead.

Labour starts the day before my due date and in the beginning the pain makes me glad – it's only physical, much easier to bear than emotional agony – and I feel a perverse sense of satisfaction as it gets increasingly worse.

But the pain lasts for two days and two nights and eventually becomes so immense and overwhelming that I beg the gods for it to stop and scream and shout at the midwives to help me, but they only nod and smile and tell me to crouch down and finally I am pushing, pushing, pushing, the universe from between my legs, and then she is here. Sarah. Mick's daughter. My baby girl.

And I don't know whether it's the glorious cessation of pain, or some kind of hormonal rush, but I feel a deep and overwhelming sense of love and gratitude. For my baby girl, for Mum and Philippa who have helped me bring her into the world, for the midwives, for all humanity. I feel – as I haven't felt since Mick died. And I lift my daughter, still slimy and wet from her birth, and hold her against my chest and I whisper a quiet prayer to Mick, a solemn promise, to protect and love her for ever. To keep her safe.

39

Robbie smiles. At first his smile is tentative, almost fearful, but when I smile back and nod, he beams, shakes his head, laughs. And in the next moment he is in front of me, his hands in mine.

'My God. Katherine. It's you. I can't believe it. It's really you.'

Close up I can see that he looks older – of course he does, it's been five years – and it suits him. His face has become more masculine, squarer, more rugged somehow.

'Mummy, Mummy, who's that man?' Sarah is tugging at my leg, looking up at Robbie curiously. He crouches down so that his face is level with hers.

'Hello. I'm Robbie. I'm an old friend of your mummy's.'

Sarah tilts her head to the side, gazes at Robbie sympathetically. 'But you don't look old. You don't look like my Nan and Pop.'

Robbie laughs and Sarah, unable to resist the lure

of the hill, collects her toboggan and begins dragging it back up.

Robbie and I stand side by side, watching her. 'She's beautiful,' he says. 'Gorgeous.'

'Yes. She looks like her father.'

'And you.'

There are a billion and one things I'd like to tell him – a conversation that could go on for hours – but right here, right now I can think of nothing to say, not a word. And we stand there, the two of us silent, until he puts his hand on my arm.

'I've got to get back to work. I can't really stop like this.' He turns to look at the crowd of people behind us. 'They're waiting.'

'Sure,' I say, not meeting his eye. 'Of course.'

'It was great seeing you,' he says. 'A bit of a shock.'

'Completely unexpected.' Now that I know he is going and I am safe, I can look him squarely in the eye. 'A lovely shock, though. It was great seeing you too.'

He squeezes my arm, nods, turns away. I am about to follow Sarah back up the hill when he calls my name.

'Yes?' I turn back.

'Are you busy later? Tonight? Do you want to have dinner?'

We agree that it would be best to have dinner in my cabin so that Sarah's routine isn't disrupted.

Robbie arrives at six-thirty with the ingredients for

a meal. Sarah has already eaten and had a bath and is tucked up on the sofa in her pyjamas watching a DVD.

Robbie sits next to her and talks about the characters in the movie while I open a bottle of wine. We sit at the small round dining table, opposite one another.

At first we are awkward and overly polite and our conversation feels forced. We talk of the weather, of work, of things neither of us really cares about, but eventually, finally, Robbie mentions Alice's name.

'Did you miss her? That first year when you were in Europe?' I ask him.

'Yes.' He nods. 'I did, despite everything she'd done. I missed her a lot. At first, before she died, I was tempted to come home. I kept thinking that I just wanted to be with her, no matter what she'd done. And then there was no point. I didn't even come back for the funeral. I couldn't handle it.'

'No. I know. I didn't go either.' And I look down at my hands, which are clasped tightly together in my lap. I'm ashamed, now, of my spite, my anger. 'I just hated her so much by then that it would have been hypocritical. I was glad she was dead. I couldn't go to her funeral and pretend to grieve. I hated her.'

'Katherine,' Robbie says, and I look up at him. He shakes his head, smiles tenderly. 'Of course you hated her. It was only natural. It was her fault that Mick died, everyone knew that. You were pregnant and really happy for the first time in years and she ruined it for you. Of course you hated her. I hated her for that too.'

'Did you even consider coming back for her funeral?' I ask him.

'No. Not really. My dad called me and told me that she'd drowned. He saw it in the papers and he ended up calling your mother. She told him everything – about Mick, about Alice's brother Sean, and the whole connection with Rachel, and it was just so shocking, so disgusting . . . I couldn't face it. It made me question everything, my entire relationship with Alice, all those months the three of us were friends. Was it all just some kind of sick game? Was anything real? I was so angry with her. I couldn't have come.'

'I wondered that too. Whether any of it was real or not. The whole friendship – I mean, did she secretly hate me the whole time? Was she just waiting until she could get her revenge?' I shrug, smile bitterly. 'I certainly chose the wrong school, didn't I? Of all the schools in Sydney I had to choose Drummond. Where Alice went.'

'But how did she even know you? How did she know who you were?'

'She must have recognised me. From a photo, I guess. Her parents found all this stuff in her flat after she died. A whole file on the court case. Newspaper clippings, court transcripts, the lot. There were photos of me and Rachel in the papers. She must have seen me walk into Drummond High and thought all her dreams had come true. She knew who I was and what had happened all along.'

'Jesus. It's so creepy. So wrong.'

'Yep.'

'I'm sorry,' he says, suddenly leaning forward and looking at me intently. 'I'm sorry now that I didn't come back. I should've come back and helped you, been a better friend. I should've come back for your sake.'

'No.' I shake my head. 'You couldn't have done anything. You couldn't have helped. It wouldn't have made any difference.'

Robbie looks down. He is quiet and I'm afraid that I've hurt his feelings.

'Robbie?' I say. 'Are you okay?'

'Yeah. Just thinking of all the time I wasted because of her. Of all the time I wasted missing her, wanting her, when none of it, absolutely none of it, was real. I'd have been better off loving a rock.'

I laugh. 'At least you wouldn't have expected anything from a rock. It couldn't have disappointed you.'

'True.' And though he is smiling, his eyes are wet with tears. 'And my dad, you know. I didn't speak to him for a year because of her. And it was stupid, a complete waste; the thing with Alice wasn't even his fault, he was set up, like the rest of us. And I stayed angry with him, even when I'd heard that Alice had died. I don't even know why now. And that still pisses me off, you know, that year of us not being friends. Because of her.'

'It's funny, though,' I say, and I look over at Sarah who is now asleep on the sofa, her thumb in her mouth. 'I regret so much about that time and I wish, almost every day, that things had turned out differently. But I can never really regret meeting Alice, can I? If I hadn't met her I would never have met Mick. I wouldn't have had Sarah. How can I regret that? It's impossible to wish your own child away.'

'Yeah. I don't know. Obviously you have to regret that Mick died. He was innocent, completely uninvolved. But you can't regret Sarah. It's weird, isn't it? Everything to do with her was weird,' he says, his voice bitter. 'It was all screwed up.'

'You're still angry?' I ask. 'You still hate her?'

'A bit,' he says. He smiles ruefully. 'But only when I think about her. Which isn't that often any more. What about you? Are you still angry?'

And as I think about it, look into myself, examine the tender spots within and search for the deep, hot core of anger that burned for so long, I realise it has gone. 'Not any more. I think I just feel a whole lot of pity for her.'

Robbie raises his eyebrows. 'Really?'

'I know it might sound very insincere. All new-agey. But she didn't know how to care about anyone but herself. And her brother, I suppose. She wasn't taught to love. Her own mother didn't love her. Imagine what that must be like.' I look over at Sarah, whom I love more than life itself. 'And then she lost the one person she cared about. She was empty inside. Heartless. Living like that would be miserable.'

Robbie nods, but doesn't look convinced.

'I can see it,' I continue, 'in Sarah. She watches me, copies me. If I'm kind, she's kind. If I'm loving, then so is she. Imagine not having any influence like that. Imagine not being taught to love other people. It would damage you horribly.'

'Maybe,' Robbie shrugs. 'Maybe that explains some stuff about her. But that doesn't completely absolve her. Not in my eyes. Other people have it worse and grow up to be decent human beings.'

We are quiet for a while, both of us preoccupied with our private thoughts.

'Anyway, I've missed you,' I say eventually. 'I didn't realise how much until tonight. But I've really missed you. So much.'

'And me you,' he says. 'The only difference is that I knew how much I missed you. From the day I left.'

'But you didn't try to stay in contact?'

'No.' He shrugs. 'Before Alice died I deliberately

348

didn't contact you. I just thought it would make it too hard to stay away. Talking to you. Missing you. Missing Alice. And then after Alice died I was in shock. I was depressed, I think. A bit. And then after a while, I just didn't know if you'd want to hear from me. I had heaps I wanted to say, though. I wrote a hundred long emails that I ended up deleting.'

'I wish you'd sent them,' I smile.

'Me too.'

And we smile, keep our hands clasped together, drink our wine.

Robbie cooks dinner, and we talk for so long, so late into the night, that I invite him to spend the night with Sarah and me in the cabin. He sleeps in the big bed next to me. It's not sexual. Robbie wears a T-shirt and a pair of my pyjama bottoms, I wear a modest winter nightie. But we hold hands as we go to sleep and it's nice to have a warm adult body in the bed next to me, good to feel a little looked-after. And when Sarah comes in the middle of the night she laughs delightedly to find him there and insists on snuggling down between us.

I watch Robbie – his eyes half-closed – adjust Sarah's pillow, pull the blankets up over her, smile tenderly.

Robbie makes breakfast, scrambled eggs and toast, and the three of us eat companionably at the table together.

'Are you going to be my new daddy?' Sarah asks out of the blue, her mouth full of eggs.

'Sarah!' I try to laugh it off. 'Don't be silly.'

But Robbie doesn't act shocked, or contradict Sarah, he simply smiles. And I'm glad that he doesn't look at me because I can feel my face burning hot.

I walk him out to his car when it's time for him to go. Sarah clings to his leg, begs him to stay.

'I can't,' he says, laughing. 'I have to teach people to ski. I have to help keep them safe on the mountain.'

'When are you coming back?' she says. 'I'll let you go if you tell me when.'

He looks at me – and in his look there is a question, a choice – but I've already made my choice, I made it the day Mick died, and I will not let the world hurt me again.

I turn away, bend over to pick Sarah up and bury my face in her hair so that I don't have to meet his eye. 'Robbie's a very busy man, darling,' I say. 'He doesn't have time to come back here.'

'Aunty Pip, Aunty Pip!' Sarah pushes open the door and lets it slam shut behind her as she runs straight down the path to meet Philippa. Philippa beams and scoops her up, envelops her in an enormous hug.

'Baby-cakes,' she says. 'I've missed you.'

Philippa is taking Sarah to the zoo for the day while I fill out university applications. Sarah will be starting school next year and I will have time, finally, to continue my studies.

Philippa walks up the driveway and we embrace. We go inside and she collects Sarah's things – her water bottle, her hat, her favourite doll.

'I'll bring her back at about three. We might have lunch at McDonald's or something. A treat,' she says.

'McDonald's?' Sarah bounces with excitement. 'Really? Can we, Mummy? Can we?'

'What a good idea,' I say. 'You lucky thing.'

We take Sarah out to Philippa's car and buckle her into the baby seat that's there just for her. When I've said goodbye to Sarah and closed the door, Philippa reaches out, a scrap of paper in her hand.

'This is from Robbie,' she says. 'It's his phone number. He wants you to call him.'

'Oh.' I don't take the paper. Instead I tuck my hands into my jacket pockets. 'You saw him?'

'He called. He wants to see you. He really wants to see you, Katherine.'

'No.' I shake my head. 'No. I don't want to. I can't.'

'Why not?'

'I just . . . I just don't want to.'

'You don't want to? Or you're too scared to?'

'I dunno.' I shrug. 'Scared, I guess.'

'Why?' Philippa lifts her eyebrows. 'Because he might die?'

'No. Of course not. No.' I shake my head and rub my eyes. I just wish she would hurry up and go. Leave me alone. 'Maybe. All right. Yes. I don't know.'

And then she steps forward, takes my hand in hers, speaks quietly and gently.

'Do you ever think about the kind of example you're setting for Sarah?'

'What do you mean?'

'Never taking any risks. Being so cautious and afraid all the time.'

'Afraid? Really?' I turn to look at Sarah in the car. She is busy talking to her doll, fixing her hair. 'Is that how she sees me?'

'Not yet, but she will when she's older.' Philippa squeezes my hand, smiles kindly. 'If you don't try to be happy. If you don't live your life with some courage.'

And it's that word that does it. Courage. I take the scrap of paper from her hand and push it deep into my pocket. I bend down and kiss Sarah goodbye through the car window.

Courage.

'Hello?' He answers almost immediately. But I find myself unable to say a word. I'm suddenly terrified. I hold my hand over the mouthpiece and use all my energy just to keep on breathing.

'Hello?' he says again, and then, 'Katherine? Is that you? Katherine?'

It takes a moment to find my voice but when I do it

is more controlled, more substantial than I'd expected. 'Can you come over, Robbie?' I say. 'Today?'

'Yes,' he says. 'I'll be there soon. I'll be there as quickly as I can.' And he doesn't try to play it cool or hide his enthusiasm and I remember how much I like him, how funny and kind and good and generous he is. And I know, without a doubt, that I've done the right thing.

ACKNOWLEDGEMENTS

A heartfelt thank you to Jo Unwin, who is not only a brilliant and indefatigable literary agent but is also a talented editor and an inspiring, warm and generally fantastic individual.

To my editors – Sarah Brenan in Australia, Kate Miciak in the US and Julia Heydon-Wells in the UK – thank you, thank you and thank you for helping to make this book so much better.

To Erica Wagner at Allen and Unwin – thank you for being brave enough to be the first editor in the world to acquire rights to *Beautiful Malice* – I imagine it must be a scary thing to take a chance on an unknown author.

A million thanks also to my sister, Wendy James, for her generous and helpful reading of everything I've ever written and for being the very first person to tell me I could write.

And to the people who were kind enough to read my book in draft form: Mum and Dad, Prue James, Haidee Hudson, Sam Ackling and Kath Harris: thank you! Your encouragement was, and is, invaluable.

A special thanks to Jake Smith-Bosanquet for all his hard work selling the book around the world and another special thank you to agent Sally Harding, for her earlier encouragement and faith. Thank you also to my little sister, Emma James, for reading, and for always being so incredibly optimistic.

Of course, a gazillion thanks and a million kisses to the wonderful bloke I live with, Hilary Hudson. He deserves a medal for putting up with my crazy obsessiveness these past few years and for bringing me so many perfectly made cups of tea.

And to our sons, Charlie, Oscar, Jack and Jimmy — thank you for the happy chaos.

ff

Faber and Faber – a home for writers

Faber and Faber is one of the great independent publishing houses in London. We were established in 1929 by Geoffrey Faber and our first editor was T. S. Eliot. We are proud to publish prize-winning fiction and non-fiction, as well as an unrivalled list of modern poets and playwrights. Among our list of writers we have five Booker Prize winners and eleven Nobel Laureates, and we continue to seek out the most exciting and innovative writers at work today.

www.faber.co.uk – a home for readers

The Faber website is a place where you will find all the latest news on our writers and events. You can listen to podcasts, preview new books, read specially commissioned articles and access reading guides, as well as entering competitions and enjoying a whole range of offers and exclusives. You can also browse the list of Faber Finds, an exciting new project where reader recommendations are helping to bring a wealth of lost classics back into print using the latest on-demand technology.